DEADLY INTENT

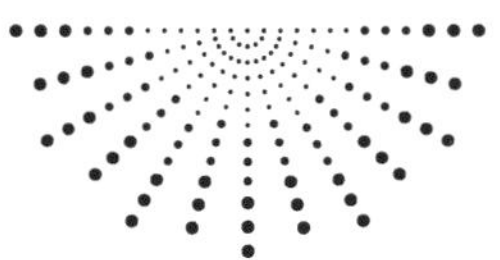

D S BUTLER

Deadly Obsession
Deadly Motive
Deadly Revenge
Deadly Justice
Deadly Ritual
Deadly Payback
Deadly Game
Deadly Intent
Lost Child
Her Missing Daughter
Bring Them Home
Where Secrets Lie

CHAPTER ONE

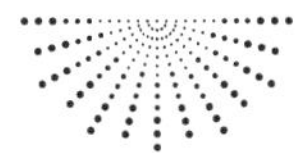

ASHLEY BURROWS SQUIRMED against the hard wooden board. How could she have been so stupid? So trusting? She wasn't a kid any more. She was twenty-one years old and should have known better. But he seemed so normal… so nice.

Her throat ached from the hours she'd spent sobbing. But there was no point in crying. It wasn't getting her anywhere. She needed to get out of there.

He'd taken her clothes, though hadn't taken her underwear, and tied her wrists and ankles with cable ties before leaving her in the loft. His house was in the centre of a row of terraces. The neighbours were so close. At first, she'd tried to scream—sure someone would hear her—but no one had come to help.

How long had she been there? Days at least. It was hard to tell in the attic space because there were no external windows. The only light came from a dim solitary light bulb hanging from one of the rafters. Spider webs, thick with insect remains, draped over the rafters. She shuddered.

Though her wrists were fastened together with cable ties, he had at least kept her arms in front of her body so she could drink from the bottle of water he'd left. She reached for it awkwardly, plastic crunching as she gripped the bottle. She swallowed only a mouthful before putting it back down. There was only a third left, and she didn't know when or even if he would bring her more water.

The floor of the loft was only partially boarded and the rest was exposed insulation material—fibreglass, she thought. That was probably what was making her eyes and skin itch and burn. A few boxes and black bags were scattered in the corners. She'd been so tempted to look inside, thinking they might contain something that would help her escape, but so far she'd been too scared to look. The boards creaked loudly whenever she moved, and she was terrified of him coming back.

Tears welled in her eyes again. Why hadn't she said no? Why had she agreed to go to his house when she hardly knew him?

Her mum would be worried sick. Would she have reported her missing yet? Of course, she would. The police would be looking for her. It wouldn't be long now. Everyone would have known something was wrong when she hadn't turned up for work. She'd been working there for a year and had never been so much as a minute late.

Ashley curled up on her side, bringing her knees to her chest. The grain of the board beneath her felt rough against her exposed skin. She'd been lying and sitting for so long her body ached. Her shoulder blades and hip bone felt bruised. But the muscle cramps and aches were nothing compared to the desire to scratch her skin. The itching was driving her crazy.

She needed to think, to clear her mind and focus on a way out of this, but the incessant need to scratch overwhelmed everything else. Her hands twisted under the restraints until her fingernails connected with the skin on her forearm. She scratched and the relief was instant, but it only lasted seconds before the burning itch was back.

She shivered. Though her skin was hot to touch, she felt so cold and exposed lying there in her underwear. She rubbed the long red welts on her arms where she had scratched and scratched until her skin bled. Red pinpricks of blood still dotted the pink crisscrossed lines. What had he done to her?

After he'd blindfolded her, he'd babbled on, spouting a load of nonsense. He'd talked about making history and had said that together they were going to change the world. An absolute nut job. Why hadn't she seen it earlier?

To make matters worse, he'd actually apologised. As though she would forgive him for what he'd done. She hadn't replied, of course.

He was mad. That much was obvious. It was just a shame it hadn't been obvious before she'd agreed to come to his house, but it wasn't really her fault. He'd changed. In an instant, the friendly, smiling, non-threatening guy had turned into a ranting madman with rage in his eyes.

The first day in the loft had been the worst. Since then, he'd left her more or less alone apart from delivering sandwiches, cups of soup, and water.

The loft space smelled of urine from the bucket he'd left in the corner. The last time he'd come to change it, she'd been asleep and had woken to see him standing over her. Though he hadn't touched her—that time—the mere proximity of him sent her heart thundering in her chest and left her lungs gasping for air. She must have passed out because when she woke again, he was gone, and the bucket was empty.

Her fingernails raked along her skin. What had he done to her? He'd done something. He must have. This itching couldn't be just down to the fibreglass insulation. The day he'd taken her, he'd covered her head with a hood, and she'd felt him put something over her arms. It hadn't lasted long, only minutes—long, terrifying minutes—and shortly after that the itching had started.

Ashley's shivering grew worse. She couldn't sit and wait for the police to find her. There was nothing linking her to this man. They'd met through a support group. That's why she'd thought he understood, that he was on her side.

She pushed herself up onto her hands and knees and shuffled towards the black bags and boxes, flinching as the board creaked beneath her.

She paused, hearing banging from below. He was home.

Ashley didn't move, listening hard. Was he coming up here?

She cocked her head. She could hear whistling. Anger made her clench her teeth. He was down there, whistling away happily as though everything was normal and fine.

She inched forward again, heading for the nearest black bag. She tugged on the plastic until it fell over. A white t-shirt and a shopping bag fell out. It was her bag. It was her stuff!

She felt a spark of hope. There was her small pink clutch bag, too. Breathing heavily, she put both hands inside the clutch and tried to feel around.

Please, please, please let my phone still be in the bag.

Her fingers closed around her purse. If that was still there, then surely…

Her heart leapt as she felt the cold case of her phone, but in her haste to pull it out, she lost her grip, and the phone clattered onto the board.

Oh no.

She turned, watching the loft hatch. Had he heard? He'd stopped whistling.

Her heart pounded.

He could be on his way up here right now. She didn't have much time. Grabbing the phone with shaking hands, she flipped it over to look at the screen. It hadn't broken. But the screen was black.

She fought against the need to scratch her arms again, trying to focus, and pressed the on button. But nothing happened.

The battery was dead.

It had been there all the time, and she hadn't realised. The phone had sat in that bag with its battery draining away, along with her chance of escape.

With a sob, she threw the phone back at the bag. That was it then. He'd won. There was no way she was getting out of here.

Viciously, she scratched her arms and then stopped when she heard footsteps below. She wrapped her arms around herself, trying to hide her bare skin. Her limbs trembled.

Ashley held her breath as the loft hatch began to open.

CHAPTER TWO

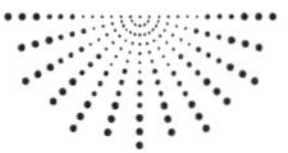

Dr Wendy Willson looked at her patient list and sighed. She had a busy morning ahead, and now she had two new additions to her patient list. Great. That was all she needed. The extra appointments would eat even further into her lunch hour. Not that she resented treating patients who needed her care. She usually spent her lunch break finishing off paperwork and chasing up test results.

She glanced again at her patient list and felt a flicker of irritation when she saw the first name on the list. She always tried to be sympathetic and thorough with all her patients, but this particular patient was a *problem*.

She'd had dealings with him before, as had most of the doctors in the practice. It was unusual for a week to go by without a visit. Privately, just between the doctors at the practice, they referred to him as *the hypochondriac.* Cruel, perhaps. But he turned up week after week with new complaints, demanding they run tests and prescribe unusual medications.

He probably spent most of his free time researching symptoms on Google.

The Internet was a problem with certain patients. Health education was a good thing, but the information on the Internet wasn't always correct, which wasn't helpful for doctors. The number of her patients who now turned up with a self-diagnosis, or more accurately *misdiagnosis*, was verging on dangerous.

She wondered what it would be this time with the hypochondriac. Parasites, perhaps? That seemed to be his current favourite fixation.

She closed the file on her computer for her previous patient and then pressed the intercom to call him in.

Nervously, she waited, busying herself at the keyboard. He had a way of making her feel on edge, uncomfortable. When he started reeling off research studies to back up his self-diagnosis, Wendy couldn't help feeling inadequate. Which was quite ridiculous. She'd spent seven years in medical school and then had further training to become a GP, and she'd been working in this practice for five years. Wendy was very good at her job.

She'd dealt with many varied conditions, but as every practising doctor knew, you had to rule out the most obvious things first, and parasites were not a common cause of disease in the Western world. He could be convincing though, and it was tempting to prescribe something just to shut him up.

Dr Farquhar, who headed up the practice, had told her conspiratorially that he always gave the hypochondriac a prescription for something—usually an emollient cream or vitamins, something that would do him no harm, but Wendy didn't think she could do that. It wasn't right to prescribe something when it wasn't required.

When the door opened, Wendy forced a smile. "Hello again."

Immediately, he frowned. She had said the wrong thing by drawing attention to his frequent visits.

She pushed on. "Take a seat and tell me what's wrong."

"I need antibiotics, a broad spectrum one." He sat in the chair opposite Wendy and met her gaze steadily.

No preamble this time, Wendy thought. He's clearly already decided not only what's wrong with him but also what treatment is required.

How about I, the only person in this room with a medical degree, decide what medication you need? Wendy wished she could say that out loud. Instead, she nodded and said, "I see. What do you need the antibiotics for?"

His facial features tightened and Wendy half expected him to say it was none of her business. Finally, he said, "I've got a rash. I think it's bacterial."

"Let's take a look shall we?" Wendy said and stood up to put on some protective gloves. "Where is it, this rash?"

He held out his arm. When he turned his arm over, she saw a line of red bumps that ran across his pale skin.

Snapping her gloves on, Wendy leaned forward to take a closer look. At least he wasn't making it up this time. It wasn't an *imaginary* symptom. That said, it didn't look like a bacterial infection to her.

"Have you changed your washing detergent recently? Perhaps used a new shower gel?"

He gave a harsh laugh looked at her through narrowed

eyes. "I'm not an idiot, Doctor. No, I haven't changed anything."

Wendy held back the response she would like to have given him and said, "It's not bacterial."

"How do you know that? You haven't even taken a swab!"

"I don't think we need to take a swab. It will probably clear up on its own. It looks to me like it could be bite marks. Do you have any animals?"

He looked thrown by the question and then shook his head. "No, I don't have any animals. Why do you ask?"

Wendy peeled off her gloves and put them in the bin. "They look a little like flea bites."

He looked down at his arm with fascination. "Fleas?"

"I'm not saying that's what it is for sure. And it doesn't mean your house is dirty because fleas can come into the cleanest of homes," Wendy added hurriedly. She sat down beside her computer. Reluctantly she began to type. "I'm going to prescribe you a special cream to treat the rash. Keep the area clean and dry, and if it hasn't improved in two weeks, come back and see me."

"What kind of cream? An antibiotic cream?"

Wendy tried not to roll her eyes. "It's a special cream, specifically for rashes. An emollient cream."

He was quiet for a moment, processing the information.

She really hoped he would take the prescription without argument. There was no way she was going to prescribe antibiotics when he didn't need it. She could get in big trouble for that.

"I don't know..." he said. "I really think it needs antibiotics."

"I can't prescribe antibiotics unless I'm sure you need

them," Wendy explained. "There's been a lot of research about antibiotic resistance. It would be very dangerous if antibiotics lost effectiveness due to overexposure, so we only prescribe them when absolutely necessary."

"That's ridiculous." He leaned forward suddenly making Wendy jump. "Most antibiotics are used in factory farming. Surely you've heard of that. Maybe they should stop giving them to animals before they try to limit human use!"

Wendy murmured something noncommittal and gave her computer screen her full attention.

It wasn't enough to deter him.

"Are you listening to me? You doctors are all the same." He stood up, towering over her.

He wouldn't physically attack her, would he? Not here in the surgery, surely.

Wendy glared back at him. She shouldn't let him intimidate her. He was nothing but a bully. But then… there *was* something wrong with him. These imaginary conditions were a cry for help, and as a doctor, shouldn't she be a little more compassionate?

"Sit back down, please," she said in a firm voice, usually reserved for her three-year-old son. "I think we need to revisit the possibility of referring you to a mental health specialist."

He practically exploded. "There's nothing wrong with my head." He tapped his temple. "All I need is you lot to do your job properly and I'd be fine." He clenched his fists, and his mouth contorted with anger. "Why do you never listen? Don't you think patients are the best judge of their own bodies?"

"Sometimes, but—"

"This is ridiculous. I've been coming here for years, and you've still not found out what's wrong with me."

Wendy was tempted to say that was because *physically* there was nothing wrong with him. His problems were usually purely mental. On this occasion, he did have a rash, perhaps insect bites, but it was nothing that wouldn't heal on its own. Week after week, he was using up her time, and the time of all the doctors in the surgery, time which could be better used for patients who really were physically ill.

"It's easier for you to say I'm crazy than to actually try and help me."

"That's not true," Wendy said.

"Yes it is. It's the current trend in the UK. The hot topic. Everyone has mental health problems. I bet half the waiting room is filled with people who want you to sign them off work for depression or a breakdown."

"Depression is a very serious condition."

"Sure. But most of them lot out there are only pretending they've got it so they don't have to work for a living."

Wendy shook her head. There was no use arguing with him like this. It was true that many of her patients visited to discuss mental health issues more often than they ever had in the past, but Wendy thought that was a positive step forward.

"Look, I know this is hard, but if you could talk to somebody about your anxiety—" Wendy began.

He interrupted. "My anxiety? I'm not anxious."

"Your anxiety relating to your medical conditions. The brain can be a funny thing. It can convince you something's wrong when in reality you're perfectly healthy."

He gave a roar of outrage and thumped his fist on the desk.

Wendy pushed herself back in her wheeled chair as far as she could go. Then stood up, pulling the chair in front of her as a makeshift shield. "Calm down!"

"How am I supposed to keep calm when you won't even listen to me?"

"Losing your temper won't help. You need to talk to someone."

"Forget about it," he growled and stalked out of the room.

Wendy leaned heavily on the back of the chair and took a few deep breaths. For a moment, she'd thought he might hit her. They didn't prepare you for that sort of thing when you went to medical school.

After a few more calming breaths, she walked back to her desk, wheeling the chair behind her. She picked up her pen and scrawled on her notepad: *delusional parasitosis?*

Then she picked up her phone and dialled the direct number for Dr Farquhar.

CHAPTER THREE

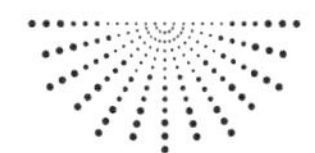

He stormed through the waiting room. He had to get out of there before he really lost his temper. Things escalated quickly when he lost his rag, and there was too much at stake right now to risk that.

He stepped over a child playing with a red car on the floor. His mother was too busy looking at her phone to notice the little boy was now sucking on the toy. Very hygienic.

He yanked open the door, only to find an elderly woman blocking his way. He held his breath, manners dictating he hold the door open for her. But she took forever, shuffling and leaning heavily on her walking frame.

I don't have all day, he thought impatiently, but then regretted it. Her slowness wasn't her fault. She'd been let down by the medical profession just as he had. He'd seen her at the surgery before. She'd been with her daughter then, and they'd been discussing the length of time she'd been on the waiting list for a hip replacement.

So he hid his frustration as well as he could and gripped the door as she'd managed to shuffle through the doorway, muttering apologies. Of course, the sulky looking teenager, sitting in the seat nearest the door, didn't bother to get up and offer his chair to the elderly lady. That was just typical of society today. Nobody cared about anyone else. Doctors included.

He should have known he'd be in trouble when he got put on Dr Willson's list. That woman had never liked him. He'd have had more luck with Dr Farquhar. Perhaps he should have insisted on seeing the male doctor. At least *he* didn't cower in fear when presented with facts.

But that didn't solve his immediate problem. He needed the antibiotics. Perhaps he should have known the rash wouldn't be enough. They were all cracking down on the amount of antibiotics prescribed these days. He'd heard a radio programme about it just last week. Of course they didn't mention the fact that over eighty percent of the world's antibiotics were actually used on farm animals. He doubted the industry would be interested in reducing those. It would eat into profits, and that would never do.

Finally when the old woman got out of the way, he pushed his way out of the waiting room and stepped outside into the germ-free, fresh air. He took a couple of calming breaths. His anger had made him feel dizzy. He pressed his fingers to the edge of his wrist to check his pulse rate. Just as he thought. Ninety bpm. That was all the doctor's fault.

The public was so trusting. They hardly ever questioned the way doctors like to pump them full of drugs these days – even though for many of the drugs there was very little evidence they actually worked.

They were the ones either prescribing or gobbling up the drugs, but everyone saw *him* as the crazy one. When really he was the only one who was actually looking at things logically.

The most frustrating thing was, no one would help him. He tried talking about it to friends, people he'd met on the forums or in the meet-up groups, but they shut down or changed the subject. Their smiles would grow guarded and their eyes shifty as they tried to come up with a way to extricate themselves from the conversation. Still, what did he care? He didn't need them. All the great discoveries of science had been ridiculed at first. Scientists had been thrown in jail for daring to go against the grain. No one believed them at first, but history would view him as a genius. The person who finally put the human race on the right track.

But his lack of antibiotics was a serious setback. He could try to buy them online and get them shipped in from somewhere like India, but there was a chance they'd get held up at customs, and the shipping would take far too long. By the time the antibiotics arrived, it would be too late.

He shuddered as he thought of what might happen. They'd blame him. It didn't matter that his intentions were good, that he never wanted to hurt anyone. All they would care about was the outcome.

Suddenly feeling weak, he staggered a few steps to the bus stop and sat down. Across the street, a group of teenagers were screeching and calling to one another, pushing and shoving each other while far too close to the road. Idiots.

At the other end of the bus stop, a bald man lit up a cigarette and took a deep drag. The light smoke spread around him, mingling with the smell of fried bacon from the cafe just along the street.

The smell of a bacon buttie carried by a youngish man, wearing a leather jacket and a backpack, made him feel hungry. He'd left home without eating breakfast. It was hard to eat when a life was on the line.

He rubbed his face in his hands and tried to think. He could try a natural remedy—tea tree oil was good for treating infections. It couldn't hurt anyway. Maybe he could use that as a last resort.

As he wafted the smoke away from his face, he considered something he'd read recently, an article about online doctors. That could be worth a try.

Feeling a glimmer of hope, he pulled out his mobile phone and searched the Internet for an online doctor. As he scrolled down the screen, his eyes widened in surprise. There were loads of them.

He picked one at random and went through the instructions, which told him to install an app and then select an appointment. Each appointment was ten minutes long, and as a first time user, he had a fifty percent discount. The idea behind the NHS was wonderful, but this could be the way of the future, he thought as he tapped on the screen. Who wanted to wait weeks for an appointment when this app told him the next available appointment was in five minutes?

He filled in the required medical form asking for his medical history and family history and then ticked the box confirming he had no known allergies to any medications. The form was accepted almost immediately, and he was asked to select an appointment.

There was an opening available in one minute. Perfect. He selected that appointment and then waited, staring at the virtual waiting room screen. Now, this was something exciting. A real innovation. Healthcare when you needed it! He didn't see how the doctor would be able to examine him over the Internet, not that he minded on this occasion. Actually, he was glad. It would play straight into his hands.

The screen changed suddenly, and a moment later, he was looking at the online doctor, an Asian man with thinning hair who looked about forty.

"How can I help?"

A little embarrassed about talking to the doctor in public, he held the phone closer to his mouth. "I need some... er... antibiotics for an ear infection."

"I see. And what are your symptoms?"

He licked his lips. "Pain and my ear feels hot to touch. I get ear infections a lot, so I know how it feels. I went swimming a couple of days ago and think I must have got some water in my ears."

The doctor on the screen was nodding. That was a good sign, wasn't it?

"Any discharge?"

He hesitated. What should he say? Did you get a discharge with an ear infection?

The doctor looked directly at the screen and raised his eyebrows.

"Um, it feels a bit wet, but no discharge."

"Okay, good. Do you have a temperature?"

Suppressing a smile, he nodded. He knew the answer to this question. You usually had a temperature if you had a bacterial infection. "Yes, it is a bit high. It was thirty-eight this morning."

"Have you ever had any reactions to medications?"

"No."

"All right, it sounds to me like you do have an ear infection. I'm going to prescribe a seven-day course of amoxicillin. I'm going to disconnect now, but if you stay in the app, you'll receive your prescription, and you can go to one of our registered chemists to pick it up. Is there anything else I can help you with today?"

He shook his head. "No, that's all. Thank you very much."

The doctor disconnected, and he saw that his appointment had only taken four minutes. Well, that was efficient.

It took a few moments for the prescription to arrive in the app, and then he scrolled through the settings trying to find out where the registered chemists were located.

He should have guessed there would be a downside. Even the nearest chemist would take a convoluted journey and would mean at least three bus changes to get there. By his calculations, the trip would take nearly forty minutes minimum. Ridiculous.

But, it had to be done. He didn't have a choice. If only people knew what he put himself through for the greater good.

Maybe he should write a journal and fill it with all his trials and struggles. Then the history books would remember him accurately.

He checked the time on his phone just as a bright red bus hissed to a stop in front of him. Typically, it wasn't the bus he needed. He suppressed a sigh and checked the timetable for the next number seven.

Three minutes. Not too bad. He just hoped he'd be back home before things turned really bad.

CHAPTER FOUR

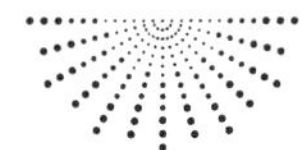

DS Jack Mackinnon ignored the sweat stinging his eyes and steadily made his way up the staircase. It was mid-July, and London was gripped by a heatwave.

He loosened his tie and took a shallow breath. The smell of stale cooking filled the claustrophobic stairwell. Rectangular windows allowed light to flood in on every level, but they were all sealed shut. It was like an oven and seemed to get hotter as they climbed higher.

Buddleia Tower, part of the Towers Estate in the City of London, was much the same as all the other blocks of flats, filled to capacity and in need of repair. Both lifts were out of order, displaying "sorry for the inconvenience" signs. The signs had been defaced with graffiti, presumably by an angry resident.

Two uniformed officers climbed the stairs in front of Mackinnon, and six more followed behind. Less than twenty minutes ago, the team received a tip-off that the young girl they'd been looking for over the past eight days was located in a flat on the eighth floor of this tower block. He and DC Brown had been working this case relentlessly, and now finally they were close to a breakthrough.

The missing girl was eight-year-old Aleena Khan. She'd been snatched from her front garden in broad daylight. But no one had seen a thing, or at least no one was willing to tell the police what they'd seen. Aleena's mother had left her daughter playing for just a few minutes as she prepared the child some pasta for her tea.

Over and over again, Maria Kahn had told them Aleena was only out of her sight for seconds at a time because she had a good view of the garden from her kitchen window. One minute Aleena was happily playing with a skipping rope, and the next, the garden was empty.

Rather than waste time checking with the neighbours and walking around the local estate, Maria Kahn had called the police straight away. She knew her daughter had been taken. And she knew that because she knew who had taken her.

As with any potential child abduction, the police were swift to react, but in this case, the investigation was unusual because Maria was confident she knew who had taken her daughter.

Two years ago, Maria had divorced Aleena's father, Asad. It hadn't been an amicable split. The court awarded Maria full custody of Aleena, and Asad was only permitted visitation rights once a fortnight. He hadn't taken that well at all. For the first year, those visits had been supervised, but that requirement had been relaxed six months ago.

After looking through the paperwork, Mackinnon thought Asad Khan was lucky to be granted any visitation rights at all.

He'd seen reports from social workers as well as the domestic violence reports. There'd been no proven abuse against Aleena, but several unexplained bruises had been recorded by social workers before the couple had separated.

How a full-grown man could hurt any child, let alone his own daughter, beggared belief.

Once they reached the seventh-floor landing, Mackinnon paused and looked around, taking in the determined faces of the officers in the team. DC Charlotte Brown met his gaze with a nod. Sergeant Brian McDougall, the officer in charge of the uniformed tactical unit, stood to one side and checked his radio. Then he said, "Cleared. Let's move quickly."

They continued to climb the final set of stairs.

For eight days, Aleena had been missing, and for every one of those days her mother had been put through the worst kind of torment. They'd been keeping a close watch on the ports to make sure Aleena hadn't been smuggled out of the country, but there had been no sign of her or her father.

Aleena's mother had been panicked and breathless as she told them she was convinced her husband was going to try to take Aleena to Pakistan, to his family. If they left the UK, there was every chance she would never see her daughter again.

Mackinnon really hoped it didn't come to that.

"His whole family will be in on it. That's just what they're like. They'll take her from me. I know they will," Aleena's mother had sobbed.

Asad hadn't been seen since his daughter disappeared, despite an intensive police search.

Just when it seemed he'd disappeared from the face of the earth, they'd had a tip-off. Asad had been spotted entering Buddleia Court twenty minutes ago.

It made sense, because his brother, Badar, lived at number 81 Buddleia Court.

Badar was a slippery customer. He insisted he had no idea where his brother and his niece were, assuring the police he was desperately worried about them. He was appropriately sorrowful, even mustering up a few tears as he spoke about his "dear, sweet niece." He'd offered cups of tea when they'd visited and was quick to tell them how much he appreciated the effort the police had put in to search for Aleena.

If Mackinnon had learned anything from his time with the City of London Police, it was an understanding of how manipulative some individuals could be. Some people lied without shame or remorse.

He wasn't convinced Badar was telling them the truth, and his gut instinct told him to trust Aleena's mother over the girl's uncle.

The officer in front of Mackinnon jerked to an abrupt halt. Looking around the officer's bulky uniform, Mackinnon saw a young boy of five or six. He had dark skin and closely cropped black hair.

The youngster's brown eyes were wide as he stared up at the police officers. "What's happening?"

Mackinnon quickly assessed the situation. The boy was alone. Not a good idea at any time, but especially not now when a young girl had recently been snatched from the area. They were working under the assumption that Aleena had been taken by her father, but that didn't mean it was safe for any child to wander around alone.

"Where do you live?" Mackinnon asked.

"Upstairs," the boy said, pointing upwards with his index finger.

"And where are you going?"

"Downstairs to play. My mum said I've watched too much TV."

Mackinnon guessed the boy often played downstairs on the grassy area outside the flats. But it wasn't sensible for a five-year-old to be out there unsupervised.

They had no intelligence to suggest Aleena's father would be armed, but there were no guarantees. Cases like this had a habit of surprising you.

He told the boy to go back upstairs to his mother and stay inside. No doubt the mother would be out demanding to know what was happening within the next few minutes, so they needed to act swiftly.

Mackinnon nodded to the uniformed officer in front of him. "Let's go."

The officer wore gloves and carried the Enforcer battering ram known as the big red key. They had brought it just in case Badar decided he didn't want to answer the door, but Mackinnon hoped that wouldn't be necessary. He was glad he hadn't had to carry the battering ram up the stairs though. It wasn't a light piece of kit, and unsurprisingly, the officer was sweating heavily.

Quietly, they gathered on the landing outside number eighty-one, and Charlotte asked, "Everything all right?"

Mackinnon nodded. "Yes. Are you ready?"

Charlotte gave a short, confident nod.

Sergeant Brian McDougall knocked on the door as Mackinnon pulled the warrant out of his pocket.

Aleena's uncle, Badar, opened the door. He had a narrow, thin face, and his upper teeth protruded, giving him a rabbit-like appearance. He stared up at Mackinnon and blinked.

Then his gaze darted between the other officers gathered at his front door.

Badar cleared his throat nervously. "What is all this?"

"We have a warrant to search your premises," Mackinnon replied, holding up the paperwork.

"Why? I'm a law-abiding citizen. I know my rights. I forbid you to enter! You can't come in here."

"We can, Mr Khan. That's what the warrant is for," Charlotte explained patiently. "And I think you know why we are here."

Badar licked his dry lips and folded his arms over his chest, blocking the doorway. Was he really going to try and stop them entering the property?

Sergeant McDougall gave him a hard stare, which caused Badar to have second thoughts. He lowered his arms and shuffled to the side.

"I don't know what this is about. It's persecution," he said as the officers filed past him into the flat.

"We are looking for, Aleena, your missing niece. You know where she is, don't you, Badar?" Mackinnon said.

Badar was sweating now. "No, I don't. And you won't find her here. You should be out there looking." He waved his arm in the general direction of the landing window.

"We just need to have a look around your flat to satisfy our curiosity," Mackinnon said. "If you haven't done anything wrong, you don't have anything to worry about."

"That's not how it works! The police target us because of the colour of our skin. You should be out there chasing real criminals."

Mackinnon ignored him and stepped inside the flat.

It was spacious, more so than he'd expected. He knew from

the plans they'd quickly downloaded before leaving the station that the flat had three bedrooms. The hallway was wide, and the rooms were bigger than most of the modern flats on the Towers Estate.

Mackinnon walked down the dark hallway towards the brightly lit kitchen at the end of the flat. Charlotte had already started to search one of the bedrooms, and three uniforms were in the living room.

"Found anything?" Mackinnon asked Sergeant McDougall, who was pulling open kitchen cabinets.

"Not yet."

Mackinnon frowned. Had they been too late? The tip-off had only been twenty-five minutes ago at most. And they had a unit stationed outside, watching the tower block. There were only two routes out of the block of flats and both were visible from the road.

The only other possible exit was out of a window or the balcony, but they were eight floors up. Surely, Asad wouldn't have risked trying to escape that way?

He left the kitchen and walked through the living area, opening the balcony doors. The balcony was small, six by four foot. A dried-up, shrivelled pot plant sat on the floor, but other than that it was empty.

Mackinnon leaned on the railings and looked down at the small square of grass below. There was no way Asad could have escaped this way. The balconies were too far apart. He'd have to be an extreme athlete to make the jump, and even then, it would be risky.

He heard laughter and looked down to see the young boy they'd run into on the stairs. He was alone, staring up at the balcony, waving.

Mackinnon sighed. It looked like his advice had been ignored.

"I've found her!" Charlotte called out.

Mackinnon walked back through the flat.

Charlotte poked her head out from one of the bedrooms. "She is in here, Jack. She was hiding behind the wardrobe."

As Mackinnon walked through the doorway, the young girl shivered and took a step back, pressing herself against the wall as though she hoped to disappear.

She was small and slight. Glossy black hair hung either side of her face, and her dark brown eyes looked haunted.

Mackinnon stopped a few feet away from the child. The last thing he wanted to do was traumatise Aleena any more than she had been already.

He attempted a reassuring smile. "Aleena? We've been looking for you. Your mum will be very glad we found you."

Aleena didn't speak. She just stared at Mackinnon, her eyes big and shiny with tears.

Badar burst into the room. "That's not Aleena! That's her cousin, Liann. She is my daughter."

Mackinnon turned just as Aleena's uncle pushed his way past him.

"What lies are you telling them, child?" he asked fiercely, putting an arm around Aleena's shoulders and pulling her tightly against him.

The little girl froze.

Mackinnon shot a glance at Charlotte. The girl looked exactly like Aleena.

Charlotte shook her head. "I'm sure it's Aleena."

"Nonsense," Badar said through gritted teeth. "I'll have to ask you to leave. You're upsetting my daughter."

Mackinnon noticed a slight shift in Badar's gaze. It was merely a momentary flicker, but it was enough.

Badar had looked at the bed. Why?

Mackinnon kneeled on the carpet and lifted the duvet, exposing the bottom of the divan bed.

It had storage beneath in the form of two large drawers.

"What are you doing?" Badar's voice was panicked.

If he hadn't been sure he was on the right track before, Mackinnon was convinced now. He yanked open the first drawer, only to find it filled with spare bedding and towels. Then he tugged the second drawer. It was harder to open, stiffer, and definitely had something heavier inside.

Mackinnon pulled the drawer open wide, revealing Asad's hiding place. Aleena's father was curled up in a ball. He blinked at the sudden light.

"So that's where—" Charlotte started to say, but before she could finish her sentence, Asad launched himself out the drawer, barrelling into Mackinnon and sending him off balance.

Mackinnon crashed back into a chest of drawers, which smashed against his ribs painfully as Asad made a dash for the front door.

He'd taken them all by surprise and managed to leg it down the hall before anyone stopped him.

Mackinnon gave a growl of frustration. He'd been caught napping, but there was no way he was going to let Asad get away. He pushed himself to his feet and ran after him.

CHAPTER FIVE

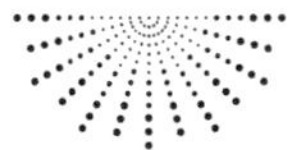

"Oh, no, you don't," Charlotte said, holding out her arm to block Aleena's uncle's exit from the bedroom.

Badar had grabbed the child by the arm and pulled her along behind him, intending to follow his brother out of the flat.

"You have no right to detain me here. This is *my* daughter." His voice was higher pitched than usual, and the tendons in his neck strained as he shouted.

"If this child is your daughter, then you'll be able to provide some evidence. Where is her mother?"

"At work," he snapped.

"Do you have your daughter's birth certificate? Passport?"

He started to shake his head, but then his eyes lit up and he nodded. "Yes. I have her passport."

"Good. Can I see it?"

Badar nodded but didn't let go of the little girl's arm.

Charlotte had been searching for Aleena for the past eight

days. She'd looked at her photograph so many times the girl's face was imprinted on her brain.

It wasn't possible for two girls to look so alike, was it? Badar claimed this young girl was Aleena's cousin. But they looked *identical*. Charlotte could have sworn this was the missing child. But Badar was insistent, and if he did have a passport that proved this girl was his daughter, they would be back to square one in their hunt for Aleena.

Charlotte walked past a couple of officers, who were looking through notes and scraps of paper on the telephone table, as she followed Badar and the girl into the kitchen.

Badar opened the second drawer beneath the kitchen counter and then lifted his hand and crooked a finger at Charlotte, beckoning her closer. She suppressed a shudder. He gave her the creeps.

The little girl was shivering even though they were in the heights of a heatwave and the flat was sweltering. Was she scared of Badar?

He rifled through the drawer, pushing aside takeaway menus and an instruction manual for a microwave, and then proudly pulled out a burgundy-coloured passport.

He handed it to Charlotte with a smug grin. "There you go. Is that proof enough? Perhaps you could gather your colleagues together and get out of my flat. It's a disgrace that you've come here at such a time. You're persecuting my family when *we* are the victims. My poor niece is missing. You should be looking for her."

Charlotte glanced at the child, who was looking at the floor. Even if this child wasn't Aleena, there was something seriously wrong. She was scared. Anyone could see that. But if this was her home and Badar was really her father, then why would she be afraid?

Sergeant McDougall's voice carried through from the hallway as he instructed one of the officers to remove the sofa cushions.

Charlotte flicked through the passport, looking for the photograph page, and was surprised to see the same young face staring at her. So this *was* Aleena's cousin. She was the spitting image of Aleena.

Unless...

Charlotte frowned, snapped the passport shut and looked Badar directly in the eye. "You and your brother planned this all along, didn't you? It wasn't a spur of the moment thing, at all. You've been planning this for months."

The smug smile had left Badar's face, and he blinked at her, licking his dry lips. "What are you talking about?"

Charlotte held up the passport. "This. You got this passport five months ago to help your brother smuggle his daughter out of the country. What better way to do it than under the name of *your* daughter. Where is your real daughter? At school?"

Badar opened his mouth and muttered something incomprehensible.

Charlotte kneeled down, so she was at eye level with the child. "Is your name Aleena? I need you to tell me the truth, so we can take you back to your mum."

The child slowly raised her head and gave a small nod.

It was enough for Charlotte. She stood up. "We're going to be taking Aleena back to her mother. If you keep up the pretence that she is your daughter, then we will do DNA testing to prove otherwise. Of course, we will also check with your daughter's school and ask your neighbours."

Badar pushed past her and slammed the kitchen door. Charlotte looked up to see him brandishing a knife. He must have taken it from the kitchen drawer.

She carefully pushed the child behind her, blocking Aleena from the knife, and put her hands up. "Don't do anything stupid, Badar."

It didn't take Mackinnon long to catch up with Aleena's father. Asad's smoking habit made him tire quickly. For Mackinnon, it was the most satisfying collar he'd had in a long time.

As he slammed into Asad, sending him sprawling onto the ground, whoops and heckles sounded from group of teenagers hanging around a souped-up BMW, but he ignored them, pulling Asad roughly to his feet and reading him his rights.

"Was that Aleena in your brother's flat?"

"No comment. I'm not saying anything until I have a lawyer," Asad wheezed.

"Suit yourself," Mackinnon said. "Just so you know, her mother's been worried sick."

"Why should I care about that old slapper. She isn't fit to be Aleena's moral guardian. Did you know she had affairs with not one but two men while we were married?"

Mackinnon did know that, only because Aleena's mother had tearfully confessed. Over the past eight days he felt he'd learned every murky secret in her life.

Rather than take Asad back to the flat, he led him straight

to the squad van, so he could be transported straight to the station.

As he handed Asad over to the officers, one of them said, "It's all kicking off upstairs. The uncle's got a knife."

Mackinnon felt a stab of panic. He'd been so intent on chasing down Asad, he'd underestimated the brother. They had nothing on file for Badar. He had no history of violence.

"Has anyone been hurt?"

"No, but there's a tense stand-off. He's in the kitchen with the kid and DC Brown."

Mackinnon took off at a run.

Sergeant Brian McDougall hammered on the door. "You all right in there, DC Brown?"

"We are okay at the moment," Charlotte said, trying to keep calm.

She had stepped back, getting as much distance between her and Badar as possible in the small kitchen. With enough space, if Badar attempted to stab or slash at her with the knife, she had room to move and a chance to grab his arm.

"This isn't going to end well unless you put that knife down," she told him. "There's no way you can get away with this. Your flat is crawling with police officers. Your brother will have been caught by now. It's over, Badar."

He scowled. "You're just saying that. He's probably escaped."

Charlotte shook her head. "No, he hasn't."

She spoke with confidence, knowing that Mackinnon would run himself into the ground before letting a suspect escape. He'd worked this area for a long time and knew all the cut-throughs and alleyways where a suspect could hide.

"Aleena doesn't need to see her uncle holding a knife. Put it down," Charlotte said.

He still held the knife in front of him, though not as aggressively as before.

Charlotte sensed he was weakening. "Aleena's mother just wants her little girl back. How would you feel if someone had taken your daughter?"

"It's not the same. Her mother is a disgusting…" He broke off shamefaced as Aleena began to cry.

Charlotte was still tense. He wasn't angry any more, but he was still holding the knife. She needed to get him to put it down.

"Just put the knife on the kitchen counter and we'll both leave the kitchen, okay? If you don't, today's going to get a whole lot worse for you very quickly."

With a sigh he put the knife down, and Charlotte felt a rush of relief.

She opened the kitchen door. "We're going to cuff you now, Badar, and take you to the station to answer some questions."

Badar nodded as Charlotte stood back to let Sergeant McDougall do the honours.

Aleena's small hand gripped Charlotte's. She smiled down at the child. "Everything's going to be all right now. We're going to take you home."

Sergeant McDougall had handcuffed Badar and was leading him along the hallway when Mackinnon appeared in the entrance to the flat.

"They told me there was a knife incident. I thought…" He trailed off and then added, "All under control?"

"Yep," Sergeant McDougall nodded at Badar. "I'm taking him downstairs now."

Mackinnon turned to Charlotte as Aleena closed her eyes and turned her head into Charlotte's waist. It must have been overwhelming for the poor kid.

"What happened?"

"I found a passport with Aleena's picture and her cousin's name. It looks like Maria was right. They were planning to take Aleena out of the country," Charlotte said, wishing her hands would stop trembling.

"I'm glad everyone's okay," Mackinnon said. "For a minute there, I really thought…"

"Yeah, things escalated pretty quickly." She tried to smile, but her face felt numb.

After Aleena had been reunited with her mother and the initial reports had been filed, Charlotte and Mackinnon grabbed a takeaway coffee, intending to walk back to Wood Street Station together in the sunshine.

He was concerned Charlotte was putting a brave face on things. Though, she insisted she was fine.

He took a sip of his steaming hot coffee, and as the hot sun beat down on the back of his head, he wondered whether he should have opted for an iced coffee like Charlotte.

"Nice?" he asked, nodding at the fancy whipped cream concoction Charlotte was holding.

"Very nice. Creamy and extremely sweet, and it probably contains my entire recommended calorie allowance for the day." She grinned.

Mackinnon delved in his pocket for his mobile phone when it began to ring. He glanced at the screen. "It's DI Tyler."

"Nice result, Jack," Tyler said when Mackinnon answered. "It didn't go down the way we expected, but it was a good result all the same."

"Yes, it got a bit hairy there for a while when the uncle decided to wave a knife around, but DC Brown handled the situation. Aleena is back with her mother, so we're calling it a win."

"And so you should," Tyler said. "I think a celebratory drink is in order."

"So do I, are you buying?"

Tyler muttered something about feeling unwell and then hung up.

Mackinnon laughed. "Tyler's pretty pleased with the outcome. Probably not pleased enough to put his hand in his pocket though." He took another sip of coffee. "How are you feeling now?"

He was, of course, referring to the incident with the knife. Events like that tended to stick with you. They might not result in a physical injury, but mentally they could still scar an officer.

Charlotte shrugged. "I'm not going to lie, it was terrifying. But I don't think he really intended to hurt me. He was panicking."

Mackinnon nodded. Sadly, in many cases of knife crime, the incident wasn't preplanned but the result of someone lashing out due to panic or anger.

They were almost back at the station when his phone rang.

"I bet that's DI Tyler again. He's probably just thought up a great excuse as to why he can't buy the drinks this evening." Charlotte grinned before taking a slurp of her fancy coffee.

But when Mackinnon looked at his phone, he saw it wasn't DI Tyler. "It's DCI Brookbank."

He answered the call. "Are you calling to congratulate us, sir?"

"Sorry… for what?" The DCI's voice was gruff.

"The Aleena case, sir. We've just reunited the young girl with her mother."

"Oh, yes. Well done. Very good. But unfortunately that wasn't why I was calling, Jack."

Mackinnon frowned and shot a glance at Charlotte, who was busy draining the last of her coffee.

"DI Tyler's been taken ill, and I'm short of officers at the moment. I need you to be SIO temporarily on a case."

"I hope it's nothing serious."

"Food poisoning. It's come on very suddenly. I just hope it's not norovirus. Officers will be dropping like flies."

"I hope it's not as well, sir."

"Now, about this case. The body of a young woman has been dumped behind a Chinese restaurant on Gravel Lane. Can you attend?"

Mackinnon stepped aside as two men in suits and fancy shirts with contrasting collars strode towards him. "Absolutely, sir. I'm with DC Brown. We'll head there now."

"Good. Thank you. And Jack…"

"Yes?"

"Prepare yourself. It sounds like a nasty one."

CHAPTER SIX

WHEN THEY REACHED the crime scene, it was two p.m. The alleyway had already been cordoned off, and a screen had been erected to hide the body from passers-by walking along Gravel Lane. The narrow alley ran between the Supreme Chinese Takeaway and Linda's Launderette. Litter dotted the ground. Yellowing leaflets, drink cans and empty crisp wrappers had been blown into a pile against the wall. A large graffiti mural, spray-painted in garish pink and fluorescent green, contrasted against the white rendered wall of the launderette. The vent just above Mackinnon's head pumped out hot, steamy air.

The uniformed officer, standing beside the crime scene tape nodded when they approached. Looking a little green around the gills, he attempted a weak smile as Mackinnon and Charlotte held out their IDs.

"You're the SIO?" he asked, looking up at Mackinnon and pushing his damp hair back from his sweaty forehead.

Mackinnon nodded. "Temporary SIO."

"Poor kid. We were first on the scene, and it's not a pretty sight. At first, I thought she'd overdosed. But the pathologist isn't so sure. He got here before you because he was leaving another crime scene just around the corner when he got the call."

Mackinnon and Charlotte donned protective coveralls, overshoes, and gloves to minimise contamination of the crime scene. As always, Mackinnon struggled to fit his large frame in the pale blue suit.

Cursing under his breath and tugging uncomfortably at the suit, he waited for the officer to detach the crime scene tape and allow them access to the scene.

"I hate these suits," he grumbled.

Charlotte looked down at her own baggy suit. "It's good to know there are some benefits to being short."

They walked along the alley, and as they got closer, Mackinnon saw the corpse was propped up against a large communal bin. Her legs were positioned straight out in front of her, and her torso pressed back against the blue plastic side of the bin. At first glance, it did look like she could be an overdose victim. Maybe she'd only been intending to get high, but the strength of the drugs was too much for her. Had she sat down, intending to wait until the sickness passed only to find the hit had been too much for her system?

Her hair was dark blonde and hung around her face in lank clumps. She was tiny, almost childlike. It was hard to judge exactly from her position, but Mackinnon guessed she couldn't be much taller than five foot and probably weighed about seven stone. She was thin, but not unhealthily so.

The pathologist, Dr Duncan Blair, was crouched over the

young woman's body. Although Mackinnon knew him by reputation, he hadn't worked with him before. When he saw Mackinnon and Charlotte approach, he straightened his tall, lean frame and nodded. "The photographers are almost done, and I'm nearly finished here, but we didn't want to move her until you'd attended the scene."

Now standing directly in front of the young woman's body, Mackinnon got a better look at her blotchy skin and noticed long scratch marks criss-crossing her arms.

"Thanks," Mackinnon said. "I appreciate it."

It helped to see the victim in situ. Of course, there were crime scene photographs, but that wasn't the same as seeing the victim in real life. It got under your skin, but that was all part of the job. Photographs allowed too much detachment in Mackinnon's opinion. The crime scene itself made death uncomfortably real, and when you were trying to get justice for the victims of crime, that was important.

Her clothes seemed odd. She was only wearing an oversized blue T-shirt. It swamped her small body, and there was no sign of her skirt or trousers nearby.

"So do you think it was an accidental death? Did she walk down the alleyway alone, or did someone dump her here?"

He crouched down, taking a closer look at the woman's body. The strongest smell in the alleyway was that of fried food coming from the Chinese takeaway next to them, so Mackinnon guessed she hadn't been here long. On a hot day like this, a body started to decompose quickly.

He noticed along with the scratch marks there were circular, red marks around the woman's wrists. Had she been tied up?

He pointed them out to the pathologist. "Ligature marks?"

The pathologist nodded thoughtfully. "Yes, it appears that way to me." He frowned. "It's a strange one. At first glance, it does look like she overdosed, and I can't immediately see another cause of death. There are no external injuries apart from these marks on her arms. But the ligature marks do suggest that something happened to this poor woman. She still has her underwear on, but the T-shirt looks far too big for her."

"I wonder what caused those other marks on her arms?" Charlotte asked.

"The scratches?" Mackinnon asked. "They could be self-inflicted. Incredibly itchy skin can be a side-effect of some drugs can't it, Dr Blair?"

Dr Blair nodded. "It can, but there are also these small bumps on her arms." His hands were encased in blue nitrile gloves, and he pointed at some of the raised spots on the victim's arm. Some of the marks were pink, and others were red with the hint of yellow, suggesting infection.

"Yes, I was wondering what caused them," Charlotte said. "It looks like some kind of rash?"

"Perhaps," Dr Blair said but didn't seem convinced. "I should be able to tell you more after I've done the post-mortem. We'll be able to tell if she was on any drugs. She hasn't been here long. My guess would be she died three hours ago at most."

"Do you think she died here?"

"Possibly. I can't say for certain."

Mackinnon looked down at the woman and wondered what had happened to her. She looked so young. "Did you find any ID on the body?"

The pathologist shook his head. "As far as I know, no bag, phone, or wallet has been found in the vicinity."

Mackinnon stepped back, narrowly avoiding a puddle. For the past week, it had been twenty-eight degrees or above and hadn't rained. He didn't even want to think about the contents of that puddle.

As the crime scene team moved about laying down markers and taking pictures, Mackinnon looked around for the crime scene manager. He felt hotter than ever and slightly claustrophobic standing in the narrow alleyway.

There was a high-pitched yelp that made everyone turn. The source of the noise was a small black cat yowling in displeasure as the officer standing guard beside the crime scene tape had tried to shoo it away.

With no regard for crime scene procedure, the cat promptly scampered up the alleyway before springing up to climb over a wire fence and disappearing among the weeds.

There were a few chuckles and bursts of nervous laughter as the sudden appearance of the interloper lightened the tension.

But Mackinnon didn't laugh.

He wasn't used to being the SIO, and it suddenly hit him that *he* was responsible for finding out what had happened to this poor young woman. Did she have a family? Had she been reported missing? Or was she an addict whose family had long since washed their hands of her?

He stretched his fingers, his hands sweaty beneath the blue nitrile gloves, and turned to Charlotte. "I think the first thing we need to do is to talk to the owners of the takeaway and the launderette. We want to know if anyone saw anything and also find out if they've got functioning security cameras." He pointed at a white security camera fixed above the side door of the Chinese takeaway. "With any luck, that's not just a deterrent but a working camera."

Charlotte nodded. "I'll do that now. I'll talk to the owners of the restaurant and the launderette myself and organise a uniform door-to-door of the other businesses in the area."

Mackinnon nodded at the rear of the alley towards the wire fence and the weeds growing through it, mostly made up of young buddleia plants. Buddleia seemed to sprout everywhere, even occasionally out of brickwork. "Good. I'm going to take a look around the back of the alleyway. I'm wondering if she came from the street or from back there."

DC Charlotte Brown knocked on the front door of Supreme Chinese Takeaway. She'd had no luck at the launderette. The woman working the morning shift said she hadn't seen anything out of the ordinary and they had no security cameras. It was past lunchtime, and though she could hear noise coming from inside the takeaway as well as smell the spices and hot oil from the kitchens, the door was locked.

When there was no reply, she knocked again.

Finally a young Chinese woman opened the door. She had bobbed, shiny black hair, and her eyes narrowed in irritation as she unlocked the door.

"We're closed. Don't open again until five."

Charlotte held up her ID. "Are you the manager?"

The woman shook her head. "I'll get my father."

She led Charlotte inside and pointed to the seats in front of the large window. Charlotte didn't sit down but instead slowly paced the small waiting area in front of the counter while watching the people walking past on the street outside.

A moment later a man appeared behind the counter. He had an open, friendly face. He smiled. "I'm Chen Lin, the manager. How can I help?"

"The body of a young woman was found in the alleyway next to your premises this morning." Charlotte paused to judge his reaction.

The smile slid from his face. "What happened to her?"

"That's what we'd like to find out. I wondered if you or any of your staff heard or saw anything unusual this morning?"

"I didn't hear anything. Sorry. It's usually quite noisy in the kitchens when we are working. We start prepping for lunch about ten."

"Do you have CCTV?" Charlotte asked. "We noticed the camera above your side entrance that leads out onto the alleyway."

He nodded. "We do. I can show you now. You're welcome to take it with you."

"Thank you," Charlotte said following Mr Lin as he led her behind the counter and through into the kitchens.

Inside the large kitchen, there were two people busily clearing up. One was Mr Lin's daughter, who'd originally opened the door. The other was a young Chinese lad, who Charlotte guessed to be in his late teens. Acne scars peppered his skin.

They both watched Charlotte with curiosity, and she guessed they'd listened in to her conversation with their father.

"This is my daughter, Ran, and my son, Sung," Mr Lin said. "They both work with me. It's a family business."

"I'm DC Brown," Charlotte said. "Did either of you hear or see anything out of the ordinary this morning?"

Sung nodded and paused in his wiping down of the stainless steel worktop. "I did."

Charlotte looked at him sharply. "What did you see?"

"I think I saw the man who killed her."

"You did not!" His sister rolled her eyes.

"This is serious," Charlotte said. "If you saw something, I need to know."

"He's been watching too much TV," Ran said. "We didn't see anything."

"Quiet, Ran. Let your brother talk," Mr Lin said, removing his apron.

"If he wasn't the man who killed her, he was acting very suspiciously." Sung shot his sister a superior glance. "It was about eleven a.m. I was standing outside, having a cigarette because Dad won't let me smoke inside."

"It's against the law, Sung," Mr Lin said, shooting Charlotte an apologetic smile.

"Well, I was outside smoking," Sung continued, "and I saw a man with a big bag, like the type you'd take to the gym only bigger. He went down the alley. I wondered what he was doing because it's a dead end. I said good morning and he ignored me. I did think about keeping an eye on him, but Dad had given me a long list of things to do in the kitchen this morning." He gave his father an accusatory look.

"How big was this holdall?"

"Huge, and very heavy. He was quite a big guy, but he was struggling with the weight of it.

"Do you remember what he looked like?"

He shrugged. "Not really. I got the impression he didn't want to be seen. He was white, and that's about the only thing I can tell you. He was wearing a hoodie and tracksuit bottoms, I think, or maybe jeans." His forehead crinkled as he tried to remember. "Sorry, that's all I can recall."

"That's very helpful. Hopefully he's been caught on your CCTV."

"You're welcome to take a look," Mr Lin said. "It's time-stamped, so we can start by looking at around eleven a.m."

He ushered Charlotte into a small office area just off the kitchen and pulled out a wheeled computer chair so she could sit down. He perched on the table beside her and accessed the CCTV through his desktop computer.

Satisfied that it was very unlikely the victim could have come from the other end of the alleyway since there were no holes in the fence and the thick buddleia stems and long wild grass showed no signs of recent trampling, Mackinnon walked back to have a chat with the crime scene manager.

While he was talking to the crime scene manager, Dr Duncan Blair joined them to announce he had finished his preliminary examinations. "We'll get her back to the morgue now, DS Mackinnon. If that's all right with you?"

Mackinnon nodded. "When do you think you'll be able to get to this postmortem?"

Dr Blair grimaced. "I've got them lined up, I'm afraid. Just before I got this call, I attended a scene at the Towers Estate. An elderly lady died in her flat, and her body had gone undiscovered for three days. So I'm sorry, DS Mackinnon, but she and three others are in the queue ahead of your case."

"I don't suppose you could prioritise this one? I have a bad feeling about it. It's unlikely she caused the ligature marks on her wrists herself, which means we could be looking for a murderer."

Dr Blair shrugged. "I don't make the rules. If you need the PM to be prioritised, you'll have to get your boss to bump it up the queue through official channels."

Mackinnon felt a flash of impatience. Though most of the time he enjoyed his job, feeling he was making a difference, he didn't enjoy the bureaucracy. Surely common sense dictated a suspected murder victim should get priority over an elderly lady who appeared to have died from natural causes. But he knew it wasn't Duncan Blair's fault. He was just following procedure, and Mackinnon would have to do the same. When he got back to the station, he'd ask Brookbank to prioritise this young woman's postmortem.

Taking one last look at the victim, Mackinnon's gaze fell again on the bumps in her forearms. "Do you think those marks could be injection sites?"

"Unlikely. Injection sites are usually hidden between fingers or toes, or at least on the underneath of the arm." He chewed on his lip and then said, "You see how some of the bumps are yellowish? That indicates infection."

"An infected rash? An allergy?" Mackinnon guessed.

Dr Blair shook his head as he looked down at the woman's body. "I don't think so. If I had to put money on it, I'd say they look like insect bites."

CHAPTER SEVEN

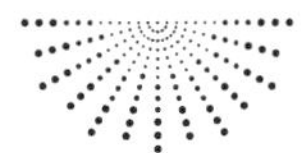

BACK AT WOOD STREET STATION, Mackinnon leaned back in his chair and looked glumly at the mounds of paperwork on his desk. He still had to file piles of the stuff for the Aleena case, but he'd have to get to that later. This new case was his priority.

He didn't like putting off paperwork. He preferred to fill out forms and write statements while the details were still fresh in his mind. Not that he could ever be accused of *enjoying* paperwork. That was one of the downsides of the job.

He'd already tried to see Brookbank, as he was eager to get the postmortem underway as soon as possible, but Brookbank's new assistant, Janice, said he was having an important phone call with the Commissioner and couldn't be disturbed. She promised to call him as soon as the DCI was free.

Mackinnon stared at the phone on his desk, which stubbornly remained silent.

The loud hum of the air conditioning, which never seemed to work properly, was annoying. It was still too hot. It was never quiet in the open-plan office. There were always phones ringing and the constant murmur of voices.

Mackinnon got up and opened a window. Well, he opened it as far as he could. Health and safety rules meant the windows were prevented from opening more than two inches.

It made no difference to the hot, stuffy air.

He took a drink from his water bottle and scrolled through the reports on his computer screen, searching the police database for recent reports of missing women aged between fifteen and thirty. Distressingly, there was a long list of them, and that was just in this area. If their victim came from outside London, they'd have to widen the net, and things would get even more complicated.

He was sure Brookbank would agree to prioritise the case, especially when Mackinnon told him they had a witness who'd seen a suspect carrying a large holdall into the alleyway.

Unfortunately, despite Charlotte's best efforts, the CCTV had been a bust. The angle of the camera had been too high, and they'd only managed to get a glimpse of the top of their suspect's navy-blue hood, but Brookbank wouldn't ignore the witness report.

Mackinnon had given Charlotte and DC Collins the unenviable task of scouring through all CCTV from businesses along Gravel Lane. He was still waiting for the outcome from the door-to-door enquiries. Surely someone else had to have seen the man in the navy blue hoodie carrying the large holdall.

If the holdall had been as heavy as Sung Lin stated, chances were their suspect would have used a vehicle. If they could get the vehicle's registration number, they may be able to get an ID.

Finally the phone rang, and Mackinnon snatched it up.

"Jack, the DCI's free now if you'd like to come up," Janice said.

"Thanks, I'll be right there."

He took the stairs two at a time, eager to get to Brookbank's office. He felt oddly nervous. This case was already weighing heavily on his shoulders. But he had no reason to think Brookbank would turn down his request.

They hadn't always got along well in the past, but Brookbank was a good police officer. He wouldn't let personal differences get in the way of an investigation.

Brookbank called out a gruff, "Enter," after Mackinnon rapped on the door.

"Take a seat, Jack," the DCI said. "Sorry to keep you waiting. How did it go?"

"We've got a witness. At approximately eleven a.m. a man was seen carrying a large holdall into the alley where our victim was found. So far, we haven't been able to get any CCTV images to back up the witness report, but I think her body was dumped there, sir. I strongly suspect foul play."

"Yes, I can see why you would. What have you done so far?"

"We've got a door-to-door enquiry going. DC Collins and DC Brown are going through the CCTV both public and private."

"Any other witnesses yet?"

"Not yet."

"An ID for the dead woman?"

"No, I'm going through reports of missing persons, but so far, nothing."

"Well, I know being SIO on a case can be stressful, but you seem to be handling it. Let me know if you have any problems," Brookbank said and then nodded at Mackinnon in dismissal.

"Thank you, sir," Mackinnon said, "There actually is something you can do for me."

Brookbank looked up. "Oh, what's that?"

"The pathologist is incredibly busy at the moment, but I'd like to bump this postmortem up the queue. Their pathology department needs the request to come directly from you, though."

Brookbank nodded slowly. "I agree with your assessment that this is looking like a murder investigation, so I'll put in the request now."

Mackinnon felt a rush of relief. "Thank you, sir. I appreciate it."

He got to his feet, eager to get back downstairs and get on with the task of identifying the victim.

"Oh, and Jack…" Brookbank said as Mackinnon was about to close the door behind him.

He paused. "Yes?"

"DI Tyler will take over the enquiry when he's recovered. But I'm impressed with how you've handled the pressure so far. We should talk about you going for your inspector exams."

Taken aback, Mackinnon nodded. "Yes, thank you, sir."

When he got back downstairs, Charlotte waved him over.

"We've got him on CCTV." Her eyes gleamed. "And Sung Lin was right. It's a huge holdall, and our victim could easily have fitted inside, in my opinion. Our suspect is a white male, approximately six foot two, and I'd say around thirteen stone."

"Excellent work," Mackinnon said. "Can I see the footage?"

Charlotte nodded. "It's CCTV from a bus. The number 22. Collins got them to email the appropriate clips. Here, take a look." She used the mouse to navigate to a video file and double-clicked.

The screen filled with a video of a man just like Sung Lin had described. The video was time-stamped ten forty-five a.m.. He was dressed in a navy blue hoodie and navy tracksuit bottoms. He'd pulled the hood around his face despite the warm weather they'd been having. No one would venture out dressed like that in a heatwave unless they had something they were trying to hide.

The suspect sat with his head down, staring at the ground. On the floor next to him, blocking the aisle, was a large blue holdall. It looked like it was made from tough nylon fabric, but Mackinnon couldn't see any brand or manufacturer's label.

He sat on the lower floor of the bus, and there were only two other passengers, both female. They might be able to track them down for an interview.

The suspect shuffled his feet. He wore white Adidas trainers, but there was nothing unusual about those. When he leaned forward and gripped the seat in front of him. Mackinnon wondered if they could get DNA from the bus but instantly dismissed the idea. It would be an impossible job trying to isolate DNA from a bus where there would be thousands of different DNA types all mixed in together. They would have a better shot at getting DNA from the victim's body.

Charlotte paused the video. "This is the best image we have of him. You can see part of his nose and cheek, enough to guess he's Caucasian, but we're not going to be able to ID him from this."

"No," Mackinnon said slowly. "But we can find out where and when he got on the bus… perhaps we can trace his whole journey."

Charlotte nodded. "Collins is already on it."

"Great stuff."

As they were waiting for Collins to send over more clips from the CCTV footage, Mackinnon made some coffee. He put a full mug on Charlotte's desk, knowing that it would be stone cold before she remembered to drink it, and then headed back to his own desk to resume his attempt to identify the victim.

He loosened his tie, undid his top button, and tried to ignore the uncomfortable heat as he scrolled through all the recent reports of missing young women.

He'd been at it for forty minutes when he suddenly stopped scrolling.

He focused on the photograph the police had been given by the worried parents of the missing woman.

Ashley Burrows, twenty-one. She'd been missing for ten days.

The photograph showed Ashley smiling, with shiny blonde hair, glowing smooth skin, and bright eyes. The contrast between the young woman he'd seen this morning and the woman in this photograph was huge, but he was sure it was her. The shape of her eyebrows, her chin, her jawline…

It was her.

They had an ID. Their victim now had a name. Ashley Burrows.

CHAPTER EIGHT

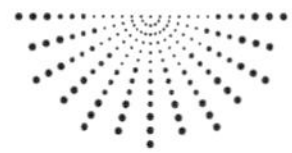

MACKINNON AND CHARLOTTE made it to York Square in Limehouse just before three p.m. Ashley Burrows's parents lived in one of the three-storey houses set around the green square.

Mackinnon had arranged for the family liaison officer, Kate Squires, to meet them there. She was experienced and would be a great help in making this difficult time go as smoothly as possible for Ashley's parents.

"I hate this part of the job," Charlotte said, leaning back in the passenger seat and staring straight ahead, watching a group of teenagers hanging around in the gardens.

"I know how you feel."

It had taken them over ten minutes to find a parking space, and even then they were only supposed to leave the car there for thirty minutes. Perhaps they should have taken the Underground, but it was a hot day, and Mackinnon didn't want to arrive at the Burrows's house crumpled and sweaty. It seemed disrespectful.

In the small amount of time he'd had before heading to Ashley's parents' house, Mackinnon had discovered as much as he could about Ashley. Social media made that side of the job much easier these days.

Mackinnon saw Kate walking towards the car in the rearview mirror and straightened his tie. "Ready?"

"Yes."

They both got out of the car and waited for the family liaison officer to approach.

"Sorry, have you been waiting long?"

Despite the heat of the day, Kate Squires looked fresh and smartly dressed. She wore a navy trouser suit, a crisp white cotton blouse, and low heels rather than her standard uniform.

As Mackinnon shrugged his jacket on, he wondered how she managed to look so smart in this heat.

"Not too long. It took us a while to find a parking space."

"I guessed it would. That's why I took the Underground."

Limehouse Station was only around the corner, so she hadn't had to walk far, but looking so cool after travelling on the tube was pretty impressive. Thanks to the hot weather they'd been experiencing, the Underground felt like an oven for most of the day.

"So, what do the parents know so far?" Kate asked as all three of them began to walk towards the Burrows's residence.

"Only that we want to speak to them concerning their daughter's disappearance. I think news like this is better delivered face-to-face."

Kate nodded. "Absolutely. I agree. There's no nice way to do it, but delivering the news in person shows more respect."

"I'd like to take the opportunity to take a look around

Ashley's bedroom if her parents have no objection," Charlotte said.

"Good idea," Mackinnon said as they crossed the road to walk in the shade.

"She still lives at home?" Kate said before correcting herself. "Sorry, lived at home?"

"Yes, she did. So her parents reported her missing the first evening she didn't come home," Mackinnon said. "That was ten days ago."

Ashley Burrows's body had been found that morning, and it was clear her death was relatively recent, which meant they needed to account for those nine days between the evening she went missing and today. Had she been held captive? It was looking more and more likely.

They stopped in front of the Burrows's glossy red door, and Mackinnon rang the doorbell.

"I can break the news if you'd like," Kate offered.

It was a hard job, and Mackinnon wasn't usually the type to take the easy way out, but Kate would be the officer offering the family support afterwards, so he accepted her offer.

The door opened, and a slim woman with heavily highlighted hair blinked at them. It was dark in the hallway and hard to make out her features. Despite the dim light, Mackinnon could see the family resemblance. Like her daughter, Maxine Burrows was very petite.

"Can I help you?"

Mackinnon introduced himself, and they all held up their IDs.

Maxine put a hand to her chest. "Is it bad news? It is, isn't it?"

"Could we come in, Mrs Burrows?" Mackinnon asked.

She nodded and called for her husband. Gripping the door so hard her knuckles turned white, she asked again, "Is it bad news? Please, just tell me."

After they stepped inside, they stopped beside the staircase.

A slim, bald man with thick, dark-rimmed glasses hurriedly made his way down the stairs. "What is it?"

"It's the police," Maxine said. "It's about Ashley."

Tim Burrows took charge, ushering everyone into the front room. Kate and Charlotte took a seat on the sofa, Mackinnon sat in the armchair beside them, and Maxine collapsed into the armchair opposite. Tim pulled over a chair from the dining table at the other end of the room, but he didn't sit down straight away. Instead, he leaned heavily on the back of the chair.

"What happened?" he asked, his face tense.

"I'm very sorry to tell you that we found the body of a young woman this morning. We believe it's Ashley," Kate said.

Maxine let out a guttural groan and then began to sob. Her husband moved beside her and squeezed her shoulder.

"What happened to her?" he asked. "Was it an accident?"

"We don't believe so," Mackinnon said. "But we are still working to determine the cause of death."

"Where did you find her?" Tim asked, dropping his hand from his wife's shoulder.

"Not too far from here. We found her beside a Chinese restaurant called The Supreme Chinese on Gravel Lane. We believe Ashley was moved there after she died."

"So you're saying she was murdered? Somebody killed

her?" Maxine raised her head and glared furiously at Mackinnon.

"We think so."

"Who?"

"We don't know yet. Can you think of anyone who could have done this? A violent ex-boyfriend? Someone paying her unwanted attention?"

"No, it doesn't make any sense. Everyone loved Ashley. She wasn't seeing anyone after breaking up with Noah, and he would never hurt her," Tim said.

Charlotte straightened. She had her tablet on her lap, ready to take notes. "When did Noah and Ashley break up?"

Maxine replied, "About a month ago."

"They were always breaking up and getting back together," Tim said. "They've been together since they were sixteen. Noah is a good lad. He's never been violent."

"I see," Mackinnon said. "Well, we'll arrange to talk to him too, in case he can provide any further information."

"Are you sure it's her?" Maxine asked suddenly, a spark of hope in her eyes.

Mackinnon had attended several death notifications and people's reactions were never predictable. Some wailed and screamed, others took the news silently, but the hope the police had got it wrong was one thing that was usually consistent.

"We are very confident that it is Ashley. You will be asked to identify the body."

"I'll do that," Tim said. He pulled his glasses off and rubbed a hand over his face.

"Kate is your family liaison officer. She will be available to answer any questions you might have. I know this is a terrible shock and the last thing you want to do is answer questions right now, but we really want to find out what happened to Ashley."

Both parents were silent.

"Did anything unusual happen in the days before Ashley's disappearance? Had she had trouble at work? An argument with a friend?"

Maxine shook her head, and Tim said, "No. Everything was perfectly normal. She was happy and planning a holiday to Costa Brava next month. There was nothing in Ashley's life that was dangerous. She was a good kid. Never took drugs, hardly ever drank. She was very health-conscious, always on at me to quit smoking." His face crumpled, and he rubbed his eyes.

"It must have been a stranger. Maybe someone followed her home from work," Maxine said. "You'll be able to see that on CCTV, won't you?"

"We are looking through the CCTV, yes," Mackinnon said. He decided not to press them on more questions right now. After they'd had a chance to think, they could remember something important. Random killings were nowhere near as common as some people thought. Most murder victims were killed by someone they knew.

"We haven't located Ashley's bag or mobile phone. Did she have a bag and phone with her when she left for work?"

"Yes," Maxine said. "She never left the house without her iPhone. She had loads of bags, but she was using a pink shoulder bag from River Island the day she went missing."

"Did she have a laptop?"

"Yes, but she wouldn't usually have taken that with her. It's probably in her bedroom."

After they'd answered some of the parents' questions, Mackinnon asked permission to take a look around Ashley's bedroom.

"Yes, I'll show you her room," Tim said. "She actually used the whole basement. There's a small kitchen, bedroom and bathroom, so it's relatively self-contained. It's impossible for young people to get a place around here now."

"It really is difficult," Charlotte agreed, and they followed Tim downstairs, leaving Kate to comfort Maxine.

It was darker and cooler in the basement area of the house. The bathroom was tiny. A white porcelain toilet, shower, and sink all crowded the small space.

A thin partition wall had been put up to divide what was once a single large basement room into a bedroom and kitchen.

"You're welcome to stay while we search," Mackinnon said, "but we won't take anything of Ashley's without your permission."

Tim stood in the doorway of his daughter's bedroom, not daring to step over the threshold. His eyes flickered about the room. "I'll leave you to it and go back upstairs to see if Maxine's all right."

After he left, Mackinnon and Charlotte pulled on gloves and set about methodically going through Ashley's belongings. It was a typical young woman's bedroom, although it was a little tidier than he'd expected. The walls were painted a light grey, matching the carpet.

There was no sign of the laptop.

As Mackinnon went through the chest of drawers, Charlotte looked under the bed and found plastic storage cases.

The drawers were crammed full of clothes, except the top

drawer which was filled with perfumes and make up. On top of the chest of drawers was a large freestanding mirror, with small photographs stuck on the frame with blutack.

He selected one to take a closer look. It was of Ashley and a young man, approximately Ashley's age. He was standing beside her with his arms around her waist. Noah, perhaps? He should be their next port of call.

Using his phone, he took pictures of the other photographs. They would need to speak to all of Ashley's friends as the investigation went on.

"Found anything?" Mackinnon asked, putting his phone back in his pocket.

"A lot of random stuff but nothing really useful," Charlotte said, still rifling through the boxes.

Mackinnon moved over to the built-in wardrobes and grimaced at the tightly packed clothes inside. It would take ages to have a proper look through all the clothes. He started with the coats first, checking the pockets.

He'd been searching for a few minutes when Charlotte suddenly said, "Bingo!"

He turned.

Charlotte held up a thick notebook with a blue cover decorated with pale butterflies. "It's a diary."

Mackinnon stopped what he was doing and looked over Charlotte's shoulder at the book. Ashley's diary. Did it hold all the answers?

Charlotte flipped through the pages. "It seems pretty mundane stuff… about work, mostly. Let's ask her parents if we can take it back to the station. It's going to take a while to read."

"Okay. Let's finish up here and then—" Mackinnon broke off as his mobile phone buzzed in his pocket.

It was a text message from DI Tyler. He was back at work, which meant Mackinnon was no longer acting SIO.

"Something important?" Charlotte asked as she replaced the lids on the storage boxes and pushed them back beneath the bed.

"Yes. Tyler's in charge of the investigation now, and he wants a briefing."

CHAPTER NINE

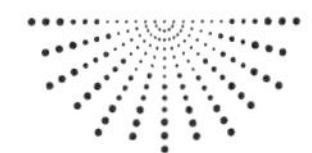

MACKINNON AND CHARLOTTE left York Square after getting contact details for Ashley's workplace and close friends, as well as her on and off again boyfriend, Noah Thorne. Kate Squires stayed with the Burrowses. She would remain with them, answering their questions, for as long as they needed her.

Mackinnon breathed a sigh of relief after they returned to the car and found they'd escaped without a ticket, despite spending far longer than the allowed thirty minutes.

It was four p.m. when they reached Wood Street Station.

"Her parents were adamant there was no one in her life who would hurt her. Do you think they're right about it being a random killing?" Charlotte asked as they climbed the stairs, heading for DI Tyler's briefing.

"Unlikely," Mackinnon said. "But I suppose we can't rule it out."

"She works as a travel agent, so that would bring her into

contact with a lot of people," Charlotte said, frowning. "Maybe her connection with her killer was through work rather than her personal life."

"Possible," Mackinnon said. "We'll definitely want to speak to her boss and colleagues."

"We could do that next?"

"We'll have to follow Tyler's lead. It will be his decision as to what we do next."

"Oh, yes. I suppose it will."

Mackinnon thought it should have been a relief handing over responsibility to Tyler, but he felt strangely possessive over this case and reluctant to step down as acting SIO. DI Tyler could be unorthodox at times, but he was an officer who got results. Ashley Burrows's case would be in safe hands, and Mackinnon would still be involved in the investigation, so his reluctance was odd. It was more a feeling than a logical, thought-out reaction.

Officers had already gathered in the incident room when they arrived. DI Tyler was at the front of the room standing beside a large whiteboard. He called the room to attention as Mackinnon and Charlotte entered.

Mackinnon went to the corner of the room and got himself a drink from the water tower as Tyler started to talk.

"First up, I want to say I'm very impressed with this department's work on the Aleena Khan case. Excellent police work. Now, I've gathered you all here because I want you to give your focus to our new investigation. DCI Brookbank has kindly brought in more officers to help." He nodded at two men and a woman Mackinnon recognised from the fraud squad. "We'll go around the room and you can update me. I'm late into this investigation, but from what I've heard, DS Mackinnon has done a great job so far, so let's keep it up. DC Collins, how are you getting on with the security camera footage?"

Collins slowly spun around on his chair to face the detective inspector. "I've managed to track our suspect on his bus journey. He embarked and returned at the same bus stop, on Mile End Road. I've been coordinating with the Met on the CCTV, and with any luck, I'll be able to use the footage to track where he went after he got off the bus. We know Ashley Burrows went missing ten days ago. She was last seen at five thirty at her place of work, Flyaway Travel Agents. I'd like to follow her route using security footage, but I could really do with an extra pair of eyes."

"DC Webb," Tyler said, scanning the room for the officer. "I'd like you to help DC Collins with that."

DC Webb gave a barely disguised groan. Trawling through camera footage was no one's idea of a good time, but in this day and age, it was often vital for a conviction.

"DS Mackinnon, I understand you and DC Brown have just got back from visiting Ashley's parents."

Mackinnon nodded and set his paper cup on the table in front of him. "Yes, they were understandably very upset. We left Kate Squires with them acting as the FLO. They had no idea who would want to harm their daughter. According to them, everyone loved Ashley. They gave us contact details for some of Ashley's close friends as well as her ex-boyfriend, Noah Thorne. We took a quick look at Ashley's bedroom, and DC Brown found a diary. I think it's worth taking a more thorough look at her bedroom in case we missed something in our quick search."

"Interesting. Is there anything in the diary that could help our investigation?"

Charlotte held up the diary, which she'd placed inside an evidence bag. "I had a quick look through, but I haven't had a chance to read the whole thing yet."

"All right. Give the diary to Evie." Tyler nodded at Yvonne Charlesworth, one of the police support staff Mackinnon had worked with many times. She was a hard worker and extremely thorough, the perfect choice to go carefully through the diary, looking for important evidence.

Charlotte walked over to Evie to give her the diary somewhat reluctantly. He knew she got on well with Evie and respected her, but Charlotte's natural curiosity made her want to be the one to read the diary.

"Thank you, DC Brown. I'd like you and DS Mackinnon to go to Flyaway Travel Agents after the briefing. Talk to her boss and the rest of the staff. Find out if something happened at work recently that struck them as odd. We need to find out as much as we can about Ashley's life. It's just after four, and the travel agents shuts at five thirty, so you should have time. When you're done there, I'd like you to go and speak to Noah Thorne."

Tyler wrapped up the meeting by assigning further tasks, and as the officers filed out of the room, he approached Mackinnon and Charlotte.

"Thanks for covering, Jack."

"Not a problem. How are you feeling now?"

"Still a little shaky. I can't stomach anything but water. Other than that, I'm tickety-boo," Tyler said wryly.

"I hope it's not contagious," Charlotte said. "It could be a stomach virus."

Tyler shook his head slowly. "No, I can promise you it wasn't that."

"How can you be so sure?" Charlotte asked, not looking convinced and keeping her distance.

Tyler sighed heavily. "If I tell you, you keep it to yourselves, understood?"

Mackinnon and Charlotte nodded.

"Last night I thought it would be a good idea to cook Janice dinner."

"Janice? Brookbank's new assistant?" Charlotte asked.

"Yes. Anyway, I really put the effort in. Got a Nigella Lawson cookbook and everything. I'd been shopping and remembered everything for the recipe apart from the prawns, but then I remembered I had some in the freezer. I put them on the draining board to defrost… for a few hours."

"That wasn't a good idea in this heat," Mackinnon said.

"Yes, I realise that now. Anyway, that's how I got sick. And I also managed to give Janice food poisoning, so I think I have royally screwed up that fledgling relationship."

"She might soften towards you after she's feeling better," Charlotte said.

"Maybe," Tyler said glumly. "But I don't like my chances." He glanced at his watch. "Anyway, enough about my depressing love life. You two better get to the travel agents."

Flyaway Travel Agents was on the corner of White Horse Road and Wakeling Street. It was within walking distance of York Square, and Mackinnon wondered if Ashley had usually walked to work alone. He made a mental note to ask Kate Squires later.

Flyaway Travel was printed in large yellow letters on a blue sign above the door. An A3-sized poster was in the window, listing bargain flights, and there were tempting pictures of white sandy beaches, blue skies, turquoise seas and palm trees hanging in the window too.

Mackinnon and Charlotte stepped inside the small office. On the right, there were four separate desks, only two were occupied. Each desk was approximately two foot behind the one in front.

The heat was stifling as the sun shone directly in the large window.

A tall woman got up from the furthest desk and made her way towards them. "Detectives?"

Charlotte had called ahead so the manager was expecting their visit. They introduced themselves and showed ID.

"I'm Heather Brooke, the manager here." She gave them a broad smile, but there were tears in her eyes.

She had a deep tan, and Mackinnon wondered if she took advantage of the frequent holiday deals or if her tan was out of a bottle.

She tucked her dark hair behind her ears. "I was so sorry to hear about Ashley. She was a lovely girl."

The other woman in the office kept sneaking glances their way but didn't introduce herself.

"Is there somewhere we could talk?" Mackinnon asked.

"It's probably best if we talk here, if that's okay with you? There is a small kitchen and toilet at the back of the office, but nowhere really we could sit and talk in private." She gestured to the other woman. "This is Sadie Griffith. She was close to Ashley, so you'll probably want to talk to her too."

Sadie didn't make eye-contact and fidgeted in her seat.

Heather sat back down behind her desk and Mackinnon and Charlotte sat in front of it.

"How long had Ashley been working for you?" Mackinnon asked.

Heather rifled through a drawer and pulled out a blue file. "She'd been here about eighteen months. This is her personnel file. I don't think there's anything useful in it but you may as well have it just in case."

Charlotte took it and thanked her then pulled out her tablet to start making notes.

"Had Ashley been upset about anything recently?" Mackinnon asked.

"Upset?"

"Issues with her boyfriend perhaps? Or maybe troublesome customers?"

Heather blinked and looked surprised at the question. "I'd assumed it was some kind of mugging gone wrong. Are you saying she was killed by someone she knew?"

"We're still in the early days of the investigation," Mackinnon said. "I know it's difficult, but we need to ask these sorts of questions."

"I understand, but Ashley was such a sunny, happy young thing. I can't believe anyone would want to hurt her."

"Sadly, murder doesn't discriminate. Even happy young things can become victims," Charlotte said.

Mackinnon shot a surprised glance at Charlotte, but her head was bent over the tablet as she made notes.

"Right. Of course, sorry," Heather said. "It's just all such a shock."

"Have you had any problems with customers recently?" Mackinnon asked trying to get the interview back on track.

"No. We haven't had any trouble. As you can see, it's only a small office, so I'm sure I would have noticed if Ashley was uncomfortable or having a problem with a customer."

"Did you ever meet her boyfriend, Noah Thorne?"

"Yes, a few times. He'd sometimes meet Ashley after work, and they'd go out to dinner. I think they were on a break at the moment, though."

"Had she been upset about that?"

"Not really. They were always breaking up and getting back together. She was too young to settle down if you ask me."

"Do you know why they broke up this time?"

Heather thought for a moment and tapped a finger against her chin. Her nails were long and painted a bright pink. "I'm not sure what caused the breakup this time. Sadie? Do you have any idea?"

Sadie looked nervous. Mackinnon guessed she was approximately the same age as Ashley. A long, lank fringe covered her high forehead and obscured most of her eyes. Small spots covered the lower part of her cheeks.

She shrugged. "Just the usual. Noah was going out drinking too much. Ashley didn't like it. She was a bit of a health nut."

Heather nodded. "She was. Always eating fruit and rice and vegetables for lunch. She was a vegan. She went to the gym three nights a week too."

"Do you know which gym she used?" Mackinnon asked.

"One on Mile End Road. Fitness First, I think," Sadie said and chewed on her lip.

Mackinnon didn't reply straight away. He thought Sadie looked like she had something more to tell them.

She glanced at him and then Charlotte and then finally looked down at the floor. "Things aren't always what they seem."

"How do you mean?"

"Just that on the surface, Ashley was happy and bubbly, but she actually had some problems."

"What problems?"

"I don't really feel comfortable saying. It's like not respecting her memory or something…."

"Sadie, this is a murder investigation. Somebody killed your friend, and we're trying to catch the person responsible. If you know something was bothering Ashley, you should tell us what it was."

"I don't know if it's related to what happened. It might not even be important."

"We won't know until you tell us."

Sadie chewed on her lip again and wrapped a lock of her hair around her index finger. "She'd seen the doctor recently. She hadn't been feeling well, but the doctor wasn't much help. He said it was all in her head."

"She was depressed?" Mackinnon asked.

"That's what the doctor said, but Ashley said they just write everything off as depression these days."

"Do you know if she was taking any medication?" Mackinnon asked.

"Sorry, Ashley didn't mention that."

Mackinnon tried to recall if he'd seen any bottles of pills in

Ashley's bedroom and bathroom. He was sure he would have noticed something like that. But it would be worth taking a second look.

"Anyway, I just meant that Ashley seemed like she had it all, the perfect life, but she'd been pretty down recently. She'd been attending some kind of group. Counselling, probably."

"Do you know where the group met or what they were called?"

Sadie shook her head.

"Any idea?" Mackinnon asked, looking at Heather.

"No. I had no idea Ashley had been having any problems." Heather wiped a tear away from her cheek. "It's awful. I spent all day with her at work, but I never thought… She seemed so happy."

Sadie twirled her hair around her finger and shook her head. "She only looked that way on the surface. She wasn't happy. Not at all."

CHAPTER TEN

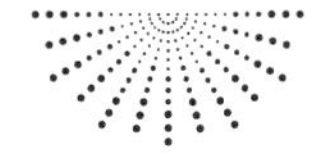

IT WAS ALMOST five thirty when Mackinnon and Charlotte left the travel agents. The traffic around the Barbican was heavy.

At six p.m. they finally arrived at the Golden Lane Estate. Noah Thorne lived on the fifth floor of Great Arthur House.

"The yellow panels are certainly eye-catching," Charlotte commented as they walked past flowers and shrubs growing in concrete tubs in the square beside Great Arthur House.

Mackinnon grinned. "It's a nice estate. I lived here for a while. There is supposed to be an amazing view of St Paul's Cathedral from the roof garden."

"Supposed to be?"

"Yes, I never got to see it. It used to be open to residents, but it was closed after a couple of suicides."

They looked up at the fifteen-storey building. It towered over the other buildings in the estate.

"Are the flats still all council?" Charlotte asked.

"No, quite a few of them were purchased under the Right to Buy scheme. Some are still council owned though."

"Do we know if Noah Thorne is a council tenant?"

"He's privately renting the flat."

"That must cost a few bob."

"Yes, he works in banking," Mackinnon said, and then catching the look on Charlotte's face added, "He's not an investment banker. He is an administrative assistant for a banking firm."

They took the lift to the fifth floor, sharing it with a woman carrying a grumpy toddler.

When Noah Thorne opened the door, Mackinnon quietly assessed him as Charlotte carried out the introductions. Noah was five foot seven and had small dark eyes and fluffy brown hair. His eyebrows were arched, making Mackinnon wonder whether he plucked them. It gave him the appearance of being constantly surprised.

His red-rimmed eyes and the way he folded his arms over his chest, protectively, showed he was emotionally fragile. He'd been affected by the news of Ashley's death, but that didn't mean he was innocent. It only meant he was upset. Being a murderer didn't preclude a person from emotion. Most killers weren't cold, calculating psychopaths. They were angry, disturbed and emotional.

"I can't believe it," Noah said as he let them in. "I knew something was wrong but hoped she'd be okay."

He led them into a sitting room that looked like the domain of a single man. There were no photographs or pictures on the wall. No cushions. There was a large flat screen TV, dark brown leather sofa with matching armchair and a huge black reclining chair.

Noah sat down on the recliner, and Mackinnon and Charlotte sat on the sofa so they were facing him.

"Do you know what happened?" Noah asked. "I just spoke to her parents, but they were hazy on the details. Still in shock, I think. Understandable."

"We are trying to find out what happened," Mackinnon said. "We only found Ashley's body this morning, so we're speaking to people who knew her and trying to find out if there was anyone in Ashley's life who could have done this."

"Killed her? No. I don't think so. Everyone loved Ashley."

There it was again. *Everyone loved Ashley.*

"Even you? You'd broken up recently. Was there any bad feeling between you?"

Noah's already small eyes grew smaller, and he frowned. "No. I mean, we had a few arguments and decided to take a break, but I still cared about her."

"When was the last time you saw her?"

Noah looked down at his lap. His fluffy brown hair fell forward covering his eyes. Was he trying to hide something?

"Two days before she disappeared," he said eventually.

"Where?"

Noah sighed and ran his hands over his face. "The thing is, I know this is going to sound bad, but I waited for her after work. I just wanted to talk."

"Why would that sound bad, Noah?"

"Because she wasn't very happy to see me, okay?" His fists clenched in his lap. "She yelled at me to give her space…and I yelled back. You may as well know because it happened on the street, and I'm sure some busybody will tell you. I didn't touch her. I would never hurt Ashley."

Charlotte was busy making notes.

"Did you have a tempestuous relationship?" Mackinnon asked.

"Not really."

"Were you ever violent?"

"No! I told you. I would never hurt her."

Noah got to his feet and paced the small area in front of the television.

"I know this is upsetting, but we need to ask these questions."

Noah shook his head and grunted. His fists were still clenched, and his face was flushed.

"Had Ashley been worried about anything or anyone recently?"

Noah thought for a moment. "No, she was fine. We only broke up because I like to have a drink and go out with my friends a lot. It was my fault. I should have been a better boyfriend."

"What about health issues?"

"Health? No, she's always been perfectly healthy."

"She's never suffered from depression that you know of?"

"No, I don't think anyone would say Ashley was depressed. She was always so happy and bubbly. Why do you ask that?"

"It was just something one of her friends said."

"Who?"

Mackinnon didn't answer his question. Noah Thorne was an interesting character. It was hard to judge a person's true nature after they'd received devastating news. Their emotions were all over the place and unpredictable. But from Noah's reactions, Mackinnon suspected he was hotheaded and quick to temper. Of course, that alone didn't make him a killer.

"Have you had any visitors to your flat over the past ten days?"

Noah's upper lip curled in anger. "I don't like where this questioning is going. I didn't have Ashley locked up here if that's what you mean. And as a matter of fact, yes I did have visitors, including Ashley's own parents. They came here last Tuesday so we could brainstorm ways we could search for Ashley. We made posters…"

Noah's voice trailed off. He cradled his head in his hands and began to sob.

After work, Mackinnon made his way to his friend Derek's flat. He usually stayed there overnight while he was working and went back to Chloe and the girls in Oxford when he had a day off. Lately, he'd been staying in London more often, not minding if he was called to cover someone else's shift. Guilt nagged at him, but he just found it easier. As Sarah, Chloe's eldest daughter, had been thrown out of college and evicted from the halls of residence, she was now back at home, and the atmosphere was not good. Sarah and Chloe were always at each other's throats.

Sarah had made it very clear she didn't like Mackinnon, although to be fair, Sarah wasn't particularly warm and friendly to anyone. Since she had come home, Mackinnon found it easier to stay in London and keep out of the way. He missed Katy, though. Chloe's youngest daughter was funny and clever. She'd taken to calling Mackinnon when she needed help with homework. Though it had to be said, he failed to answer most of her questions. He didn't remember learning half the stuff Katy asked him about when he'd been at school.

Derek's dog, Molly, greeted Mackinnon enthusiastically at the door. He had never known such a loving dog. He put the takeaway curry down on the floor to make a fuss of her.

"Evening," Derek said, walking into the hall. "Is that our dinner?"

Mackinnon reached over and handed him the takeaway bag. "It is. I got the usual."

"Perfect. I'll plate up."

Molly followed Mackinnon, wagging her tail, as he put his bag into the spare room. When he walked into the kitchen, Derek pressed a bottle of beer in his hand.

"Now, before you go off on one, the food processors in the sitting room are completely legitimate. A friend of mine bought too many, so I'm selling them on for him."

With a sigh, Mackinnon took his beer and walked into the sitting room. Stacked against the wall were at least twenty-five boxes containing top of the range food processors. "Where did you get them?"

"I told you. A friend."

Mackinnon took a sip of his beer and shook his head. "You do recall I'm a police officer?"

Derek smiled. "Of course." He clinked the neck of his beer bottle against Mackinnon's. "Let's eat."

Mackinnon ate his extra spicy Rogan Josh in front of the TV. Derek had recorded an old American football Super Bowl game. He'd been trying to follow the sport for a while now. But the rules still confused him at times.

"How's work?" Derek asked, scraping his fork to collect the last mouthful of madras on his plate.

"Interesting. I was acting SIO on a case for all of five minutes today."

"Does that mean a promotion? Extra money?"

"I wish."

"You work too hard."

"Don't I know it."

"How are Chloe and the girls doing?"

"Katy is doing great. Still top of her class. Chloe's having a hard time now that Sarah is at home, though."

"What happened to make the University throw her out?"

Mackinnon took a sip of his beer. "Stealing."

Derek dropped his fork on his plate. "What did she steal?"

"Money from a collection apparently. We're still waiting to hear if she's going to be criminally charged."

"Doesn't she know you're a police officer?" Derek asked with a smirk.

"Honestly, she doesn't seem to care. I know she's young, and she's Chloe's daughter, but it's really hard to get along with her."

"Sounds like she could have done with a slap or two when she was growing up."

"People don't slap their children these days, Derek."

"I don't see why not. My mother wasn't scared of walloping me if I did something wrong, and I turned out okay."

Mackinnon glanced at the stacked food processors and raised an eyebrow. "Yes, you're a model citizen."

Molly looked heartbroken to see that both Mackinnon and Derek had completely emptied their plates.

"Sorry, sweetheart," Mackinnon said as he took their plates out to the kitchen. "Curry is not good for your digestion." He rubbed his chest and popped a Rennie in his mouth. "It's not that great for mine either."

As he washed up the plates, he thought back through the events of the day. Collins had reported a glitch with the CCTV software, which meant there was a delay in getting the footage of their suspect and Ashley on her journey home from work on the day she went missing. The technology was fantastic when it worked. But when things went wrong, it was a disaster. He hoped the bug, whatever was causing it, would be fixed by tomorrow. Despite speaking to Ashley's parents, her ex-boyfriend and work colleagues, Mackinnon felt they were no closer to understanding what had happened to Ashley in the ten days she'd been missing.

He put the clean plates in the cupboard and then reached into his pocket for his mobile phone to call Chloe. He saw he'd missed a text message from her forty minutes earlier.

Absolutely shattered. Going to bed early. Night x

He put the phone back in his pocket and returned to the sitting room to watch the rest of the old Super Bowl with Derek.

He wasn't planning to stay up too late. DCI Brookbank had done as promised and arranged for the postmortem to be bumped up the queue. It was scheduled for first thing tomorrow morning, and Mackinnon was planning to attend.

With Molly curled up by his feet, he sipped his beer and kept his focus on the television, trying to put the case out of his mind.

CHAPTER ELEVEN

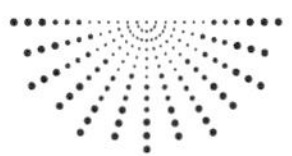

THE FOLLOWING MORNING, Mackinnon was at the mortuary before eight. He sat on the hard plastic seats outside the entrance waiting for the arrival of Dr Duncan Blair.

Within a few minutes, he caught sight of the pathologist striding down the corridor, clutching a takeaway coffee cup in one hand and a leather document case in the other.

"I see your DCI managed to get the postmortem bumped up the queue, Jack," he said as he came to a stop beside Mackinnon. "Is it still a priority case?"

Mackinnon nodded. "Absolutely. I'd like to attend the PM if possible."

"Not a problem. You might want to leave me to get the preliminary stuff out of the way first and then I'll talk you through what I found. Police officers often get squeamish when the chest saw comes out."

Mackinnon had no burning desire to witness *that* part of

the postmortem. But he did want to see Ashley's body as the pathologist ran through his report. "Shall I wait here?"

"You can, or in the hospital cafeteria upstairs. You could get yourself some breakfast."

Mackinnon took his advice and headed up to the cafeteria. The cooked breakfast smelled surprisingly good, but he held back. He didn't want heavy, greasy food sitting in his stomach just before he went to a postmortem. Instead, he ordered a black coffee and took a seat at a table by the window. Then he used his phone to check his email.

Collins had sent out an update. Apparently, they were still struggling with the bug and were unable to download and view the CCTV files. It looked like something in the system had been corrupted.

Mackinnon didn't know much about software and coding, but it didn't sound good. He hoped the system hadn't been attacked by a virus.

He would miss the early morning briefing, but could catch up with the briefing notes when he got back to the station.

When he'd finished his coffee, he returned to the mortuary. He sat on the chairs outside again but didn't have to wait long.

One of the mortuary assistants poked their head through the double doors.

"DS Mackinnon?"

Mackinnon got to his feet. "Yes."

"Dr Blair is ready for you now."

As Mackinnon walked through the double doors, the smell of disinfectant and the sickly sweet smell of death washed over him. The floors and walls were pristine, but no matter how clean the place was, the smell of death lingered.

The mortuary assistant led him into a bright sterile room.

Dr Blair was standing beside an autopsy table. He turned and waved Mackinnon over.

"Nice breakfast?"

"I decided to give it a miss."

"Probably wise." The pathologist smirked.

The naked body of Ashley Burrows lay on the autopsy table. Fluid had been caught by the raised edges of the table. Mackinnon's stomach rolled and he was glad he hadn't gone for the bacon and eggs. He'd been to postmortems before, but hadn't expected the smell to be quite as overpowering this time. The body was relatively fresh, and yet smelled really bad.

He took a step back, still staring down at Ashley's blotchy skin. "Did you identify a cause of death?"

"Sepsis."

Mackinnon tore his eyes away from Ashley and looked at the pathologist.

Dr Blair nodded. "She had an infection, probably from these scratches. Bacteria from her skin entered her bloodstream. That's what killed her."

Mackinnon had been expecting the cause of death to be trauma. But sepsis? Had it been accidental? But if so, why dump her body?

His gaze travelled back to Ashley and focused on the bruising around her wrists. It looked like she'd been restrained and that made a natural death very unlikely.

"Why didn't she go to the hospital?" Mackinnon wondered aloud.

"I don't know. That's your department. But I did find something interesting. Do you remember I said the bumps on her arms looked like insect bites?"

"Yes."

"Well, I think I was right, and I think I might know what insect caused them."

"What?"

"Cimex lectularius."

Mackinnon looked at him blankly.

"Bedbugs. You see here where the bites appear in relatively straight lines and in groups of three." He pointed a gloved finger at a trail of red bumps on Ashley's left arm.

Mackinnon looked closely and then nodded.

"That's typical of bedbugs. Each bug usually bites three times. Morbidly, some people refer to it as breakfast, lunch and dinner."

Mackinnon didn't consider himself particularly squeamish but he fought back a wave of revulsion. "Is that how she caught the infection?"

Dr Blair shrugged. "Possibly, although it's more likely the infection came as she scratched the bites. She needn't have died. A simple dose of antibiotics could have stopped the infection in its tracks."

Mackinnon wondered again why Ashley had been unable to get medical treatment. Whoever was keeping her captive, must have watched her deteriorate and known she needed medical help. He gritted his teeth.

"And the marks on her wrists?"

"As we suspected when we first saw her body, they are ligature marks, caused by plastic cable ties. I believe she was restrained for some time. We need to wait for the toxicology panel to come back, but there are no external indications of drug use."

"And the bites on her arms," Mackinnon said, "are they only localised there?"

"Yes, oddly they are only on her forearms. I suppose it could be they were the easiest access points for the bedbugs, but the insects are tiny little things and can creep through gaps in clothing easily."

"I suppose the bites caused the intense scratching and that led to the infection then," Mackinnon said, thinking aloud.

"Yes. It's likely that although she had her wrists bound, they were in front of her body rather than behind, which allowed her to scratch her arms."

Instinctively, Mackinnon rubbed his own arms. "So it looks like Ashley was held somewhere infested with bedbugs?"

The doctor nodded. "It looks that way."

There was a squeak from a gurney as another body was wheeled in next door. Over the muffled voices, he heard the sound of the hoses being turned on. He shivered. It was much colder in the mortuary than anywhere else in the hospital, but the shiver had come from a mixture of imagining the insects crawling over Ashley's skin as well as anger that Ashley had died needlessly.

The results from the postmortem had made the case more complicated. Ashley hadn't been stabbed or strangled, but whoever had been with her in the last days of her life and prevented her from getting medical treatment was responsible for her death.

He didn't know much about bedbugs, other than the fact just thinking about them made his skin crawl. That was some research he wasn't looking forward to.

They finished up talking about a few more aspects of the

postmortem, and Mackinnon left the mortuary after Dr Blair promised to get the report to him as soon as possible.

Despite the heat, Mackinnon was glad to get out of the hospital and breathe fresh London air. It was only mid-morning, but already the temperature had reached twenty-five degrees. The perfect temperature for lazing about in the garden at home, but irritating when you needed to work in central London and get about on the underground.

As soon as he started down the steps at the underground entrance, the warm stale air hit him. Removing his jacket, he draped it over his arm, but it didn't make much difference.

He got on an eastbound train and was pleased to see the carriage was quiet. Taking a seat, between a young Asian man with huge white headphones covering his ears and a middle-aged white woman, who clutched her handbag on her lap, Mackinnon pulled out his phone.

The signal was poor, but he managed to type bedbugs into the Google search engine and tapped on the first link before it disappeared completely.

An image of a bedbug appeared on his phone screen. It was reddish-brown and almost completely flat. The zoomed-in picture was a scary sight. He shuddered.

The younger bugs were a light cream colour. Further down the page was a picture of typical bite marks from a bedbug. As Dr Blair had said, the bites typically occurred in groups of three. The marks appeared to be a close match to those on Ashley's skin.

As he read further, he screwed up his face in disgust. The statistics were particularly worrying. But then again, not everything on the Internet was true. He'd be better off speaking to a real expert. Perhaps someone from pest control at the council.

He felt rather than saw the woman beside him lean a fraction closer. He glanced sideways to see she was staring at his phone. Her eyes were wide. Then she shuffled to the right, moving as far away as possible.

Mackinnon tried not to smile. That would teach her to be nosy.

The train rattled and jerked as it tore along the tunnel. The tinny music from the earphones on the man next to him was irritating. Mackinnon scrolled down the page and then, to his horror, read that bedbugs had been found on public transport. He glanced at the rough material covering the seat beneath him.

Perhaps he should have remained standing.

CHAPTER TWELVE

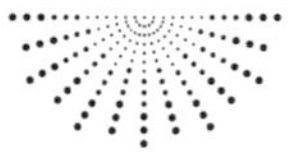

HE STARED at the bottle of whiskey in front of him. Morning drinking. How had it come to this? He was supposed to change the world, but Ashley had gone and died on him when she was supposed to be helping him in his fight against the non-believers.

He'd got the antibiotics for her, hadn't he? If only she'd held on for just a few more hours…

The unopened box of co-amoxiclav, a combination of amoxicillin and clavulanate, sat on the table, mocking him.

He poured two fingers of whiskey into his coffee mug. Everything was against him. It wasn't fair. Just when he thought he'd found somebody who might help with his plan, everything went terribly wrong.

He took a sip of the whiskey and sniffed. He'd been devastated when he'd found her body. All that chasing around for antibiotics had been pointless.

When he got back, antibiotics clutched in his hand, he'd

gone straight up to the loft, and at first he'd assumed she was sleeping. Sleeping was all she ever seemed to do. He leaned down to shake her awake and got the fright of his life when her head flopped towards him. Her eyes were wide open, unseeing and lifeless.

He screwed up his face and took another mouthful of whiskey.

He was a failure.

The next sip of whiskey made him feel a bit better, the alcohol feeding his confidence. Technically, it wasn't his failure. It was Ashley's. She was the one who'd given up.

He nodded and drained the mug. Yes, she was the failure, not him.

This was a setback. A temporary one. Didn't all the great scientists have setbacks at some point in their lives? Their achievements weren't handed to them on a plate. He poured himself more whiskey.

Grabbing the mug, he walked through to the kitchen and stood at the sink, looking out of the window. It was already hot out there. The small patch of green outside the terraced house had turned brown from a combination of lack of rain and too much sun over the past couple of weeks.

The papers were full of stories about people struggling with the heatwave. Stupid. As soon as the rain started, the heat would be forgotten, and people would be moaning about the wet weather again. People were occupied by such trivial matters. Not him, though. He had a purpose.

He set the whiskey-filled mug on the counter and scratched his arms.

They were back.

He ran to the spare bedroom and sat down at the dressing

table. He pulled the microscope towards him, yanking off its black dust cover.

He searched a drawer until he located a scalpel. Resting his arm on the dressing table, he pressed the metal against his forearm and slowly scraped his skin. He didn't press hard enough to draw blood. Having the little critters in his bloodstream was the last thing he wanted.

Carefully, he tapped the scalpel onto a glass microscope slide and put another piece of glass on top, trapping whatever he'd harvested from his skin in between the glass.

His hands were shaking as he placed the slide under the lens. After two deep, calming breaths, he peered through the eyepiece.

Plenty of skin cells, clumped together. Coloured fibres, probably from his jumper. And…

Did something just move?

He was sure he'd seen movement. Staring down through the microscope, not wanting to blink in case he missed it, he scanned all sections of the slide. His eyes began to water.

"I saw you. I know you're there," he said between clenched teeth.

After ten minutes, his eyes were fatigued and blurry. He flopped back into the chair, admitting defeat. This time they'd escaped him, but soon he'd harvest them and make a recording, so the medical profession would have to accept what he'd been saying all along. He'd discovered a new illness. A new parasite. His name would be remembered. Maybe they'd even name the little bugs after him.

The thought made him smile.

When you were absolutely convinced of something but no one else believed you, it was lonely and isolating. But one day soon, he would be proved right, and the doctors would have to apologise to him.

He'd be magnanimous, of course, and smile for the press. They'd probably award him the Nobel Prize. He giggled. That would show them. That would really rile up the establishment. Maybe they'd even give him his own lab and research assistants.

He carefully filed the microscope slide away and then tugged the dust cover over the microscope. Despite his lack of success yesterday, he felt more positive now. Giving up was not his style.

He walked into the kitchen and poured the whiskey away.

Today his primary task was finding another helper. He went into his bedroom and sat down at his PC. He went to the favourites folder and logged onto the forum, cureityourself.

He smiled. Who would be the next lucky man or woman to help with his project?

He'd prefer a woman. If things got violent, he didn't want to take a chance against someone stronger than himself. He'd learned many lessons from Ashley. People weren't prepared to help. They needed to be convinced, and that took time.

It was unlikely he'd find anyone to take part in his experiment willingly, so he would have to be careful and a little cunning. Once, his research had been accepted by the medical establishment, he would give his assistants their due and make sure their work was credited, but until then, he would keep his research to himself.

Another death would be unfortunate. But he wouldn't flinch from it. For great achievements, sacrifices were needed.

He glanced at the underside of his arm. The rash he had shown the doctor yesterday had completely disappeared. That was to be expected. He'd merely rubbed a stinging nettle leaf on his arm shortly before his appointment. Dr Wendy Willson had had no idea. And she called herself a doctor? Honestly, the whole lot of them were useless. It was scary how much faith society put in them, really.

He scrolled through the recent posts on the forum and ran his tongue over his upper teeth as he focused on one post, titled: please help!

He quickly scanned the post, his smile widening as he did so. This forum member would be perfect. He rested his hands on the keyboard and began to type.

CHAPTER THIRTEEN

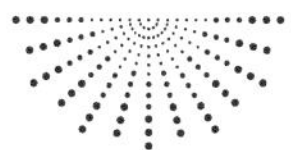

TAMMY HOLT LINED up her glass of celery juice beside a bunch of dried flowers. She had to get the layout just right if she was going to post it on her Instagram feed. The harsh sunlight streaming in through the windows was causing problematic shadows. Tammy adjusted her position and the angle of her iPhone and snapped a couple of shots.

She looked through them. Not bad, considering the angle of the sunlight.

Usually, she preferred to post in the morning, but she'd slept late today, unable to find the energy to get out of bed before eleven. So technically, her celery juice was actually lunch.

She scrolled through the apps on her phone, locating the one that contained her favourite filter. It desaturated the image just a tad and made the contrast pop. She looked critically at the finished result. It would do.

She uploaded the photograph to Instagram with the hashtags cureityourself, celerycleanse and beyourowndoctor.

Putting her phone to one side, she picked up the celery juice and took a sip. It was awful.

She gulped down half of it and then stopped before she retched. Some of the crazy fads she had used to try and regain her health were ridiculous. There had been the raw food diet, the paleo diet, before she realised meat was the last thing she should have been eating, and the fruitarian diet. At least the fruit had tasted nice. But this celery juice was the worst.

She wrinkled her nose. Celery was disgusting, but desperate times called for desperate measures.

She'd been feeling ill for the last eighteen months, and the doctors had been absolutely useless. They started out giving her a few creams for her skin rash, giving her strong anti-acid medication for the pains in her stomach, and had really splashed out by giving her an abdominal ultrasound that was inconclusive. It was ridiculous. How were they supposed to diagnose what was wrong with her without proper CT scans?

Her illness had gotten worse over the past few months, but her GP had sent her home with a diagnosis of fibromyalgia. At first, she'd been relieved to have a name given to her condition and thought now she knew what was wrong with her, she could go about trying to cure herself. That was before she'd looked into it.

Fibromyalgia. Myalgia just meant pain. And the fibro part of the word referred to fibrous tissue. So basically the genius doctor had diagnosed her with muscle pain. She could have told him that. What was the point of all that university training if they never put it to use? Unless it was an infection, a broken arm, or a cold, doctors had absolutely no idea how to help their patients.

She lifted the celery juice to her mouth again and almost gagged from the smell. She pinched her nose and swallowed down the rest of the juice. The celery cleanse was incredibly popular on Instagram and YouTube at the moment. There were so many reports of the concoction curing chronic illness, so Tammy was hopeful. Maybe natural foods would help where medicine couldn't.

Last night, she'd watched a video of a woman who'd drunk celery juice for thirty days, every morning on an empty stomach, and cured herself of acid reflux and fibromyalgia. If it got her the same result, Tammy was prepared to drink the disgusting juice for the next thirty days.

The nagging feeling she was doing this all for nothing wouldn't leave her alone, though. What if this was it? What if she was destined to spend the rest of her life in pain and too tired to hold down a job, let alone go out and have fun like a normal twenty-three-year-old.

Tammy roughly wiped away the tears that trickled down her cheeks. She'd lost count of how many times she'd cried over the previous few months. It never helped.

She'd feel less alone if just one person she was close to understood how she really felt. Her mum was sympathetic enough, but she didn't really understand. She called it growing pains, despite the fact Tammy was twenty-three and fully grown. Her sister was the worst. Just two years younger than Tammy, Julie was the healthiest person imaginable. She ran half-marathons for fun and had boundless energy. Her advice was that Tammy needed to get more fresh air and exercise.

Just for one day she'd like to swap places with her sister. Tammy huffed. She'd like to see Julie go for a jog when she felt as bad as Tammy did. Most days it was a struggle getting out of bed. Taking a shower wiped her out for the rest of the morning.

She hadn't been able to hold down a job, and her diagnosis of fibromyalgia wasn't enough to get her disability allowance, so she constantly tried to get someone to employ her. Usually, she was turned down if she made it to the interview stage, but on the rare occasion somebody thought she was employable, they soon dumped her when she took too much time off sick. She wasn't an idiot and saw the way they looked at her when she went to sign on. She wasn't missing an arm or a leg, she didn't have cancer, so why didn't she pull her finger out and get a job? That's what they all thought.

Tammy wished for just one day they had to walk in her shoes. Then they wouldn't be so quick to judge.

Her celery juice finished, Tammy walked slowly to the kitchen to make coffee. She knew the caffeine wasn't good for her, but she needed it to get through the day. The artificial boost in energy was better than nothing.

She took a quick look at her Instagram feed as she waited for the kettle to boil.

Thirty-three likes already. Not bad.

With a steaming cup of coffee in hand, she walked back to her bedroom, planning to spend a little time on the computer. Her mum was out at work, so if she felt like it, Tammy could go back to bed in a little while.

She lifted the lid of her laptop and began to type in the web browser. After she typed the first two letters, the website came up as a suggestion because Tammy visited it so frequently. She clicked the link and sipped her coffee as she looked at the new posts on the forum.

On the forum, she didn't feel like a pariah. People understood what she was going through because they were experiencing the same thing. They all had an illness that wasn't recognised by the medical profession and had no choice but to try and cure it themselves.

She smiled when she saw she had three replies to her previous post. Her name on the forum was Fibromyalgiagirl. Last night, when she was feeling in a particularly bad way, Tammy had shared her feelings. She read her post again and tears came to her eyes. It was raw and honest, and it felt good to offload her feelings. Scary, but good at the same time.

@Fibromyalgiagirl:

Please help.

I don't know what to do. I'm at my wit's end, and no one will help me. I've seen multiple doctors but now my GP refuses to refer me to anyone else, even though I feel terrible. I haven't been able to work full time for over a year and I'm only twenty-three. I'm so tired all the time and my muscles ache. I feel like my life is over and nobody will help me. No one understands. I know something is wrong, but I don't know what. I feel so alone.

Beneath her response, @justagirl had written:

I understand. Please don't feel alone. We are all in the same boat here. Keep going back to your doctor. They have no right to turn you away.

Then there was a response from @theestablishmentsucks:

Typical doctors! I'm so sorry you're going through this. Hang in there.

The last post was from @lookingforacure:

I'm so sorry to hear this Fibromyalgiagirl. I think I might be able to help. PM me.

Tammy re-read the last message. This was a forum anyone could join, so she was a little nervous about using the private messaging service, but then again, what was the harm? She hadn't used her real name, and lookingforacure certainly hadn't used his or her real name. She wasn't about to get her hopes up, but she'd be a fool to turn down the offer of help.

She hadn't private messaged anyone on the forum before, so it took Tammy a little while to figure out how to do it. Finally, she accessed the PM section of the board through the drop-down menu at the top of the website.

Her hands froze on the keyboard. There was so much she wanted to say, yet she didn't know how to put it into words. Staring at the screen, she felt like an idiot. If she shared too much, she might scare the person off. But she'd mentioned she had fibromyalgia, and lookingforacure did say they thought they could help.

She took a sip of coffee and began to type.

Hi lookingforacure,

This is Fibromyalgiagirl. Thanks for offering to help. I'm sure my post must have come across as self-pitying, but sometimes it's just so hard, you know? I'm doing a celery juice fast at the moment to see if that helps, but if you have any other ideas, I'd be very grateful to hear your advice.

Thanks.

She sat looking at the message for a moment, sipping her coffee with her finger hovering over the return key. What was she afraid of? She wanted help, didn't she?

She pressed the return key, and the message disappeared momentarily and then reappeared in her sent box.

The coffee hadn't helped much. She still felt like her brain was full of fog and she couldn't process things properly. Maybe she needed more?

In the kitchen, she fixed another cup of coffee and then grabbed a couple of biscuits. Perhaps the sugar would make her feel more human, or at least give her some energy.

When she returned to the computer, she felt her mouth grow dry when she saw she already had a reply to her PM. She clicked on the message and read:

Hi Fibromyalgiagirl,

I'm so glad you messaged me. I'm a researcher and I'm close to identifying the cause of fibromyalgia. The doctors won't tell you this, but it's actually caused by a parasite.

Tammy stared at the screen in horror. A parasite? Why hadn't that been picked up by her doctor? She began to type a reply.

@Fibromyalgiagirl: *A parasite??? That's awful. What do I do to get rid of it? Will the celery juice help?*

@lookingforacure: *the celery juice can't hurt, but it probably won't get rid of the parasite completely. I know how you feel. I've been let down by the medical profession too. They're useless, and they won't admit there's something wrong if they can't diagnose it. I just wanted to offer my help. The parasite burrows through the skin so I've been taking some skin scrapes and treating them with different solutions to see what works. I'm pretty confident I've found a cocktail of vitamins that gets rid of the parasite in just seven days.*

@Fibromyalgiagirl: *what vitamins?*

@lookingforacure: *I use quite a few different ones as well as minerals. The parasites hate it :)*

I can't give you the exact protocol because it's part of my research. I hope you understand.

Tammy shook her head. She needed this cure. Why wouldn't this person tell her what they used?

@Fibromyalgiagirl: *Please, I'm desperate. Can you help me?*

@lookingforacure: *Well, there might be a way, but I'm not sure you'd be up for it.*

Tammy started to type she'd be up for anything as long as it made her feel better, but then decided better of it. She didn't know anything about this person.

@Fibromyalgiagirl: *Try me. I really want to feel better.*

@lookingforacure: *Would you be willing to donate some skin scrapes? It won't hurt at all. I just need to scrape off the surface of your skin and look at the cells under a microscope. If I can see the parasite, I'll give you the vitamin mix that will cure you.*

Tammy's hands were shaking. She wanted to feel better, but in order for this person to get their skin scrapes, she would have to meet them, wouldn't she?

Would she be safe? Maybe they could arrange to meet in a public place. Or as they were a researcher, perhaps they wanted Tammy to go to their laboratory. She was desperate to accept lookingforacure's offer, but she had to find out more about them first.

@Fibromyalgiagirl: *Are you a guy or a girl?*

@lookingforacure: *A guy. My real name is Brendan.*

The fact he was a guy made her nervous, but he'd voluntarily given her his name. That was a good thing, wasn't it?

Unless he was lying.

Tammy gulped down her coffee, trying to clear her brain fog and find some clarity. This was important. It could be her one chance to feel better, and she couldn't screw it up.

@Fibromyalgiagirl: *I'm Tammy. I guess we have to meet up for you to get the skin scrapes?*

@lookingforacure: *Yes, we do. Look, I know this whole thing sounds a bit weird, so do you want to meet up for coffee later, somewhere public where we can chat about the protocol? I don't want you to do anything you're uncomfortable with.*

Tammy sat back in the computer chair. Surely, if he was up to anything dodgy, he wouldn't offer to meet in a public place first, would he? She could go, and if something about him was off, she'd leave. What could go wrong?

@Fibromyalgiagirl: *That sounds great. Where should we meet?*

@lookingforacure: *You pick. Your profile says you're from London. So am I.*

Tammy smiled. That was lucky. She was glad he wasn't in Edinburgh or somewhere like that. She wasn't sure she'd be able to make the trip.

The fact he was letting her pick their meeting place made her feel more confident, too. Surely a scammer wouldn't do that.

@Fibromyalgiagirl: *The Costa Coffee Shop near Whitechapel station?*

@lookingforacure: *Perfect. What time?*

@Fibromyalgiagirl: *Can you make it today?*

@lookingforacure: *Yup.*

@Fibromyalgiagirl: *Two o'clock?*

@lookingforacure: *See you then!*

He logged off, and Tammy was left staring at the screen. Her pulse was racing. This could be it. In less than a week, she could be feeling better. Holding a shaky hand to her chest, she stood up and carried her coffee cup back to the kitchen. She'd forgotten all about the biscuits, and now she was too nervous to eat.

Two o'clock! She'd better get ready.

* * *

Brendan shut down his PC. That had gone well. Easier than he'd expected. Now that he had a new assistant lined up, it wouldn't be long before he'd have the breakthrough he needed.

Tammy seemed nice enough, and he'd felt a momentary twinge of guilt while they were exchanging messages, but when he finally found the cure, she would forgive him. Sure, it would take longer than the seven days he'd promised Tammy, but all good things come to those who wait.

He smiled as he walked back to the kitchen, all thoughts of the Ashley Burrows failure purged from his mind.

CHAPTER FOURTEEN

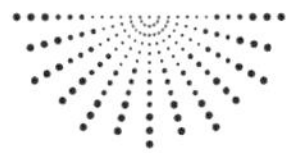

WHEN MACKINNON GOT BACK to Wood Street Station, he found someone had left the briefing notes on his desk. He sat down and began to look through them.

The CCTV was still the bottleneck. Without viewing the footage, it would be almost impossible to track their suspect. According to the notes, the tech team were putting all their resources behind the problem and hoped to have it fixed as soon as possible.

Mackinnon hoped that was true. They could really do with a break on this case.

Despite a search of the local area and door-to-door enquiries along the street near to where Ashley's body had been found, no new information had turned up. The team still hadn't located Ashley's bag or mobile phone.

Mackinnon turned the page, but before he could start reading, Tyler appeared at his desk.

The detective inspector perched on the edge of Mackinnon's desk. "Any surprises from the postmortem?"

Mackinnon nodded. "Yes, a couple. Firstly, the cause of death was sepsis."

Tyler raised an eyebrow. "Sepsis? Like blood poisoning?"

"Dr Blair thinks it was probably from the scratches on her forearms. The scratches got infected, and the infection spread to her blood. From there, it would have caused her organs to fail and her body to slowly shut down. It wouldn't have been a nice death."

There weren't many *nice* deaths. But Mackinnon hoped he died in his sleep, comfortable in his own bed. The thought of Ashley slowly growing feverish and sicker and sicker before dying in pain was not a pleasant one to contemplate.

"Poor kid," Tyler said. "So how do we treat this one? Was it an accidental death?" Tyler scratched his chin. "If it was, why would someone dump her body like that? She'd been restrained, hadn't she?"

"Yes, the marks on her wrists were consistent with being tied up for hours, probably days, with plastic cable ties, according to Dr Blair. She'd been restrained and prevented from getting medical help. Dr Blair said if she'd gone to the hospital in time, it was likely she would have made a full recovery."

Tyler nodded slowly. "Was there any sign she'd been sexually assaulted?"

Mackinnon shook his head. "None."

Tyler grunted and folded his arms over his chest.

"That surprised me, too," Mackinnon said. "I was expecting something quite different from the postmortem. But

I still think we're looking for a killer. He didn't physically take her life, but he was still responsible for her death."

"He?" Tyler queried.

"I think we're looking for a man, don't you?"

"In all likelihood. But we can't rule anything out at this stage, Jack. Thanks for attending the PM. I hate going to them."

"Not a problem. I've been going through the briefing notes, but it doesn't look like we're making much progress."

"Slow and steady. We'll get there. If we could get the CCTV to cooperate, that would be a great help." He shook his head. "In this day and age, I can't believe we're having such trouble. There are cameras everywhere."

"From the briefing notes, it doesn't sound like a fatal problem. They are working to fix it, aren't they?"

"Let's hope so. Apparently the downloaded files are corrupted, and for some ridiculous reason, they've been wiped from the main system. So somehow the lads and lasses from tech are going to have to unscramble the files if we are to have any chance of viewing them."

"Was it a computer or operator error?"

Tyler let out a long breath. "The corrupted files seem to be a computer error, but the fact they were wiped from the system is down to the operator."

Mackinnon grimaced. Whoever had wiped the files from the system was in for a serious dressing down. He was glad he wasn't in their shoes.

"And still no sign of Ashley Burrows's phone?"

"No, Charlotte has contacted the mobile phone company and has requested her call log. We should have a copy of that soon. Did you happen to see a laptop when you searched Ashley's bedroom?"

Mackinnon shook his head. "No, we did ask the Burrowses, and they confirmed Ashley had a laptop, but they didn't know where it was. It's possible it could have been elsewhere in the house. I'll give Kate a call and ask her to speak to Mr and Mrs Burrows again."

"Yes, do that."

"There was something else unusual about the postmortem. Dr Blair thinks the insect bites on her forearms were the reason for all the scratch marks on her skin. It would explain why her arms were itchy and why she scratched her skin in the first place. He thinks they were bedbug bites."

"Bedbugs?" Tyler pulled a face.

"Yes. If we presume she didn't get them at home, then perhaps she got the bites from wherever she was held in the ten days she was missing."

"Logical."

"I did a bit of reading on my way back on the tube, but I think we need to talk to a professional. If we can get a list of reported bedbug infestations in the city within the last six months or so, that might narrow down the area where she'd been held while she was missing."

Tyler nodded slowly. "That might just work. Give it a go. Who are you going to speak to?"

"I thought pest control at the council would be my first point of call and see what they suggest. I'd hope they keep records, but I'm not sure."

"All right. Follow that up this afternoon after you've spoken to Kate and have asked her to double check on the laptop."

"Will do."

As Tyler got up to leave, Mackinnon said, "Nice tie, by the way."

Tyler was wearing a dark blue tie with narrow cream stripes. It made a change from his normal, more garish neckwear.

Tyler tugged at the bottom of the tie. "Thanks. It was a present from Janice."

"How is that going? Has she forgiven you yet?"

Tyler shook his head. "I sent some flowers yesterday, but I haven't heard from her. I think the writing is on the wall for this one, Jack."

After Tyler went back to his office, Mackinnon fished out his mobile phone and called the family liaison officer, Kate Squires. She answered on the third ring.

"Kate, this is Jack Mackinnon. I wondered if you'd be able to ask the Burrowses if they know where their daughter's laptop could be? We didn't see it when we visited the house, but it could have been stored out of sight, or maybe Ashley left it at a friend's house."

"Sure. I'll ask them now," Kate said.

"Thanks. How are they holding up?"

"About as well as you'd expect. Maxine's devastated. She's crying all the time. Tim is constantly pacing the house. He's angry."

Different people reacted to grief in different ways, and most went through stages. The death of a child was something that never went away, but the nightmare parents went through in the immediate aftermath was an unbelievable strain, an experience Mackinnon wouldn't wish on his worst enemy.

"Thanks Kate. If you could get back to me about the laptop, that would be great."

He hung up the call and then used his computer to search for the details of the pest control office at the City of London.

He dialled the number of the appropriate department, and the call was answered by Lyra Gray.

"Lyra, this is DS Jack Mackinnon of the City of London Police. I have an unusual request. We have a murder victim with what we think are bedbug bites. I wondered if you or anyone in the department could tell me where there have been reports of bedbugs in the city?"

"Oh, that is an unusual request," Lyra said. "We do keep records of cases that have been reported to us, but we don't keep records of those that have been treated by private contractors."

"So there could be cases of bedbugs in the city where you wouldn't have a record of them?"

"It's possible, I'm afraid."

"Right, well, I suppose we'll have to work with what we've got first. Could you email me the records of bedbug cases in, say, the last six months in the City of London?"

"I should be able to… but, well, I have to check with my manager first. You know, people are quite fussy about privacy when it comes to this sort of thing."

Mackinnon sighed. "The results won't be made public. I just need the information to narrow down areas where our victim may have been in the days before she died. If you need to speak to your manager, I'd appreciate you doing so quickly."

"Of course. I'll check with him and then get the list sent straight over to you."

Mackinnon gave Lyra his email address and said, "I'd appreciate it. Also, I have one more request. Is there someone in your department I can speak to about bedbugs…about their habitat and behaviour?"

"Um, probably not someone in this office. The thing is, when residents get in touch to report a bedbug infestation, we give them the details of a local pest control firm, and they go in to treat the bugs. It's no longer carried out by the council itself, you see."

"What company do you use?"

"It's called A1 Pest Control. We've used them for a few years now, and they've been great. They offer council referrals a discounted rate to treat the bugs."

"I see. Could you give me the details for the company?"

Mackinnon jotted down the contact details for the pest control company and thanked her.

As soon as Mackinnon ended the call, his phone rang again. It was Kate.

"Kate, thanks for getting back to me so quickly."

"No problem. I spoke to Maxine, and she said that Ashley did have a laptop, but she hasn't seen it recently. She's going to take a look around the house and see if she can find it."

"Thanks, Kate. That's a great help. If we can locate that laptop, it may give us some desperately needed leads."

"I'll let you know if they find it."

Mackinnon thanked her, hung up, and then dialled the pest control company.

After introducing himself, he said, "I was wondering if there was someone I could speak to about the methods you use to treat bedbugs in the city."

The woman on the other end of phone stammered, "Oh…

um… I can assure you that everything is above board… All the pesticides we use are fully licenced and used in accordance with EU laws."

"It's not about that. I'm working a case at the moment where the victim was bitten by bedbugs. I'm hoping understanding a bit more about them will help me to understand where she was in the days before her death."

"Oh, I see." Mackinnon could hear the relief in her voice. "In that case, talking to one of our pest controllers wouldn't be a problem. They are all out at the moment, but you might catch them between appointments. Actually, I'm just looking through our appointment book, and Gary will have a half an hour break at four o'clock before his next job on Burdett Road. Would you be able to meet him then? I could ask him to meet you in the Lidl carpark."

"That would be very helpful, thank you."

"I'll give you his number, and you can give him a ring when you get there."

"Great," Mackinnon said, taking down Gary's mobile number.

When he hung up, it occurred to him how strange his job could be. This afternoon he was going to be learning all about bedbugs. That was something he'd never expected to have to learn, but this job constantly surprised him.

CHAPTER FIFTEEN

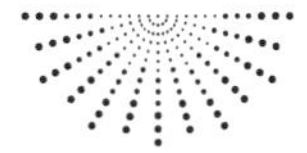

TAMMY DIDN'T THINK she'd ever been so nervous in her entire life. It wasn't just because she was meeting a random bloke from the Internet. It was because she now had the possibility of recovering her health. She had the chance to feel healthy again.

The thought made her tearful as she emerged from Whitechapel Underground and turned right.

Directly ahead, in the distance, was the Gherkin building. She weaved around the people walking towards her.

The Costa coffee shop was really close, which was fortunate because Tammy's legs were shaky. Her mouth was dry too, and her palms felt sweaty.

She'd pushed back the sleeves of her blouse to get some sun and top up her vitamin D but now tugged the sleeves back down.

She'd read that most people in the UK didn't get enough vitamin D because they didn't get much sunshine. Most people worked inside. At one point, she had wondered if her condition was related to some kind of vitamin deficiency, and her GP had run a whole panel of tests before declaring Tammy perfectly healthy.

She was too early. Her heart rate quickened as she walked past the coffee shop and headed towards the market stalls lining the pavement.

She stopped beside a stall and pretended to look at the items for sale: a selection of cross body bags. She took the time to calm down her nerves. She was over five minutes early and didn't want to get there first.

She pulled her mobile phone from her pocket and sent a quick text to her sister:

I'm just going to Costa Coffee on Whitechapel Road to meet someone who thinks they can help me feel better. They've got a whole protocol worked out. It sounds really helpful!

There, she felt a little better. At least *someone* knew where she was. She knew better than to meet a bloke from the Internet without telling anyone. She added as a quick afterthought:

His name is Brendan.

She laughed uneasily, drawing a concerned look from the stall-holder. If Brendan turned out to be a madman, at least her sister knew where she was and who she was with.

"Are you going to buy that bag? Or are you just going to pull it apart?" the stout, bald-headed stall owner asked.

Tammy glanced down and saw that she was holding one of the small bags. She hadn't even realised she'd picked it up.

She hung it back on the hook. "Sorry," she said and walked briskly away towards the coffee shop.

As usual, the place was heaving. Tammy's heart thudded.

She'd already had too much coffee today. The caffeine was adding to her jitters.

She pushed open the glass door, stepped inside, and looked around.

Was he here already? A glance at her phone screen told her it was one minute past two.

She should have asked him what he'd be wearing. Wasn't that what people usually did when they had assignations with strangers? She was starting to feel light-headed. Was that the excitement of what he could have in store for her or the fact she hadn't eaten anything apart from that disgusting celery juice?

She scanned the tables, looking for a man on his own, but couldn't see him straight away.

She walked forward just as the blender roared to life behind the counter. Cups rattled, and steam hissed from the coffee machine. Tammy's senses were overwhelmed, but she pushed on.

She squeezed past a buggy with a sleeping infant and walked further into the coffee shop. Her phone beeped, and she glanced at the screen. It was a text message from her sister.

Great. I've got a protocol that would work for you: healthy eating and exercise. I'll be at the gym at seven p.m. tonight if you want to join me as a guest?

Tammy narrowed her eyes. Sometimes she thought Julie was deliberately obtuse. Go to the gym? Was she kidding? Tammy could barely make it through the day without extra exercise on top. Come seven o'clock tonight, she would be tucked up in bed, already fast asleep.

It hurt to realise even her sister didn't understand what she was going through. She pushed the pain to one side, trying to concentrate on the future. If things went well with this protocol, she could be back to her old self in no time.

She put the phone in her handbag, and when she looked up again, she saw a tall man with brown hair looking at her.

He smiled, stood up from the table and said, "Tammy?"

"Brendan! I mean, yes, I'm Tammy. Thanks for meeting me. I wasn't sure you'd really be here. I thought maybe I'd imagined the whole thing. You know, being able to get a cure and feel better again...well, it's almost unbelievable for me."

Shut up, Tammy. You're babbling.

She clamped her mouth shut and smiled back at him.

"I know exactly how you feel," Brendan said. "I'll get you a drink, and we can talk. What do you fancy?"

"I'll have an English breakfast tea, thanks."

As Brendan went to the counter, Tammy sat down in the unoccupied seat at his table and placed her hands on her lap. She pinched the skin on her thighs as a way to reassure herself she was awake and this was really happening.

Tammy shot a shy glance at his back as he joined the end of the queue. He seemed normal enough.

He was tall and looked fit and healthy. He didn't send off any creepy vibes anyway. So far, so good.

Tammy swallowed and tried to slow her breathing. She didn't want to come off like an anxious mess. The idea of him turning her down for the treatment was too awful to contemplate. She couldn't mess this up.

When Brendan came back to the table with a tray, he smiled again and put a teapot and cup in front of her, then placed a small milk jug next to her cup.

Tammy thanked him, ignoring the jug of milk. She was

dairy free. It was another thing she'd eliminated from the diet in her ongoing futile attempt to feel human again.

Brendan sat down opposite her. "So, why don't you tell me about yourself?"

Tammy poured her tea, willing her hands to stop shaking. "I'm twenty-three. I've been ill for the past eighteen months, and it's just getting worse. I'm tired all the time. My muscles ache. My head feels like it's filled with cotton wool. I just can't function normally."

Brendan nodded sympathetically. "That has to be tough."

"It is. I mean, the worst thing is, no one really understands, and you start to think people believe you're making the whole thing up. The doctors… They run their usual tests, and when they come up with nothing, they just send me home. I feel I've been abandoned."

To her horror, Tammy felt tears welling in her eyes.

She blinked them away and raised her tea to her lips. "Sorry," she murmured before taking a sip.

"Not at all," Brendan said. "Look, I understand. Really I do. I felt just the same as you."

Tammy looked up. "And the protocol got rid of the parasites?"

Brendan nodded and gave her a warm smile. "It did. And there's no reason to think it wouldn't work for you too."

Tammy experienced a warm rush of hope. "Really?"

Brendan nodded and picked up his espresso. He took a sip and then said, "I thought it would be nice to meet in public, so you'd feel more comfortable."

"Haha, yes it gave me a chance to make sure you're not a crazy axe murderer!" Tammy gave a loud laugh that ended in a definite snort and drew looks from the tables around them.

A hot blush traveled to her cheeks. *Nice one, Tammy. Trust you to say the most inappropriate thing possible.*

"It was just a joke," Tammy said quickly. "About meeting a strange man on the Internet... Not that I think you're strange...I just wanted to say I appreciate you offering to meet up like this first."

"Of course. You can't be too careful these days."

Tammy looked uncomfortably at the people still staring at her. "Sorry about that. My sister always said I had the most obnoxious laugh."

"I don't think so. I think there's nothing nicer than a genuine laugh. So many people are fake these days."

He grinned at her, and Tammy beamed.

"I'll talk you through the process, and you can decide whether or not you trust me."

Tammy leaned forward, eager to hear more.

* * *

She felt on top of the world as they got off the bus together.

"So are we going to your laboratory or your place?" Tammy asked.

Brendan took long strides and she had to hurry to keep up.

"Unfortunately, I can't get funding for the research. I mean, the medical establishment just doesn't want to know. It's a nightmare."

Tammy nodded as though she understood.

"But, we can go to my mum's house. It's bigger than mine, and you don't have to worry because I keep the axe at my place." He winked.

Tammy's eyes widened as she laughed. "I suppose I deserved that. Will your mum be at home?"

"Probably not. Hopefully we won't get any interruptions."

Tammy walked along beside Brendan. The fact he was taking her to his mother's place made her let her guard down even more. He was hardly going to do anything dodgy at his mum's place, was he?

It was a hot day, and despite the fact Tammy's blouse was sticking uncomfortably to her back, she felt happy. Happier than she had in a long time.

The birds were singing and darting from tree to tree. She didn't think she'd ever seen so many birds in central London. She looked up at the bright blue sky and smiled. It was a good day.

When they reached Brendan's mum's terraced house, Tammy stood behind him as he carefully looked through his keyring for the appropriate key.

When he opened the door, he called out, "Hello, Mum? It's me Brendan. Are you home?"

There was no reply.

He stepped inside the dark hallway and beckoned Tammy to follow.

It was cooler in the house, and goosebumps prickled over her arms.

"We'll get started straight away," Brendan said brightly, leading the way into the sitting room.

The house smelled strange, a little stale, like nobody had lived there for a while. She pushed the thought from her mind. That was stupid. Brendan's mum lived here. Maybe she just kept the windows closed during hot weather to keep the rooms cool.

She sat down on a floral armchair and waited as Brendan went off to the kitchen.

"I won't be a minute, just relax," he called out. "I need to fix you a special drink."

"What's in it? Vitamins and minerals?" Tammy's heart gave a little jump at the thought that she might actually get the cure today.

Brendan poked his head around the door. "Sorry, no, not yet. This is just a drink containing a label."

Then he disappeared again, leaving Tammy to wonder what the label was. She tried to relax, but her whole body felt tense and uncomfortable.

Outside in the sunshine, she'd felt full of anticipation and hope, but inside in this dim room on her own, she started to feel less anticipation and more fear.

She shook her head. She was being stupid.

Brendan came back into the living room holding a glass containing a clear liquid. He held it out to Tammy.

"This is it. It's got a microscopic label in the liquid, and the label binds to the parasite. That means when I look at your skin scrapes under a microscope, I'll be able to see if you have the parasite."

"I see," Tammy said taking the glass and eyeing it warily.

"It might taste a bit weird." Brendan smiled. "But it will be worth it."

Tammy took a tentative sip. The drink had a bitter after-taste, but it wasn't too bad. It was nowhere near as bad as celery juice, anyway. She took a long gulp, and with Brendan's encouragement, finished the glass full of liquid quickly.

Brendan took the glass. "Great. We'll wait for twenty minutes or so, and then we can do the skin scrape."

Tammy nodded as Brendan carried the glass to the kitchen. She leaned back in the armchair, wondering how the label was able to get through her entire system to her skin in twenty minutes. She didn't know much about biology, but that was quite quick, wasn't it?

But Brendan was a scientist, and she was sure he knew what he was talking about. She was tempted to get out her phone and scroll through Facebook, but she thought that would be rude, so she left the phone in her bag and waited for Brendan to return.

He was taking a while. She couldn't hear any noises coming from the kitchen. What was he doing? Should she go and see if he needed some help? Maybe he had to set up some equipment for the skin scrapes.

She decided to stay still. She was feeling dizzy, probably after all the exertion plus the excitement. It had taken a toll on her.

She rested her head against the soft fabric of the armchair and closed her eyes, taking a few deep breaths. All she wanted was to curl up in bed and go to sleep. Exhaustion made her limbs feel heavy.

She wasn't sure what time it was when Brendan came back into the sitting room. She blinked. Had she fallen asleep? She really hoped she hadn't started snoring. How embarrassing.

Her eyes were blurry, and when she tried to smile at Brendan, her mouth wouldn't work properly.

Her stomach rolled, and as she sat forward, the room seemed to spin.

This was more than ordinary tiredness. There was something wrong. Had she been allergic to something in the drink? Perhaps she'd had a reaction to the label.

"I don't feel so good," Tammy said.

"Oh, what's wrong?" Brendan said, standing in front of her chair and staring down at her.

Tammy shook her head as she tried to form a sentence.

"I don't feel good," she tried to say, but her voice came out distorted and slow.

Brendan kneeled beside her and took her hand in his. "Just relax. This is how it's meant to happen."

This is how it's meant to happen? He could have warned her. She felt awful. A wave of nausea overtook her. She felt for one horrifying second she might throw up all over Brendan, but the nausea passed, leaving her with disorientating dizziness.

She tried to focus on Brendan's face, but it was blurry, distorted.

He leaned closer, putting his face only an inch or so from hers. It had to be her imagination, but she couldn't see the warmth in his eyes any more. They looked dark, soulless.

"I'm sorry, Tammy," he said quietly.

Tammy's last thought before everything went black was: *he doesn't look very sorry.*

CHAPTER SIXTEEN

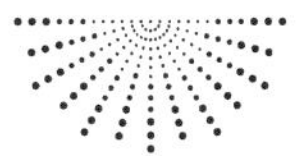

MACKINNON STILL HAD an hour and a half to kill before he needed to meet the pest control officer at Burdett Road. He stared at the mountain of paperwork on his desk, knowing he needed to get to it soon. Just because they had a new case didn't mean they could ignore the practicalities of previous ones.

He pulled out the briefing notes and wondered whether to offer Collins an hour of his time to help him chase up the CCTV.

As he got to his feet, DC Charlotte Brown walked into the open-plan office.

"Jack, Melissa West is back from Dubai this morning. I've just spoken to her and arranged to go and ask her some questions. Are you free?"

Mackinnon nodded. "I've got an hour and a half until I have to speak to pest control."

"She lives near Tower Hill Underground. It won't take us long."

"Remind me," Mackinnon said as they walked out of the station, "Melissa West? She was Ashley's closest friend according to her parents, right?"

Charlotte pushed open the double doors and they both stepped out into the bright sunlight. "Yes, they've been friends since secondary school and are still close. She only learned of Ashley's disappearance and death today. She's been in Dubai for three weeks, so she's probably going to be in shock. I don't know how much we'll get out of her."

It didn't take them long to get to Tower Hill Underground Station, although when they were locked in the oven-like carriage, Mackinnon felt the agony would never end. He wished they'd taken the bus.

They finally got out of the stifling, recycled air of the Underground and made their way to Marlyn Lodge in Tower Hill. It was a nice area, very central on Portsoken Street. A dark brown building, with large tinted windows, Marlyn Lodge was one of the few residential buildings in the area. Most of the buildings were office blocks or commercial structures.

They walked through the main entrance and under the shiny letters above the door displaying the name of the building.

They approached the concierge at the desk. "We are here to see Melissa West," Mackinnon said. Neither of them showed their IDs, as people inevitably believed the person police were interviewing had done something wrong.

"One moment," the concierge said. His uniform was rumpled, and he looked as though he was feeling the heat like everyone else, although the building felt like an air-conditioned dream after the heat from outside.

The concierge muttered a few words into the phone on his desk and then ushered them to the lifts.

"Third floor," he said, pressing the button for them and then wishing them a nice day.

"It's a relief to get out of the heat," Charlotte said rubbing the back of her neck. "It's just typical. We have about five days total of hot weather in the UK per year, and I have to work."

They stepped out into the corridor and rang the bell of flat thirty-one.

Melissa West opened the door. Her eyes were red, and it was obvious she'd been crying recently. She looked young and vulnerable. Her makeup was smudged, and she sniffed and said tearfully, "Come in. I only got back a little while ago and then… I heard the news about Ashley. I can't believe it."

Melissa led them along a short hallway and into an open-plan space. There was a small kitchen at the back of the large room, one sofa in the middle opposite a large television, and a round pine table shoved up against the window. All the furniture was white, and the floors were a pale wood.

An unopened suitcase sat beside the sofa.

"We should probably sit over here," Melissa said. "I keep meaning to buy another armchair or something, but I haven't got round to it." She pushed her hair back from her face and took a deep breath as she pulled out one of the chairs and sat down beside the table.

Despite the fact the windows were tinted, the sun still made sitting right next to the window unbearably hot. There were white slatted wooden blinds around the window, and

Mackinnon was surprised she hadn't shut them on such a hot day.

Living in a flat was always good in the winter, much warmer and cheaper to heat than a house, but on hot days in the summer, the good insulation made keeping cool a losing battle.

Melissa caught Mackinnon looking at the blinds. "I can't shut them. I've asked my landlord multiple times, but they're jammed. I'd hoped he'd do it before I got back. I know I'm on the third floor, but you feel really exposed when you can't shut the blinds at night."

Mackinnon stood up and inspected the blinds. He ran his hands over the wooden slats and found one that seemed to be at a strange angle compared to the others. He gripped the slat and pushed it back and forth until it slid into place, then reached for the cable and pulled the blinds across.

"Thank you," Melissa said, looking at the blinds with disbelief. "You made it look easy."

"I used to have similar blinds. There's always one slat that gets stuck at an angle, which means it can't move along the runner properly. It will probably happen again, unfortunately, but when you know what to look for, it's an easy fix."

"Thanks." She looked down at the table. "The officer on the phone said she wanted to ask some questions about Ashley."

"That was me," Charlotte said, pulling a small notepad from her bag. "We just need to gather as much information as we can, and Ashley's parents said you were very close."

Melissa's face crumpled. "We are… I mean, we were. I can't believe she's really gone. People are saying they think she was murdered."

"Ashley died under suspicious circumstances," Mackinnon

said. "So we are treating her death as possible murder. I wondered if you could tell us if Ashley was having any problems recently."

"You mean her boyfriend, Noah?"

Mackinnon nodded. "What can you tell us about him?"

"I didn't like him. He's not trustworthy. And he was nowhere near good enough for Ashley. He's a creep."

"Why do you say that?"

Melissa shook her head and looked down at her hands, pursing her lips together, and she paused before answering. "Just a feeling, really. You know how some men can make you feel uncomfortable?" She glanced at Charlotte. "Noah made my skin crawl. He was too over the top. Too smarmy."

Mackinnon hadn't warmed to Noah Thorne, but the fact he was smarmy didn't mean he went to the top of the suspect list. He really needed Melissa to tell them more, something concrete if they were going to look at Noah Thorne more closely. He decided to come back around to the subject of Noah and pushed the interview in a different direction. "Had Ashley been feeling unwell recently?"

Melissa looked up sharply. "Yes, but you don't think that had anything to do with her death, do you?"

Instead of answering the question, Mackinnon pushed on. "Did Ashley tell you how she was feeling?"

Melissa pushed back in the chair and studied her hands again. "Yes," she said slowly. "Ashley had been really down recently because she hadn't been feeling well, but the doctors hadn't been taking her seriously."

"Did she say what was wrong with her?"

"She kept getting headaches and really itchy skin, especially at night, which kept her awake."

"Was she attending some kind of support group?"

"Well, she didn't go to meetings, but she had a kind of support group, a forum, I think." She looked up at the ceiling as though she was searching her memories. "I can't remember what the forum is called, but she spent loads of time on it. She said the people on the forum were much better than the doctors and gave her ideas of alternative therapies and things that could help."

"That's very helpful, Melissa. If you remember anything more, especially the name of the forum, could you let us know?" Mackinnon pushed his card across the table.

Melissa glanced at it and nodded. "Of course." A tear trickled down her cheek.

"I'm sorry, I know it's upsetting to have to answer questions right now when you've only just learned of your friend's death, but we have just one more question about Ashley's laptop. We haven't yet located it or her phone. Do you think she could have left them at a friend's house?"

Melissa frowned, tucked her long hair behind her ears, and shook her head. "I doubt it. She was glued to her laptop most of the time. I told you, she was obsessed with that forum. She wouldn't have left it anywhere. She spent almost every evening on the forum for the past few months."

Mackinnon thanked her, and they got up to leave. As they walked to the door, Mackinnon tried one last time to get her to open up more about Noah Thorne. "Did Noah ever do anything to Ashley or to you to make you feel uncomfortable?" he asked, pausing by the front door.

"Nothing physical," Melissa said after a brief hesitation. "But he would hang around outside Flyaway Travel waiting for Ashley to leave work. Even when they'd broken up and she'd told him she didn't want to see him again. He was obsessive."

"Was he ever violent towards Ashley?"

Melissa shook her head. "No, not that I know of, but he would say nasty things to put her down. I told her it was psychological abuse and she should leave him, but she just said it was his insecurity and he didn't really mean it."

"All right, Melissa. Thank you for your time. You've been very helpful."

They stepped out into the corridor, and Mackinnon pressed the button to call the lift.

Melissa hovered in the doorway to her flat. "Look, I didn't trust him. I still don't. If you really think Ashley was murdered, you should look at Noah first."

"Ashley's parents seemed to think he was a nice guy," Mackinnon said as a bell chimed to signal the arrival of the lift.

As the door slid open, Melissa scowled. "That's because he's a good actor. Laying on the charm for Ashley's parents. But it's all fake. It's all an act."

Outside Marlyn Lodge, Mackinnon turned to Charlotte. "What did you make of that?"

"I think she was very upset. What she said about Noah was interesting, though. The killer is often someone known to the victim, and Noah fits that profile, all right."

Mackinnon nodded. "It's strange that Ashley's parents were both taken in by him, especially as they've known him for so long. Dads are notoriously protective, aren't they?"

Charlotte shrugged. "Usually, but if he was a good enough actor, he could have taken them in."

"He's the most likely suspect so far," Mackinnon said. "If

Ashley's parents can't find her laptop, I'm going to pay Noah a visit."

"Do you think he's taken it?"

"Possibly. If it has anything incriminating on it, that would be one reason Noah wouldn't want us to find it."

"Shall I talk to DI Tyler about a warrant?"

Mackinnon nodded and checked the time. "Yes, if you could do that when you get back to the station, that would be great. I need to go and see a man about some bugs."

Charlotte gave him a wry smile. "Rather you than me."

CHAPTER SEVENTEEN

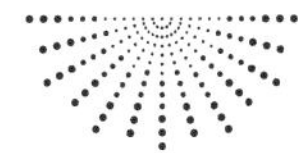

After enduring another hot journey on the Underground, Mackinnon collected a pool car from Wood Street Station and drove to East London. Dead on time, he pulled into the Lidl car park on Burdett Road and searched the spaces for a pest control van.

There were plenty of cars and one white unmarked van, but nothing to suggest it belonged to a pest control company.

Mackinnon parked up and settled back to wait. He had Gary's mobile number and could call him if he didn't arrive within the next few minutes.

He took the opportunity to check his phone for emails. There'd been a couple of updates, but nothing concrete.

With the engine turned off, the heat in the car soon became unbearable, so Mackinnon got out, locked the car, and looked around the car park again, wondering if he'd missed Gary's van the first time.

He noticed there was a man sitting in the front seat of the unmarked white van and pulled out his mobile to ring Gary.

The man in the van picked up his mobile at the same time, and Mackinnon realised the pest control company must use an unmarked van on purpose.

Gary answered on the second ring. "Hello?"

"Gary? This is DS Jack Mackinnon."

"All right. You're here, are you?" The man in the van peered out of the windscreen, and Mackinnon waved to him. He hung up and got down from the cab. Smiling cheerfully, he held out his hand for Mackinnon to shake.

"I'm told you need to find out about bedbugs," Gary said in a loud, booming voice.

"That's right. I was expecting your van to be a little easier to recognise with the company name on it or something similar," Mackinnon said, nodding at the plain white panels on the van.

Gary winked. "Well, we need to be discreet in this line of business."

He glanced over his shoulder, looking shifty as he opened the back doors of the van. To an outsider it must have looked like some kind of illicit deal was going down. The thought made Mackinnon smile.

"Well, here's the kit," Gary said, putting his thumbs in his belt loops and standing back as Mackinnon looked inside. There were multiple containers with spray pumps, the kind Mackinnon had used against garden pests like greenfly in the past. "So, you use that equipment to spray pesticides in the affected properties?"

"That's right." Gary clambered in the back of the van and grabbed a medium-sized white container with a red lid. "This is the stuff we use to kill the little blighters. It's water-soluble up to a point. Three scoops of this stuff in ten litres of water."

"It kills them on contact?"

Gary chuckled at Mackinnon's ignorance. "If only. No, they take a while to die out, especially if it's an established colony. We generally do two treatments. On the first one, we spray all the carpets, and walls, and of course the bed, and then we usually go back two weeks later to repeat the treatment. You see, if there are eggs around, they won't necessarily be susceptible to the poison. When the eggs hatch, the problem starts all over again, so the double treatment really helps wipe them out."

"I don't know how much your colleague told you," Mackinnon said, "but the reason I'm interested in these bugs is that we have a murder victim with a series of bedbug bites on both forearms."

Gary raised his eyebrows. "She did mention it. I thought it was a bit weird, to be honest. I mean, bedbugs are tiny little things, and they often like to bite you where you have contact with the mattress. That's not to say forearms don't get bitten, but for all the bites to be isolated to the forearms is unusual, particularly if it's more than one bug doing the biting."

"How would we know if there was more than one bug?"

"Well, the bedbugs don't necessarily feed every day. In fact, some people think they only need to feed every three or four days, so the fact your victim, as you said, had a lot of these bumps on her arms suggests more than one bug. Each one tends to bite three times. Not always, but that's typical."

"Yes." Mackinnon grimaced. "Our pathologist mentioned that. He said some people think of it as breakfast, lunch, and dinner."

Gary chuckled. "Yes, I have heard it referred to that way." He looked at the container in his hand and then put it back in the van. "Apparently, the things were almost eradicated back in the thirties, so I'm told, but now we're having a resurgence. We don't yet have it as bad as New York, but give it time. Things are escalating."

"So how many cases would there be in the central London area in a month, would you say?"

Gary exhaled a long breath. "I wouldn't have the first idea, I'm afraid. We only treat a small portion of them."

"But surely cases of bedbug infestations are reportable, aren't they?"

Gary shrugged. "Well, I can tell you the places I've treated in the last month. Our company reports to the council, but not all private places do, and in some cases, people decide to try and treat the infestations themselves. It can be dangerous because of the chemicals, although the really strong stuff's been banned since the eighties. If I'm honest, that's probably got something to do with the resurgence.

"There's two schools of thought. One is that we no longer use the super concentrated pesticides, which are more effective but possibly dangerous to public health, and the other one is there's a lot more international travel these days, so more opportunity for the little critters to spread."

Mackinnon let Gary's words sink in. It seemed his hope of locating where Ashley had been held for the ten days she was missing by locating bedbug sites was not going to work.

"Of course, it's not only bedbugs we treat," Gary said, taking Mackinnon's silence as an opportunity to talk. "Most of our calls are about bees and wasps at this time of year. It's been a bumper year for wasp nests. We get a lot of problems with mice and rats, too, and cluster flies can be a real problem. We get them regularly. But bedbugs are one of the worst. Because you have to spray the whole place, whereas with mice and rats, you lay a few traps, put in the poison, and you're done. With cluster flies, you get to set off a pesticide bomb in the loft."

"A bomb?"

"Yeah," Gary said. "One of these," he said, disappearing into the van and then reappearing holding a small black container. Mackinnon read the outside label: SMOKE BOMB.

"They're pretty effective," Gary said. "And it doesn't take long to set one or two of those up in someone's loft space. Spraying a whole flat or a whole block of flats for bedbugs on the other hand is very time consuming and expensive. That's why some people opt to do it themselves."

Mackinnon wondered why on earth bedbug treatment wasn't covered by the council. Surely if one flat was infested, they'd eventually spread through the whole building.

"But the council covers the cost?" Mackinnon asked.

"Some councils do. Others heavily subsidise like ours. But even that's too much for some people. Plus there's the embarrassment factor. People think it's because their house is dirty, or other people will think their house is dirty. The last case I had was one of the worst I've ever seen. It was a poor old bloke in his eighties. He had vision problems, so he hadn't been able to see them, but the carpet was practically crawling with the things when I got there. I've never seen anything like it. Usually they stay well hidden, particularly in daylight, but there were so many of them the place was overrun. We think he got the infestation from his grandson who'd been travelling around the world and had left his rucksack in the spare bedroom. I've done the first treatment. I'm going back next week for the second. He thought it was just a rash at first. Didn't help that his GP misdiagnosed the bites as a reaction to steroid medication." Gary rolled his eyes.

He checked his watch. "I'm off to do a treatment now. You're welcome to come along and take a closer look. It's an empty apartment block, so no worries about privacy on that front."

Mackinnon hesitated. The idea of voluntarily going into a flat known to be infested with bedbugs made his skin crawl. On the other hand, there was still a chance that this information could help them find where Ashley had been held captive. Though, it was looking less and less likely the more he found out about the insects.

Mackinnon nodded. "All right, then. I'll take a quick look. Thanks."

Gary nodded to the cab of the van. "Get in, we'll go now. We'll take a quick look around the place and I'll show you where they typically hide and then give you a ride back here before I start the actual treatment."

"Great," Mackinnon said, trying to sound enthusiastic as he climbed up into the cab.

The flats were an old sixties-style block that had been recently renovated. When Gary opened up the ground floor flat, Mackinnon was surprised at how nice and fresh everything looked. He knew Gary had said bedbugs had nothing to do with cleanliness, but this light, bright apartment with freshly painted walls and a soft, pristine, cream carpet was the last place he'd have expected to see the bugs.

Gary smirked. "I can tell you're surprised. But honestly, you get them everywhere. I have to admit, the worst cases do tend to be the most neglected buildings, but that's generally down to the cost. People put off getting in contact because they think the treatment isn't going to be something they can afford, and it's not clear that the council will cover it unless they are council tenants. This way."

Gary led the way into the bedroom. There was a large bed in the centre of the room. The bed covers had been stripped. Gary knelt beside the bed and pulled on a pair of latex gloves.

He beckoned Mackinnon closer. Pointing at the edge of the mattress he said, "Can you see those dots?"

Mackinnon squinted at the little black dots. At first, he thought they looked like mould. "Yes," he said.

Gary pulled back the seam of the mattress, displaying more little black dots. "It's what we call insect dirt. In this case, bedbug poo. It's one of the easiest ways to tell if a bed has been infected. It doesn't mean there's an active infestation, because they could have been eradicated, but it's a good sign to look for if you check into a hotel."

Mackinnon hadn't even thought of ever looking for signs of bedbugs when he checked into a hotel.

The surprise must have shown on his face because Gary said, "Believe it or not, it's one of the most common ways to get an infestation."

Gary slowly made his way along the edge of the mattress before giving a sharp yelp of victory and pinching something tight between his fingers. "Here we go, an adult!"

Gary held it up for Mackinnon to inspect, and though Mackinnon wanted to take a step back, he made himself look at the bug gripped between Gary's fingers. It was reddish-brown, and the most notable thing was how flat it was. It was barely as thick as a sheet of paper.

"No wonder it can creep through small gaps. It's so thin."

Gary nodded. "It's thin now because it hasn't fed for a while. After feeding they get much fatter."

Gary squashed the bug between his fingers unceremoniously and then got back to work, shifting the mattress back and revealing the slats of the wooden bed beneath.

"Lots more here," he said, but by the time Mackinnon looked, the insects had scurried back into the gaps and crevices around the frame. "The adults are hard enough to spot, but the junior bugs are a nightmare. They are a kind of cream, translucent colour, so if your bedding is white, they're almost impossible to spot."

Mackinnon scratched the back of his neck and shivered despite the warmth in the room.

Gary looked up and grinned at him. "Seen enough, have you?"

"I think I have, yes."

"I'll give you a lift back to the car park."

As they got back into the van, Gary said, "You might want to wash all your clothes at sixty degrees tonight, just in case."

"Just in case of what?"

"They get everywhere. Just in case you got some on your clothes. A little baby one or something. The heat will kill them. Wash at sixty. The best option is tumble drying, but I don't think your suit trousers will stand up to that."

Mackinnon looked down at his dark grey trousers. He felt like burning them.

"Don't look so horrified," Gary said. "It's only a precaution. It's extremely unlikely you got any on your clothes."

"Right." For some reason, that didn't really make Mackinnon feel better. "Your colleague said she's going to send me a list of places your company has treated recently, but I wondered if you remember treating a flat in the City of London within the last six months."

As they pulled into the Lidl car park, Gary screwed up his face and shook his head. "No, sorry, mate. Not me. East London's my area. Though, some of the other lads do work the City of London, so you might get some luck."

"Thanks for your help. I appreciate it." Mackinnon opened the van door.

"Not a problem," Gary said. "I just hope you catch whoever it is you're looking for."

"So do I," Mackinnon said, walking back to his car as Gary did a three-point turn and drove off.

Gary had been informative, but Mackinnon wasn't sure the information was going to get them any closer to Ashley's killer. He could only hope that one of the addresses the company had treated recently was Noah Thorne's. That would be a very interesting connection indeed.

CHAPTER EIGHTEEN

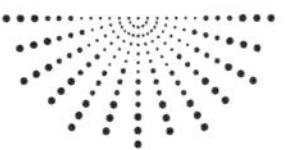

BACK IN THE CAR, Mackinnon checked his emails on his phone, keeping the engine running and the air conditioning on full blast.

A1 Pest Control had sent him the email. He clicked on it and scanned the list. It was a long list, and it would take a while to get through, but there was one address he really wanted to check out first, and that was Noah Thorne's. It was rush hour, and if he headed back to the station, he'd be caught up in traffic. There was a coffee shop just across the road, and he decided to head there to look over the list of addresses while getting a little caffeine boost.

The coffee shop was small, a traditional East End cafe. It had a large air conditioning unit at the rear, which meant it was a more pleasant temperature than outside. There were two empty tables, and Mackinnon took the one closest to the door and waited at the table to get served. He opened the word document on his phone.

A middle-aged woman with a sunny smile approached him and asked for his order. "What can I get you, love?"

"A black coffee, please."

"Anything to eat?"

"Do you have any sandwiches left?"

"No, but I can make up a fresh one. Ham or cheese?"

"Ham, please."

"Brown or white?"

Thinking of his rather unhealthy dinner last night, Mackinnon opted for brown bread. He was starving and didn't know what time he'd be able to get anything to eat later tonight. If he found a link between Noah Thorne and the bedbug bites, it was possible that they could have Noah Thorne in custody by this evening, which meant food would definitely take a back seat.

He selected 'Edit' and then 'Find' on the word document and typed in Noah Thorne's street address.

He muttered a curse when it came back with no hits. Of course, that would have been too easy. It didn't rule out Noah. He could have held Ashley somewhere else rather than his apartment. If what he had said was true and Ashley's parents had been to his place while their daughter was missing, it was unlikely he'd have kept Ashley in the flat.

Mackinnon thanked the woman who brought him a mug of black coffee. He took a sip of the scorching liquid and looked back down at the word document. The next logical step would be to check the roads around where Ashley's body was found and then follow the bus route they believed the man who'd dumped Ashley's body had taken.

Mackinnon scrolled through the digital copy of the briefing notes, which included photographs. There was a freeze-frame image of the suspect taken from the Chinese take-away's CCTV. Could the man in the hoodie be Noah Thorne?

Mackinnon stared at the image, but it was impossible to tell. It could've been anyone. The man's build and height was similar to Noah's, but the baggy clothing made it hard to tell how muscular the suspect was.

Mackinnon smiled at the woman who placed a freshly made ham sandwich on the table in front of him. It was a proper doorstep sarnie, with thick, fresh, crunchy bread and salty, smoky, thick-cut ham. Mackinnon dug in as he pondered what to do next.

Following the bus route would probably be the most sensible thing to do. That wouldn't be easy on his phone. It would be far easier on his computer back at the station. He polished off the sandwich quickly, hoping he wouldn't get instant indigestion after eating so fast, then drained the last of his coffee.

He paid the bill, which was surprisingly cheap, and left a good tip. He had just stepped outside the café when his phone rang. It was DC Collins.

"Hello, mate," Mackinnon said. "Any news?"

Instead of answering straight away, Collins asked, "Where are you?"

"Burdett Road. I've finished with the pest control expert but unfortunately haven't managed to put the pieces of the puzzle together yet. I didn't get much from him, apart from the need to wash my clothes at sixty degrees tonight."

"Sixty degrees? Why? Never mind. I'm calling because there's been a disturbance reported at Noah Thorne's block of flats, and I thought you'd want to know."

Mackinnon stilled. Interesting. Things kept coming back to Noah Thorne.

"Do we know if the disturbance has anything to do with Noah Thorne?"

"We do, Jack. Noah Thorne called it in."

CHAPTER NINETEEN

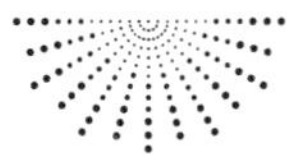

DESPITE THE HEAVY TRAFFIC, Mackinnon made it to Noah Thorne's address in good time. He pulled up outside Great Arthur House and parked beside the marked squad car.

He took the lift up to the fifth floor and on exiting saw a female uniformed officer talking to a very distraught Melissa West.

Neither of them noticed him at first, and he took a moment to assess the situation.

Melissa was sobbing, and the officer was trying to comfort her. On the floor was a half-empty litre bottle of vodka. Mackinnon pulled out his ID and approached them.

"DS Jack Mackinnon, City of London Police," he said for the benefit of the officer.

Melissa grabbed his arm. "Please, you have to help. They don't believe me, and he killed my friend."

The door to Noah's apartment was partially open, and from inside Noah's voice boomed out, unleashing a stream of expletives and vile language directed at Melissa. He yanked open the door and screamed at her. "You absolute psycho! They need to lock you up. You delusional bitch."

His face was distorted with rage and flushed red with anger. Melissa's lower lip wobbled as she took a step away from him, shrinking back against the wall.

"You killed her," she said in a shaky voice.

Another PC, a male officer, had his hand on Noah's shoulder, trying to hold him back and calm him down. "Please go back inside, sir. That sort of language isn't going to help anyone."

"It helps me. She just can't come round here shouting the odds, calling me a killer. Stupid dumb cow doesn't know anything." He sneered at Melissa. "You ought to be careful about the sort of things you say. They could come back and bite you."

Melissa wrapped her arms around her stomach and started crying again.

"That's enough," Mackinnon said coldly. "Any more of that threatening behaviour and you will be the one arrested, Mr Thorne."

Noah turned on Mackinnon, his teeth bared. "Arrest me? For what? This is the psycho you need to arrest!" he said, pointing a finger at Melissa.

She was obviously overwhelmed, distressed and very drunk. Clearly scared of Noah, she still refused to back down. "You won't get away with it."

"Get away with what, you stupid cow? I haven't done anything."

Noah turned to Mackinnon. "Tell her. I didn't do anything. Tell her I didn't hurt Ashley."

Mackinnon ignored him and instead turned to Melissa. "I think we should get you home."

She hesitated, glancing back at Noah.

"Go on, go! If you don't go now, I'm going to be severely tempted to push you down the stairs," he snarled.

Mackinnon shot Noah Thorne a look. Was he really stupid enough to threaten to do such a thing in front of three police officers?

Before anyone could say anything, he turned around and stalked back into his apartment.

"Come on," Mackinnon said gently. "My car's outside. I'll give you a lift home."

Mackinnon spent the whole journey suspecting Melissa would throw up at any moment. The officer who organised the pool cars would not be best pleased if he took back the car stinking of vomit.

Fortunately, Melissa wasn't sick on the journey. She spent most of the time staring blankly out of the window with glassy, tear-filled eyes. There had to be more to this than the fact Melissa just simply didn't like Ashley's boyfriend. She suspected Noah of her friend's murder, and she had to have a reason.

It took a while for him to get Melissa out of the car and into the lobby of Marlyn Lodge.

When he saw the state of Melissa, the concierge intervened.

"Could I take your name, sir?" he asked. He then turned to Melissa. "Are you okay? Have you been drinking?"

Supporting Melissa with one arm, Mackinnon fished his ID from his pocket with the other and held it up for the concierge. "She's had some bad news and has been drinking heavily. I'm making sure she gets back okay."

The concierge exhaled in relief. "Oh, I see. Let me get the lift for you."

It was nice in this day and age to see someone looking out for a drunk, vulnerable young woman. There were so many cases where people simply looked the other way.

Upstairs, Mackinnon lowered Melissa onto the sofa and then went to the kitchen to make coffee. There was only instant, so he put three spoonfuls into a mug and filled it to the brim with boiling water. When he took it back through to Melissa and set it on the coffee table, she was almost asleep.

"Who can I call to come and be with you?" Mackinnon asked.

He had work to be getting on with and wasn't the right person to stay up all night making sure Melissa didn't choke on her own vomit.

"I just want to be alone," she slurred.

"That's not a good idea. Where is your phone?"

"In my bag."

"I'm going to get it, and then I'm going to call your mum, all right?"

"Okay," she said sleepily and closed her eyes.

Mackinnon pulled an iPhone from Melissa's bright pink bag and then shook her gently to wake her up so she could unlock it.

He found the right contact under 'Mum' and pressed dial. He didn't relish the fact he was going to probably scare the life out of Melissa's mother. It was either a phone call from a police officer or one from Melissa slurring and not making any sense. Both would probably cause her mother to panic, but he couldn't leave Melissa there alone in good conscience.

The call answered on the fourth ring.

"Hello, darling. How was your flight home?"

"Mrs West?"

"Yes. Who is this?"

"My name is DS Jack Mackinnon of the City of London Police. I'm with your daughter at the moment. She's okay but very drunk. I was hoping you could come to her flat to be with her."

"That doesn't sound like Melissa."

"I'm afraid she had some very bad news today and has taken it hard. Her friend Ashley has died."

"Oh no, poor Ashley! I'm leaving now. Depending on traffic, I can be with you in fifteen minutes. Are you at Melissa's flat?"

"Yes."

As the minutes passed, Mackinnon coaxed Melissa to take sips of coffee, but she seemed determined to sleep it off. She was responsive when he could get her to wake up, and her eyes did focus when he could persuade her to open them. She'd probably be all right, but he wasn't comfortable leaving her until her mother arrived.

It took twenty-five minutes for Mrs West to arrive at Melissa's flat, and when she did, she was full of effusive thanks for Mackinnon bringing her daughter home.

As he made to leave, Melissa roused herself from the sofa. "Promise me you won't let him get away with this," she said, fixing him with a piercing look.

Mackinnon hesitated but was saved from answering as Melissa slumped back onto the sofa with her eyes shut.

CHAPTER TWENTY

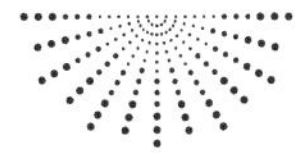

BRENDAN PEELED his clothes off in the bathroom and let them fall to the floor. Tammy was upstairs, sleeping off the second lot of sedatives he'd been forced to give her. That hadn't been his plan, but she'd really freaked out. She was strong for such a slight thing.

Brendan inspected the bruises on his shins. They were tender to touch, but the dark colour of the bruises hadn't yet blemished his skin. She'd kicked, thrashed, slapped, scratched, and done everything she could to overpower him.

He'd tried to reason with her, but it hadn't worked. He couldn't work with someone like that. Eventually, she would see that she was part of the plan, a very necessary part. But until then, she would have to learn who was boss.

Like Ashley before her, he'd been forced to bind her wrists with cable ties. It wasn't ideal. The last thing he wanted to do was to make it difficult for her to go to the toilet and to feed herself, but she'd given him no other choice. Her screeching made him worry she'd draw unwanted attention from the neighbours so he'd gagged her mouth. That was another irritation because it meant he had to help her every time she needed a drink. He didn't really have time to be playing nursemaid. There was important work to be done, and Tammy was wasting time.

She was lucky he hadn't lost his temper. He'd been tempted. Very tempted.

One well aimed punch to her stomach would have winded her and forced her to listen to him as she caught her breath.

But that would've meant they'd get off on the wrong foot, and despite her behaviour, Brendan didn't want that. He wanted them to be friends, partners.

He wasn't stupid. He knew that wouldn't happen straight away. They needed trust, and that was built slowly over time. But unless Tammy let him get a word in edgeways before freaking out, they weren't going to get anywhere.

He hadn't even had a chance to do any experiments yet. Which was very disappointing.

He leaned over the bath and added extra hot water. Steam slowly filled the room. He unwrapped a fresh packet of coal tar soap, and the scent made him gag. Not surprising, really, when there were so many bad memories attached to it.

His mum had scrubbed him all over the night he'd come home from school with a letter about an outbreak of nits in the primary class.

He'd sat in the hot bath as she'd scrubbed his skin with coal tar soap and wire wool until it was red raw.

Then she'd coated his head in medicated shampoo, even rubbing it into his eyebrows and eyelashes. Pushing the thick liquid against his eyelids until it seeped inside, burning his eyes.

"Dirty boy, bringing nits into my clean home," she'd muttered continually under her breath as she'd scrubbed his skin.

He hadn't been able to go back to school for two weeks due to the abrasions on his skin. The following day, the scratches had formed scabs, but they'd looked so shocking that his mother wouldn't let him see anyone until he was completely healed.

Luckily, that meant it was the last time she'd used wire wool on his skin, though it wasn't the last time she'd used coal tar soap and medicated shampoo.

Satisfied the bath temperature was scalding hot, Brendan stepped in, lowering one foot at a time slowly, inch by inch. The heat made his pulse shoot up, and his breathing became rapid as he slowly lowered himself into the searing hot bath. Finally submerged, he reached for the coal tar soap and began to methodically lather every inch of his body.

She'd loved him, of course. And she'd done what she'd thought was right, trying to rid him of those nasty little biting parasites. It wasn't her fault if she'd gone about it the wrong way, not really. It wasn't him she'd wanted to hurt. She'd wanted to help him, but she hadn't known how.

But thanks to Brendan's work, everyone would soon know the truth and they'd be able to eliminate all these disgusting, biting insects and their associated parasites once and for all.

Of course, all the published scientific literature said that the biting insects didn't spread disease. Brendan thought that was laughable. Mosquitoes spread malaria, ticks spread Lyme disease, yet they were supposed to believe that bedbugs, dust mites, and head lice were completely harmless.

Brendan gave a snort of disgust as he reached for the medicated shampoo.

Well, soon everyone would know the truth. That all these tiny, biting insects spread parasites that then bred beneath human skin. They didn't kill you, just made life a misery. He would be the one who led the way, the pioneer who'd determined the cause behind chronic fatigue syndrome, fibromyalgia, and numerous diseases that were classified as autoimmune but were really down to parasites.

As the water began to cool, Brendan reached for the plug and then for the shower attachment to rinse his body thoroughly of any lingering parasites.

He reached for a towel, patted his face and the skin on his arms and chest dry, and then wrapped the towel around his waist.

He paused in the hallway and listened.

All was quiet upstairs. Was Tammy still under control of the sedatives, or had she decided it was finally time to work with him and behave herself?

He considered going back upstairs to see if she needed a drink but then changed his mind.

After her behaviour today, she really didn't deserve any kindness.

Instead, he made his way downstairs and walked to the corner of the living room. He stared down at the fabric-covered case and smiled.

His mother had been annoyed about the head lice, but she'd be absolutely fuming if she could see what he'd brought into her house now. He chuckled.

Leaning down, he grabbed the fabric firmly and ripped it off, revealing the glass box beneath.

Reacting to the light, the insects scuttled into corners of the glass box.

Brendan grinned and tapped the side of the glass. "Hello, my little friends. Are you ready? I'm going to have some work for you to do tomorrow."

He watched the insects trample all over each other in an attempt to conceal themselves in the corners, but in a glass box there was nowhere to hide.

With a steady hand, he lifted the lid, reached inside, and plucked one of the flat reddish-brown bugs from the box. Then he squeezed it between his thumb and forefinger until the insect's legs stopped moving.

CHAPTER TWENTY-ONE

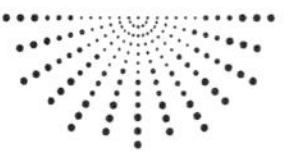

MACKINNON WAS JUST PULLING into a parking space at Wood Street Station when his mobile rang. The screen displayed Kate Squires's name.

He answered. "Any news on the laptop, Kate?"

"Yes. It's not here, but it's linked on a family account. Tim Burrows has an app on his phone, and all the devices are listed, along with their locations."

"The app tells you where to find the laptop?" Mackinnon asked as he climbed out of the car.

"It does. It says the laptop is in Noah Thorne's block of flats, Jack."

Mackinnon paused. More and more evidence was pointing at Noah Thorne.

He leaned against the car. "What about Ashley's phone? Is that linked on the app?"

"It should be, but unfortunately we haven't got a location. Probably because the battery's flat. It does have the last known location for Ashley's phone, and that was outside her place of work on the evening she went missing."

"That's really helpful, Kate. Thank you. Please thank the Burrowses as well. I believe we are actively trying to get a warrant to search Noah Thorne's property. I'll let you know how it goes."

"How much of this information do you want me to share with the parents?" Kate asked in a low voice.

"Keep the warrant and search to yourself for now. Once we get hold of the laptop, I'll keep you updated."

"All right."

After he hung up, Mackinnon called DI Tyler's direct number. He wanted to know where they were on the warrant. It looked like he might have to turn around and go straight back to Noah Thorne's flat.

Mackinnon found it difficult to keep personal feelings out of investigations sometimes. His immediate feeling about Noah Thorne was that he wasn't to be trusted, and he didn't find him particularly likeable. But that didn't mean he was a killer.

DI Tyler picked up the phone. "Jack, I hear there was a disturbance at Noah Thorne's place?"

"There was. Ashley's friend, Melissa West, got very drunk and turned up outside Noah's flat shouting the odds. She is of the opinion Noah is responsible for Ashley's death."

"And what do you think?"

"Not enough evidence to say. But I've just spoken to Kate Squires, and she tells me the parents have an app which monitors the location of all their devices, including Ashley's laptop. It's at Noah Thorne's flat. I asked him about it directly, and he denied having seen it recently."

"Very interesting," Tyler said.

"I've just pulled up outside the station. Shall I go around Noah's now and ask to see the laptop?"

"Actually, this is perfect timing. We've just got the warrant. Are you in the car park?"

"Yeah," Mackinnon said.

"Stay there. I'll be right down. I'm coming to Noah Thorne's with you, and we can execute the warrant together."

"We don't need a search team?"

"I'll arrange for one en route. But we need to get there and get hold of that laptop before he does something stupid and tries to destroy it."

Two minutes later, Tyler was sitting beside Mackinnon in the car, and they were heading back to Great Arthur House.

"What's your feeling about Noah Thorne?" Tyler asked.

"My first impression was that he was a self-centred young man. My impression of him worsened when I saw him shouting some pretty crude comments at Melissa West. He threatened to throw her down the stairs."

Tyler raised an eyebrow. "Was it a genuine threat?"

Mackinnon shrugged. "There was plenty of venom in his voice when he spoke, but I'd guess it was an angry comment made in the heat of the moment. Though you can never be too sure."

Mackinnon was well aware that it was easy to say something in anger and not mean it. He was also very aware of cases where women had been in fear for their lives and the police and authorities hadn't taken their concerns seriously, dismissing threats as something said in the heat of the moment. He didn't want to make that mistake here. It wasn't possible to really understand what motivated some people.

And there was no denying that Noah Thorne had made that threat against Melissa while in the presence of three police officers.

"I wouldn't like to say whether the threat was genuine or not," Mackinnon added.

"Fair enough," Tyler said. "Can you turn the air-conditioning up a bit? It's stifling in here."

Mackinnon shook his head as he indicated right and turned into Port Street. "Afraid not. It's on full at the moment."

"Why is it so hot? The sun's going down." Tyler rubbed a hand over his sweaty forehead.

"Well, you know the English weather. It will probably be five degrees and pouring with rain next week, and we'll be moaning about that."

Tyler gave a wry smile. "Probably."

"Any news on Janice?" Mackinnon asked.

Tyler grunted. "She did reply, finally. She said she's feeling a little better."

"Good news."

"Not for me. She's hardly likely to give me another chance after I poisoned her, is she?"

"Maybe. She sounds like a nice woman. She might give you a second chance."

"I'm not really sure I deserve one," Tyler said grumpily as they pulled up outside Great Arthur House.

Tyler looked up at the bright yellow cladding and put his hand on the door handle. "Right. Let's go and see if we can catch ourselves a killer."

Noah Thorne opened the door and blinked at the sight of the two police officers in front of him, his eyes narrowing when he recognised Mackinnon. "You again," he said, his upper lip curling in disgust. "I'm going to have you for harassment. You've got no right to keep turning up at my place and—"

"I think you'll find we have every right, sunshine," DI Tyler said, holding up his warrant card and introducing himself.

"This is ridiculous. You can't keep coming around here and disturbing me."

"Noah, we have a warrant to search your flat," Mackinnon said calmly. "I suggest you calm down and step outside so we can start the search."

"No chance. I'm not letting you in there on your own. Knowing you lot, you'll probably plant evidence."

"You're welcome to stay inside while we search," Mackinnon said, "as long as you keep your temper under control. Understood?"

Noah's head whipped around to look at Tyler again. "Well, I know you're a detective sergeant," he said, jerking his thumb at Mackinnon. "But who is this guy? He could be anyone."

"Pay attention, lad," Tyler snapped. "I just showed you my warrant card and introduced myself."

Noah pulled a face. "Oh, I'm so sorry, I didn't catch it," he said sarcastically. "I was too concerned with the unwarranted police victimisation."

"You're the victim?" Tyler asked dryly.

"My girlfriend has just died, and you're treating me in such an appalling way that—"

"Your ex-girlfriend, Mr Thorne," Tyler said. "That's an important distinction, don't you think?"

Noah's face turned bright red, and he gritted his teeth and muttered a curse under his breath.

"Please stand aside, sir, so we can search the premises," Mackinnon said.

"No!" Noah Thorne smiled, stepping forward, getting up close and into Mackinnon's personal space, and glared up at him. "Who. Do. You. Think. You. Are? You can't come in. I don't give you my permission."

"We don't need your permission," Tyler said.

Trying to diffuse the situation, Mackinnon said, "Noah, we have a warrant to search your property. Now you can do this the hard way, or you can invite us inside and tell us where Ashley's laptop is."

At the mention of the laptop, Noah fell quiet and took a step back. He looked down at the ground.

If Mackinnon had any doubts that Ashley's laptop was here and that the app had been wrong, they now disappeared.

After a brief hesitation, Noah Thorne stepped aside. "Fine, but you're victimising the wrong person. I didn't have anything to do with Ashley's murder. To be honest, I'm not even sure it *is* a murder. You haven't shown me any evidence. She could have just been mugged and killed in a random attack."

Mackinnon didn't bother to comment. If it had been a random attack, which he didn't believe, it would still have been murder. He strode inside the flat, and Tyler followed him. "Are you going to show us where this laptop is, Noah?"

Noah was fuming. He folded his arms over his chest and then let them drop to the side again as he paced the hallway. He knew he wasn't going to get out of this without showing them where the laptop was. Even if they had to tear the flat apart, they would find it.

Finally, he stalked into the bedroom, kneeled beside the bed, and opened the bottom drawer of his nightstand.

He pulled out a silver MacBook and threw it on the bed. "There! Happy now?"

"Thank you," Mackinnon said. "Now, we're going to have a little look around the property when the rest of the search team get here."

The intercom sounded. "That's probably the rest of the search team. I'll let them in, shall I?" Tyler asked and strode off down the hallway without waiting for an answer.

"If you're as innocent as you say you are, Noah, why didn't you tell me you had Ashley's laptop when I came to see you?"

"Because it's none of your business."

"We're trying to solve Ashley's murder. Her laptop could hold vital evidence."

Noah refused to meet Mackinnon's gaze, and he guessed that was exactly what Noah was afraid of. He thought the laptop did hold evidence. Evidence against him.

"Have you used this laptop since Ashley went missing?" Mackinnon asked.

"No," Noah said solemnly.

"You should tell the truth, Noah. Because the people in our tech department will be able to tell."

"I told you, I didn't. I don't know the password."

Mackinnon looked at Noah through narrowed eyes as the rest of the search team streamed into the flat.

"What's all this? You can't let all these people into my flat. It's not fair. They'll make a mess!"

"That should be the least of your worries, Noah," Tyler said.

"I don't believe this. You're just focusing on me because you're too lazy to do any real detective work. You'll never find Ashley's killer at this rate. Maybe I should tell her parents just how incompetent you really are."

Tyler stepped forward and put a firm hand on Noah's arm. "Noah Thorne, I'm arresting you on suspicion of the murder of Ashley Burrows."

Mackinnon watched in surprise as Tyler read Noah his rights. They hadn't discussed an arrest on the way here. Yes, they had discovered Ashley's laptop, but was that enough for an arrest? Obviously, Tyler thought so.

Tyler led Noah outside and into the lift.

For once, Noah was silent. His arrest was as much of a surprise to him as it was to Mackinnon.

When Noah was safely in the back seat of the car and Tyler had shut the door, Mackinnon said quietly, "I wasn't expecting that. Do you think we played our hand too soon?"

Tyler shrugged as he walked around to the passenger seat. "Maybe, but it wiped that smug look off his face, didn't it? I don't like him, Jack. He's hiding something, and we're going to find out exactly what it is."

CHAPTER TWENTY-TWO

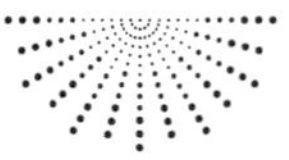

WHEN THEY ARRIVED BACK at Wood Street Station, DI Tyler took Noah to the custody suite to get him booked in, and Mackinnon took a few minutes to call Chloe.

Her voicemail cut in before she answered. He left a message.

It was going to be a long night.

Now they had Noah Thorne in custody, they needed to come up with an interview plan to make the most of the time they had with him. He would need appropriate breaks, and they wouldn't be able to start interviewing him until his solicitor was present.

Mackinnon dialled Derek's number to let him know he'd be late.

"No problem," Derek said. "You've got your key, haven't you?"

"Yeah. I'll try to be as quiet as possible when I get home. Oh, and can I use your washing machine?"

"Oh, sure... why?"

"An interesting job today. I spoke to a pest controller and went to a flat infested with bedbugs. He recommended that I wash all my clothes at sixty degrees."

"What? You've got to be kidding. You can't bring them back here."

"It's only a precaution. Besides, if I had picked anything up, they'd probably have dropped off before now."

"Fantastic. If you introduce bedbugs into my flat, you're paying to get rid of them, right?"

"Yeah, I'll pay. But I'm sure you've got nothing to worry about." Mackinnon self-consciously scratched his elbow and then studied the skin, checking for bumps and bite marks, but there was nothing.

"All right, it's programme four on the washing machine for a sixty-degree wash."

"Cheers. Is there anything you need me to pick up on the way home?"

"No, I've got a date tonight, so I might be back even later than you if I'm lucky."

"All right. So I may or may not see you later. Have a good night."

Mackinnon hung up and then tried Chloe again. This time she answered.

"Sorry, Jack. I was on the landline."

"That's all right. I thought I'd try and get you before I go back into the station. It's going to be a late one."

"Good or bad?" Chloe asked.

"Good, hopefully. We've arrested a suspect."

"Right, that's good."

"Is everything okay? You sound distracted."

Chloe sighed. "I had a row with Sarah yesterday, and she didn't come home last night."

"Oh." Mackinnon didn't really know what to say. The fact that Chloe had had yet another row with her eldest daughter wasn't really a surprise, but despite Sarah's prickly nature, she was still Chloe's daughter. Like any mother, Chloe constantly worried about her children.

"She's probably fine, just punishing me," Chloe said. "But I wish she'd let me know she was all right."

"Any jobs on the horizon?" Mackinnon asked hopefully. Since Sarah had now been turfed out of university, it seemed logical she would be on the lookout for a job. So far, she didn't have a conviction for stealing the money, so he hoped it wouldn't hinder her employment prospects.

"You've got to be joking. What she does is lie in bed till midday and then spend the rest of her time smoking in the garden and sniping at Katy and me. You know what she's been like recently."

Mackinnon did. He'd never known sisters to be so different. Katy was studious, hard-working, and a very loving child, whereas Sarah was prickly, difficult, and sometimes plain nasty.

"Do you need me to come home?" Mackinnon offered. He felt guilty for hoping Chloe said no.

"I'll be fine," she said. "I'm just going to have a hot bath, probably drink a bottle of wine, and get an early night."

"All right. Well, call me if there's any more news. Otherwise, I'll speak to you tomorrow."

"All right. Take care. Bye."

Mackinnon hung up and shoved his mobile in his pocket. There was a time when he would look forward to getting back to Oxford and spending time with Chloe and Katy, but since Sarah had moved back home, things were different.

Logic told him that Sarah would be fine. She'd been out of contact many times in the past. But he couldn't push away the niggling worry that this time, she could be in trouble.

He turned, pushed through the double doors, and headed back inside Wood Street Station. He passed Charlotte on the way.

"Heading home?" he asked.

She nodded and smothered a yawn. "Yes, I hear you and Tyler arrested Noah Thorne."

Mackinnon nodded. "Yeah, it came as a bit of a surprise to me, to be honest. I think it might have had something to do with Tyler's bad mood, recent food poisoning, and his being upset about Janice. Noah's attitude was the last straw."

"Do you think we've got enough on him to make any charges stick?"

"It depends on what we find on that laptop. Hopefully Tyler can push that through urgently, and we'll get some answers."

"Who is going to be interviewing him?"

"Tyler and me, I think. So I'd better get upstairs and help prepare the interview plan."

"Good luck, I'll see you tomorrow," Charlotte said, yawning again and walking towards the exit.

CHAPTER TWENTY-THREE

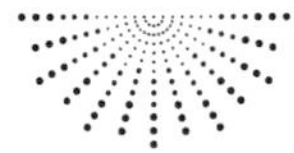

CHARLOTTE STEPPED out of the lift, turned left, and pressed the doorbell.

She was supposed to have arrived at her Nan's flat over an hour and a half ago, but she hadn't been able to get away.

Nan answered the door. "Hello, darling. You look tired."

"I am," Charlotte said as she stepped inside. "We've got a big case on at the moment, which is why I'm late. Sorry."

"Well, I've got just the thing for you. I picked up pie and mash from Maureen's in Chrisp Street today. I thought you deserved a treat." As Nan walked up the hallway, she turned back and looked at Charlotte over her shoulder with a smile. "I recorded Corrie for you, too."

Charlotte beamed. True, she was an adult, but she still enjoyed being spoiled by her Nan. "Perfect."

"The pie's in the oven, so I just need to heat up the mash and liquor."

Charlotte went to the bathroom to wash her hands as Nan used the microwave to heat up the liquor.

When she returned to the kitchen, Charlotte said, "You didn't wait for me, did you?"

Nan shook her head as she carefully removed the steaming hot liquor from the microwave. "No, I ate mine hours ago. Here you go."

Nan handed her the pot of liquor, and Charlotte poured it all over the pie and mash, then added lashings of vinegar on top. It smelled divine.

She carried the piled high plate through to the living room on a tray.

"How have you been?" Charlotte asked as she settled on the sofa.

Nan sank into an armchair. "Good, thanks, darling. I met one of my old friends for coffee this morning. Haven't seen her in nearly twenty-five years. Funnily enough, she's moved back to London, so now she's living just around the corner again."

"That's good," Charlotte said. "Mostly you hear about people moving *away* from London."

Nan nodded. "Yes, most of my friends moved away years ago. But I was always a Londoner at heart. I don't mind a visit to the country, but any longer than a week or two and I get homesick."

Charlotte smiled. She was just the same. She dug into the pie and mash as Nan used the remote to start Corrie playing on the television.

Nan had a fan going in the corner of the room which gave some respite from the heat. They sat in comfortable silence watching the soap as Charlotte ate her dinner.

Though Charlotte was comfortable and enjoying her meal, something was bugging her.

Mackinnon hadn't seemed his usual self tonight. She was pretty sure that had something to do with his partner's daughter. Sarah, as Charlotte's Nan would say, was a proper little madam.

It was times like this when Charlotte was glad she was single and childless.

Since he'd met Chloe, Mackinnon's life seemed to have been taken over by her children. It couldn't have been easy for him adapting to a ready-made family, although from the sounds of it, Katy sounded like a lot of fun. But Sarah—Sarah sounded like trouble.

Charlotte polished off the last of the pie and gave a deep sigh of satisfaction.

She turned to smile at Nan. "That was absolutely gorgeous. Thank you."

She took the tray back out to the kitchen, scraped off the remaining mash into the bin, and washed the plate.

She wondered how Mackinnon and Tyler were getting on questioning Noah Thorne.

In most cases, the killer was someone known to the victim, and Noah Thorne fitted the profile, but to Charlotte, it seemed like they were missing something. Some vital piece of the puzzle. Perhaps when they finally managed to view the rest of the CCTV, they'd get their answers.

CHAPTER TWENTY-FOUR

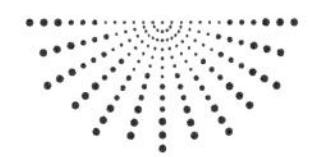

THE FOLLOWING day at seven thirty a.m., Dr Wendy Willson sat in the meeting room of the doctor's surgery.

The practice manager sat in the chair beside her. Dr Melling and Dr Todman shared a joke as Dr Farquhar called the meeting to order.

Wendy waited patiently as the practice manager described the new telephone system she was having installed next week.

Then she listened to Dr Farquhar as he covered the statistics on new patients and the urgent care and referrals they had dealt with last week.

They had a brief discussion about the new procedures implemented for the COPD clinic, and finally Dr Farquhar turned the floor over to the rest of the doctors.

"Does anyone have any issues they would like to discuss?"

"I do," Wendy said. She'd attempted to speak to Dr Farquhar about her concerns over Brendan Maynard. But Dr Farquhar had dismissed her, undermining her fears.

Wendy felt if she brought it up now, in the meeting, in front of the practice manager and the other doctors, Dr Farquhar wouldn't be so quick to dismiss her.

Dr Farquhar turned his hooded eyes on Wendy. "Yes. What would you like to share?"

Wendy wasn't certain, but she thought there may have been a warning in Dr Farquhar's tone.

But the subject was too important to ignore.

"I'd like to discuss one of my patients. Brendan Maynard."

Dr Farquhar gave a subtle shake of his head. "But Wendy, we've already talked about that patient, and he's been moved over to my list, hasn't he?"

Wendy tried to control her irritation. Dr Farquhar knew as well as she did that even though Dr Farquhar was now his named GP, when Brendan visited the surgery, he would see whichever Dr was free, and that included Wendy, especially as Dr Farquhar now only worked three days a week at the practice.

"I still believe my concerns about Mr Maynard should be addressed."

"I see," Dr Farquhar said in a tight voice. "In that case, please continue."

Wendy cleared her throat. "I believe Brendan has mental health problems, and—"

Before she could continue, Dr Todman intervened, "Oh, I know who you mean. The *hypochondriac*."

Wendy gave a small nod and continued. "I think it's more than that. He's convinced there's something wrong with him. I believe he has delusional parasitosis. He thinks he has parasites living beneath his skin, and when I wouldn't give him antibiotics, he got extremely agitated and was... threatening."

"Was he violent?" Claire, the practice manager asked, shifting in her seat so she turned to face Wendy.

"He slammed his hand against my desk and shouted, and I felt…afraid," Wendy admitted. "I don't know whether he would ever be violent towards me or anyone else, but I know at that moment, when he was in my consulting room, I was scared."

"I see," Claire said. "You are absolutely right to bring this up in the meeting. We'll need to make a full report and have a separate meeting just on Brendan. I think we'll go back over his files, consult with Dr Farquhar and the other doctors, and decide how to proceed."

"I really don't think that's necessary," said Dr Farquhar. "But I think it's best if we say going forward, Brendan can only see a male doctor."

Dr Melling narrowed his eyes. "I can't say I'm happy with that. I agree with Claire. We need to have an in-depth meeting, go through Brendan's records, and decide how to proceed."

"Absolutely," said Claire. "We don't want to put any of our doctors at risk, or any of our other staff, including the receptionists and practice nurses. There could be liabilities for the practice, Dr Farquhar."

Dr Farquhar narrowed his eyes and gave a little huff. "If that's how you all want to proceed, then fine. I think it's an overreaction, but better safe than sorry, I suppose."

Wendy smiled with relief. She was glad the doctors and practice manager were taking her concerns seriously. Whether Brendan would ever be violent towards anyone wasn't the main point. He needed help, more help than his GP could offer, and he had to be referred to a mental health unit.

Dr Farquhar ended the meeting and dismissed the doctors.

As Wendy got up and left the room, she felt a hand on her shoulder. It was the practice manager.

"Could you tell me more about this delusional parasitosis?" Claire asked.

"Oh, yes. I've never seen a case before now. But it's when a patient is convinced they're infested with parasites. Usually there are some physical manifestations like an itch or a rash. It could manifest in multiple ways, but the patient puts it down to a parasite. Fortunately, it's not very common."

Claire nodded. "And you think Brendan Maynard is suffering from this condition. Does it usually associate with any other mental health conditions?"

"It can do. In fact, I'm quite worried about Brendan. He seems very angry, and he really needs help. More help than we can give him."

Claire smiled. "Thanks, Wendy. If you could dig out your notes and his records and give them to me this afternoon, I'll see about preparing the final report, and then we can arrange a meeting."

"Absolutely. Thanks for taking my concerns seriously."

"Of course, I do. It's my job. I hope you always feel you can come to me with any issues that arise," Claire said.

Wendy walked to her consulting room feeling like a weight had been lifted from her shoulders. Finally, Brendan Maynard would get the help he needed.

CHAPTER TWENTY-FIVE

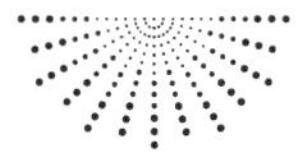

When Tammy Holt woke up, she was disorientated. At first, she thought she was at home in her own bed, but she couldn't work out why her shoulder and hip hurt so much and why it was hard to breathe.

It took a few seconds for the truth to sink in. She wasn't at home in bed. She was still stuck in the loft space of that maniac, Brendan—if that was even his real name.

Her head felt like it was filled with rocks, heavy and bruised. It even hurt to move her eyes. Breathing through her nose was her only option because he'd gagged her. She forced herself to look around, making sure he wasn't there, but she was alone.

The last time she'd woken, it had been stuffy and hot. Now the air was cool, frigid against her bare arms and legs. He'd taken her clothes, muttering something about experiments and leaving her in her underwear. She shivered and stayed still, straining to hear any sounds, like traffic from outside or neighbours talking, but it was silent. She couldn't even hear Brendan moving downstairs. Had he gone out? Maybe this was her chance to escape. But how would she get out of here with her hands bound with cable ties?

She rolled onto her side, and as she did so, her stomach flipped in protest. She felt bile at the back of her throat and panicked. She couldn't throw up, not now. She still had the gag in her mouth; she would choke to death.

She fought to control her rapid breathing, to focus on anything other than the sickness rolling around in her belly. It had to be a side-effect of whatever drug he'd given her. She tugged at the gag until it lowered to her chin and she could take a deep breath.

Tammy whimpered. She was terrified and furious at the same time. Why had she agreed to meet a man she'd only communicated with over the Internet? What was wrong with her? Hadn't she read the horror stories of young girls doing the same and getting murdered and raped?

She took another deep breath and tried to sit up. It wasn't easy. Her muscles felt weak, and she couldn't get a good grip on anything with her hands bound together. When she managed to sit up, she took a few shaky breaths and tried to clear her mind. She needed to focus. Somehow, she needed to come up with a plan to get out of there.

Why hadn't she waited instead of rushing ahead to meet him? She'd mentioned the meeting to her sister, but she'd only given Julie Brendan's first name. What good was that? They'd never track him down with only a first name to go on.

Pushing herself onto her knees, she shuffled against the bare wooden boards and looked around the attic space. Where were her phone and bag? Were they still downstairs? How would he explain that to his mother when she got home? Maybe he'd hidden them. Perhaps that was her chance. She just had to wait until Brendan's mother came home, and then she could scream and raise the alarm.

Tammy frowned. What time of day was it? Perhaps his mum had already been home and gone back to work. She had no idea if it was daytime or the middle of the night. The only light in the loft came from a single light bulb.

She tried to rotate her shoulder. It felt dead, as did her hip from where she'd been lying on the hard boards.

She blinked in the gloom and looked into the corners of the attic. A few boxes and black bin bags were stacked in one corner but nothing that looked useful. Perhaps there was something in one of the boxes she could use as a weapon against Brendan. She could take him by surprise, overpower him and get out.

She shuffled towards the bags closest to her.

What did he want from her? How long had she been there? At least since last night... or was that yesterday?

She shook her head. There was no point trying to figure it out. It was impossible.

She'd been terrified when he'd come up to the attic last night. It was hard to believe she'd just gone willingly with him only a few hours before. Now it was clear he was completely deranged. She could see the madness in his eyes. How could she have missed it before?

She'd fought back when he'd got too close, and it'd made him angry. But she would do it again. If he killed her, they would find his skin cells under her fingernails, and his blood contaminating her body when forensics found it.

She shivered at the thought. He wouldn't get away with this no matter how it ended. He would pay.

She shuffled forward painfully, her knees scratching against the rough wood. The small movement left her out of breath and her mouth dry by the time she reached the first black bag. She pulled it forward, and the contents spilled out.

For a moment, Tammy didn't move. She just stared down at the things that had been stored in the black bag.

A shiver of terror ran down her spine. The objects might seem innocuous enough to everyone else, but to Tammy, they told her something she really didn't want to accept.

There were clothes and a handbag, but they didn't belong to Tammy. One was a short denim skirt from Topshop, and the pink bag was from River Island. Something a young woman would wear… items someone Tammy's age would wear.

Tammy didn't want to think about it, but the idea pushed its way into her head regardless.

Tammy wasn't the first woman Brendan had kept up here.

Tammy whirled around when she heard a noise behind her, too fast, and she slid painfully onto her hip.

Her heart was thudding as she heard wood sliding against the boards.

It was the hatch. He'd come back.

It was Brendan.

Her mouth was so dry she couldn't swallow, and her gasping breaths made her panic as she raised the gag to her mouth, scared of Brendan's reaction if he saw she'd removed the gag.

Her skin crawled as Brendan's dark head appeared in the hatch opening.

He smiled at her. "Hello, Tammy, I hope you're in a better mood today."

Tammy just stared at him. She wanted to be strong and tough, but she was shaking and couldn't stop.

"I've got something to show you," Brendan said. He lifted a large box through the hatch. It was covered with dark red material. He easily lifted himself into the loft, all the while keeping that sickening grin plastered on his face.

"Well, don't you want to know what it is?"

Tammy shook her head fiercely. No, whatever he had in that box, she did *not* want to see it. As he stepped closer, she recoiled, pushing herself back along the wooden boards.

"I hope we're not going to have a repeat of last night, Tammy. It won't get you anywhere. You're my partner now. I'm afraid you don't have a choice, but I hope you'll realise as time passes just how important your role is."

Tammy glanced at the other woman's clothes that had spilled out along the wooden boards.

Brendan followed her gaze. "That was your predecessor, Tammy. Let's hope you cooperate, and you won't end up the same way."

Tammy felt her breathing quicken, and her heart was beating so fast, she thought it was going to explode. He came closer and closer until he reached out, his fingers grazing her cheek.

Tammy froze as he tugged the gag away from her mouth.

"That's better. Now we can have a proper conversation. I'm sure you have a lot of questions for me."

"Please let me go," Tammy said.

"I can't do that yet," Brendan said. "But I want you to

know you're really important to me. We're going to be working together, as a team."

"Working on what?" Tammy asked, looking behind Brendan to the open hatch.

Could she get over there before Brendan stopped her? Could she get down the ladder and to the front door before he caught her?

No, even if she hadn't been drugged and suffering the after-effects of a sedative, she still wouldn't have been able to beat Brendan. She'd need to disable him somehow first, find something to hit him with.

"What are you thinking about, Tammy?"

Horrified that Brendan might be able to read her intentions, Tammy rapidly shook her head. "Nothing. I don't understand what you want from me."

"I know, it's a bit overwhelming, but in time you will realise I'm doing this for a good reason."

Tammy looked at him in horror. He genuinely thought he was in the right here. He thought abducting someone was just fine, a normal, everyday occurrence. There was no chance she would get out of this by reasoning with a madman.

"I just want to go home. Why can't I help you with whatever it is you're doing but still live in my own house and sleep in my own bed?"

Brendan pondered that for a moment. "I'd like to do it that way too, Tammy, but I'm afraid I can't trust you yet. You won't always be locked up here in the attic. Once we get to know each other a bit better, then maybe you can sleep in my mum's room."

Tammy blinked in confusion. "Your mum's room?"

Brendan nodded. "I don't see why not."

"But isn't your mum using it?"

"Sadly, my mum passed away a few months ago. She left this place to me. She adored me."

Tammy stifled a sob. So much for trying to raise the alarm and alert Brendan's mother. She should have paid attention to her instincts when she'd first walked into the house. She'd smelled the damp neglect in the stale air. She should have realised the house didn't have anyone living there.

"Right, if you're feeling a bit better today, perhaps we'll move onto the first part of the experiment."

"Experiment?"

Brendan carefully walked over the wooden boards and picked up the box before bringing it back over to Tammy. He set it down beside her, and with a flourish, he removed the red cover.

Inside the box, there were hundreds of small, brown insects scurrying around the glass.

Tammy screamed.

CHAPTER TWENTY-SIX

BRENDAN STALKED down from the attic, fuming. Tammy had completely overreacted again. He was well aware that this would be a shock to anyone's system. And he was prepared to give his assistants a little leeway.

Tammy was acting like a spoilt brat. This time, she'd come at him so fast he had had no chance to react, and her fist had connected just below his eye.

Of course, Brendan would never hit back. She was a girl after all, and his mother had taught him never to be violent towards women. But he'd been severely tempted. No doubt, he'd have a black eye by this time tomorrow. He put the glass insect cabinet back in the living room and threw the red cloth over it.

Just for once, he'd like someone to appreciate the work he had planned. Perhaps that was where he was going wrong. He'd thought people suffering from diseases that doctors couldn't name or diagnose would be more willing to understand, but perhaps he should have taken a scientist or doctor. At least they'd have some basic understanding of the scientific method behind Brendan's plan.

He shrugged. Well, if Tammy didn't work out, next time he'd get someone with more than a basic understanding of science.

He was practically shaking with rage as he left the living room and went into the kitchen, pouring himself a long glass of water.

He'd intended to give Tammy some water and to make her a nice breakfast, but he wouldn't do it now. She didn't deserve it. There really was no excuse for violence.

He gulped down the water and looked outside at the yellowing lawn. It looked like it was going to be another hot day. Tammy would soon regret her actions. It would be hot up there, and she'd be very thirsty soon.

Perhaps that would teach her to be nicer to him next time.

His plans for the day had been completely derailed by Tammy's outburst. He'd intended to gradually introduce her to the theory behind his science, but he could tell he wouldn't get any sense out of her now. There was nothing for it. He would have to leave her until tomorrow and hope she saw sense then.

In the meantime, he had plenty to keep him busy.

He left the kitchen and entered the small dining room downstairs that his mother had kitted out as a study for when she worked from home. The computer was still there, as well as a printer, a comfortable computer chair, and a large desk. Brendan settled himself in front of the computer and opened up a file on the desktop.

He selected the image and clicked on 'Print' from the file

menu. He'd go for a hundred today. That was a nice round number.

He closed his eyes as the printer hummed into life.

He'd been excited to get Tammy on board when her reaction was disappointing, but he needed to remember that Rome wasn't built in a day, and this kind of experiment took time.

Besides, his income had been dwindling over the past few weeks, especially after Ashley.

He frowned when he thought about Ashley. She was a total failure. He could only hope Tammy would be better, although going by the start, it looked like he may have picked another dud.

He plucked one of the printouts from the printer tray and looked at the leaflet. In full colour, it had the name of his company: Express Pest Control.

Beneath the logo, it had some nice pictures of mice, bedbugs, and fleas and underneath that, his slogan and his contact number.

He pulled some white envelopes from the drawer and began to fold the leaflets in half, stuffing the leaflet into each envelope.

Most people would just put the leaflet through letterboxes. They wouldn't bother with an envelope, but Brendan liked to do things differently. He had a very important reason for using an envelope.

When the printer had spat out the last leaflet and he'd stuffed the last envelope, Brendan gathered them all together and carried them back through to the living room. He set the envelopes down on the coffee table and then went to his bedroom to get a pair of gloves and a pair of tweezers.

Then he uncovered the glass cage and the lid. The insects rushed to the sides, trying to escape.

Brendan lowered the tweezers and plucked an insect from its fellow bugs. He placed it in the envelope and then quickly sealed the envelope with Sellotape.

He smiled. One down, 99 to go.

It was ingenious, really. A very clever plan, even if he did say so himself.

He'd go out to a neighbourhood nearby and put the envelopes through a variety of different letterboxes. When the owner of the house opened the envelope, they probably wouldn't notice the small bug. They'd read the leaflet, perhaps put it along with the junk mail ready for recycling, and go about their business.

The little bug would make itself at home.

That night, it would come out from its hiding place, scurry along to the closest sleeping body, and tuck in.

After a few nights of bites, when the house owners realised that this wasn't a simple gnat bite or mosquito bite, they'd get in touch with a pest control company, hopefully remembering the leaflet they'd put in recycling, before grabbing it and giving Brendan a call.

He was generating his own business.

Brendan chuckled as he plucked another insect from the glass cage and put it into another envelope.

CHAPTER TWENTY-SEVEN

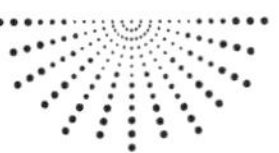

MACKINNON AND DI TYLER worked steadily on the interview plan for over an hour. Noah Thorne had been booked in, and they were awaiting the arrival of the duty solicitor before they started the interview.

They only had a limited time before Noah was entitled to a rest break. They couldn't question him all night. If the case against Noah Thorne went to trial, they couldn't risk his defence team declaring he was put under undue pressure without adequate time to rest.

Mackinnon scanned the list of handwritten questions. "How did Evie get on with Ashley's diary?" he asked. "Did she find anything we could use in the interview?"

Tyler looked up from the paperwork. "She's made some notes. I'll forward them to you later. It didn't give us the break we'd hoped for, but Ashley mentions Noah frequently and not always in favourable terms. From her descriptions, he sounds domineering and controlling. A man who wouldn't take no for an answer. She said he'd been cheating."

"Any mention of physical violence?"

"He grabbed her and left bruises. Unacceptable, and it could easily have escalated."

Mackinnon checked his watch. "And the laptop? How soon can we expect a result from that?"

Tyler gave a heavy sigh. "It's outside normal working hours, so there's only one person manning the tech department tonight. He's going to look at it for us, but I doubt we'll get any answers from the laptop before we interview Thorne."

Mackinnon nodded and shuffled the scattered paper in front of him into a pile. "So we don't have much to work with."

"Not yet."

The phone on Tyler's desk rang, and he got up to answer it. From his replies, Mackinnon got the gist of the conversation. The duty solicitor had arrived.

They headed downstairs together. Tyler had booked interview suite three. The so-called suite was in fact a small windowless room, not much bigger than the stationery cupboard, and Mackinnon wasn't looking forward to spending time inside the claustrophobic space. He hoped Thorne found it as uncomfortable as he did and wanted to spill the beans and get out of there as soon as possible.

Outside the interview suite they exchanged pleasantries with the duty solicitor, Barbara Wood.

She'd already been inside and conferred with her client, so Tyler led the way into the small room. Thorne was already sitting at the table, shoulders hunched, staring silently down at the scratched laminate tabletop.

The uniformed officer, who'd been stationed in the room to keep an eye on Thorne, gave them a polite nod as he left.

As Mackinnon had expected, the room was stuffy and far too warm.

Barbara Wood sat next to her client, and Mackinnon and Tyler sat in the seats opposite. Four bottles of water had been laid out on the table.

A red light blinked on the small camera in the corner of the room. Tyler checked there was a tape in the audio recorder, then pressed record. Mackinnon pushed bottles of water towards the solicitor and Thorne before opening his own bottle and taking a sip of the lukewarm water. Tyler began the introductions for the benefit of the tape.

As Tyler spoke, Mackinnon took the opportunity to study Thorne. He looked considerably less confident now. Reading his body language, Mackinnon judged he was stressed and scared. Would he talk? It was impossible to know at this stage.

They didn't have much time until they'd need to break for the evening so Noah had adequate time to rest, and Mackinnon hoped their carefully planned interview questions were effective and they'd get answers before they had to call it a night.

"Today, we found Ashley Burrows's laptop in your bedroom, Noah." Tyler pushed a photograph of Ashley's laptop across the table. "Could you tell us why you had it?"

Noah scowled. "Technically, you didn't find it. I *gave* it to you. I took it out of the drawer myself and handed it to you."

Tyler ignored the pedantic reply and asked again, "Why did you have it?"

Noah shrugged. "Ashley must've just left it at my place, and I forgot."

"You forgot? That seems unlikely. DS Mackinnon asked you if you'd seen the laptop recently, and you insisted you hadn't."

"So, I've got a bad memory. That's not a crime."

"Obstructing justice *is* a crime," Tyler said pointedly.

"That's not the charge put to my client today," Barbara Wood said sharply.

Tyler nodded in acknowledgement. "Could you tell us what you were doing the day Ashley went missing?"

"I was at work. I didn't finish till six thirty."

They didn't have an exact time for Ashley's disappearance. Only that the last time anyone was known to have seen her was at five thirty when she'd left Flyaway Travel Agents. Noah had a good alibi until six thirty, but that didn't mean he was in the clear.

"How would you describe your relationship with Ashley?"

Noah shifted in his seat and glanced at the solicitor. "Do I have to answer that?"

"Not if you have something to hide," Tyler said before the solicitor could respond.

"I don't," Thorne snapped. "I just don't like what you're implying."

"I'm not trying to imply anything, Mr Thorne. I just want the truth."

The duty solicitor gave Thorne a small nod. He exhaled a long breath and then said, "She was my girlfriend. We had a few arguments and broke up, but we still talked. We were still friends."

"When was the last time you spoke to Ashley?" Mackinnon asked.

He'd already asked Thorne this on a previous occasion and was interested to hear if his answer would be consistent.

Thorne blinked. "Um, the last time I saw her was just after she left work two days before she disappeared."

"And what happened the last time you saw her?" Mackinnon asked.

Thorne's features tightened in annoyance. "You already know the answer to that."

"Please tell us again for the benefit of the tape."

Thorne leaned back in his chair and folded his arms over his chest. From the sulky expression on his face, Mackinnon thought he might refuse to answer, but eventually, he said, "We argued."

"What about?"

"I wanted to apologise and asked her if we could go somewhere to talk, but she was really angry."

"Why was she angry?"

"I have no idea. Maybe she'd had a bad day at work. All I know is she was completely unreasonable and snapped at me."

"Is that something Ashley usually did?" Tyler asked.

"No…" Thorne looked up at the ceiling before continuing. "Usually she was sweet and kind. She was nice to everyone."

Mackinnon noticed the softening of Thorne's voice when he spoke about Ashley and wondered if the interview questions they'd planned were focusing on the wrong track. Maybe they should have directed the questions to exploit his affection for Ashley rather than trying to provoke him into snapping and revealing something he wanted to keep secret.

"Was it because she found out you were cheating?" Tyler asked.

"What? I wasn't. That's a lie. Who told you that?"

Tyler shrugged. "You must have said or done something to make her snap at you."

"I didn't. You weren't there. You have no idea what you're talking about."

"That's why we are asking you the questions, Noah. So we can understand," Mackinnon said.

Thorne didn't look up but kept his arms tightly folded around his body, clearly not in the mood to open up.

"What was on the laptop? Something you didn't want us to see?" Tyler asked.

Noah shrugged. "What? No. There was nothing. I don't care what you find on the computer. It's nothing to do with me. It's Ashley's laptop."

"So you didn't take her laptop in an effort to prevent the police or Ashley's parents from looking at it?"

A slight sheen of sweat had appeared on Thorne's forehead. It was hot in the interview room, but Mackinnon thought the sweat was down to stress rather than simply the heat.

Noah wiped his brow. "I couldn't care less about the stupid laptop. I told you. It's nothing to do with me."

Everything about Noah Thorne's body language told Mackinnon he was lying.

But they weren't getting anywhere, and they were running out of time. Soon they'd need to take a break. Mackinnon decided to take a slightly softer approach. It wasn't in the interview plan, but the plan clearly wasn't working.

"Noah, I know you want to find out who hurt Ashley as much as we do. We have to ask these questions. They might be difficult to answer, but we need to ask them to help our investigation. You may know more than you think."

Thorne's gaze flickered up to meet Mackinnon's, he stared at him for a moment or two, and Mackinnon met his gaze steadily.

He wanted to give Thorne the impression they were all in this together. He needed him to believe they were all on the same side.

"This must be incredibly hard for you, but we need to find out why you kept the laptop. You have to understand that it makes you look guilty."

"But I didn't hurt Ashley, I swear."

"Then you need to help us prove that. You need to start telling us the truth, Noah."

Thorne leaned forward, resting his elbows on the table and cupped his face in his hands.

No one spoke for a moment.

"All right." Thorne lowered his hands and looked at Tyler and then Mackinnon. "I know I'm being difficult, but it's because I didn't hurt Ashley, and I know you're trying to prove that I did."

"No," Mackinnon said. "We're trying to find out who hurt Ashley and why you took her laptop."

Thorne clenched his jaw, and Mackinnon wondered if he was going to deny taking the laptop once again, but he didn't.

"I…I was feeling guilty," he began with a slight stammer. "I behaved really badly, and now it's too late to tell Ashley I'm sorry."

He wiped away the tears from his eyes roughly.

"What did you do, Noah?" Tyler asked in a calm voice.

"I took her laptop. We met up to talk, but it wasn't going

well. I tried to apologise, but she said she'd moved on. I was angry. When she went to the ladies, I took the laptop out of her bag and put it in my rucksack." He shook his head. "It was a really stupid thing to do. But she was always online, and I thought maybe… I don't know what I thought…" He trailed off, looking miserably at the bottle of water in front of him.

"Did you think she'd written something incriminating about you on the laptop?" Tyler asked.

Thorne shook his head. He picked up his bottle of water and took a long gulp. "No, it wasn't that at all." He hesitated for a moment before adding, "If you must know, I thought she might be cheating on me. She was always on that stupid laptop, and I thought maybe she had some kind of online relationship going on."

"She couldn't have been cheating on you if you'd broken up," Mackinnon said.

Noah shrugged. "I thought maybe something was going on before we broke up. I thought it could be the reason she ended things."

"And when you got hold of the laptop, did you find anything?"

Thorne sighed miserably. "I couldn't access it. I tried to follow some instructions I found online to hack the computer, but it didn't work, and I think I ended up resetting the computer somehow." He looked up at Mackinnon. "I promise I didn't mean to do it, but I think I wiped Ashley's computer." There was silence for a few moments. Thorne sniffed, blinking away tears, and Tyler and Mackinnon digested the information.

Thorne thought he'd wiped the hard drive, but the app had still been working, allowing them to locate Ashley's laptop, so, perhaps it wasn't a complete reset. If Noah had been trying to hide something from the police, he could be in for a nasty shock.

"Don't feel too bad, Noah," Mackinnon said. "We know certain apps were still functioning as of a couple of hours ago. So I don't think the computer was wiped clean. Besides, it's amazing the level of detail our tech team can extract even when a file has been deleted."

Thorne paled, and he lifted a shaky hand to his mouth. "They can do that?"

Tyler nodded. "Yes, they can. Let's take a break now. Can we get you something to eat, Mr Thorne?"

If Mackinnon hadn't known better, he'd have thought the concern in Tyler's voice was genuine.

Unsurprisingly, Noah refused the offer of food. He looked sick to his stomach. He was definitely worried they would find something incriminating on Ashley's laptop.

CHAPTER TWENTY-EIGHT

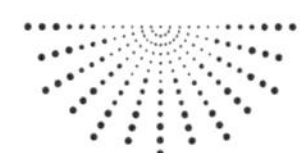

THEY LET Noah Thorne go before midnight.

Mackinnon and Tyler sat in the open-plan office area sipping strong coffee.

"Do you really think it's him?" Mackinnon asked.

"I don't know. There's something I don't like about him, something that sets off alarm bells, but we don't have enough on him yet."

Mackinnon couldn't help wondering if they played their hand too soon by bringing Thorne in before they'd gathered the evidence they needed. "We've got the laptop. That should give us something. Did you see the look on his face when Thorne realised he may not have covered his tracks as well as he thought?"

Tyler nodded thoughtfully and took a sip of his coffee. "I did. He looked scared. Extremely scared."

"I hope we're right, and he didn't manage to wipe everything from the laptop. The fact that the tracking app was still linked to the laptop gives me hope."

"I agree." Tyler checked his watch. "Which reminds me, we've not heard anything back from the tech department. I'll follow up with them before I go home."

"What about the search team we left at Thorne's place? Did they find anything in his flat?"

"Not as much as I'd like," Tyler said. "They found some items we believe belonged to Ashley. We'll have to get her parents to identify them tomorrow. Clothing mainly. There was a drawer full of her clothes in Thorne's bedroom. That could be viewed two ways. It could be innocent, stuff she kept at his place while they were dating, or it could be seen as Thorne keeping mementos." Tyler put his cup on the table and shook his head. "There's something about Noah Thorne that sets my teeth on edge."

Mackinnon felt the same. Though he wasn't yet convinced Thorne had held Ashley captive and prevented her from getting the treatment that could save her life, he thought Thorne's defensive reactions and anger were signs of a troubled personality.

As Mackinnon checked his phone, to see if he had news from Chloe regarding Sarah's disappearance, Tyler got up, drained his coffee and headed to his office.

He said over his shoulder, "I'll get you a copy of Evie's notes on the diary."

"Thanks," Mackinnon said, scrolling through his messages. He had one from Charlotte, wishing him luck in the interview and a positive result. It was too late to reply.

There was nothing from Chloe so he guessed that meant Sarah hadn't returned home.

After he got a copy of Evie's notes from Tyler, Mackinnon left Wood Street and headed back to Derek's place for the night. He stopped at a 24-hour supermarket, bought a paella ready meal and a tiny bottle of red Shiraz. He was tempted by the full bottle but opted for the smaller glass-sized one in the end. He needed a clear head tomorrow.

Once settled in an armchair at Derek's, with Molly napping at his feet, Mackinnon looked over the sections of Ashley's diary Evie had transcribed.

It was quiet apart from the muffled sound of Derek snoring. Mackinnon smothered a yawn and began to read.

2nd April.

Noah is being a complete idiot again. He followed me as I walked to work this morning, chatting away even though I was ignoring him. He just doesn't get it. He wants everything to be on his own terms. Sometimes he's so persistent he scares me.

4th April.

Sadie caught me crying at work today. It was embarrassing, but she was actually really kind. I've been a bit wary of her in the past because she is so quiet and watchful. She observes conversations rather than participates, and I thought she was a bit odd. I wasn't sure what to make of her. She was really sweet today and told me not to worry about Noah. She said he wasn't worth it. I think she's probably right.

6 April.

When I got home tonight, I found Noah in the living room talking to my parents. Of course, they don't know what he's really like and think I'm absolutely mad for dumping him. Sometimes, I think nothing would make them happier than me and Noah getting hitched. Over my dead body.

8 April.

Noah sent me a note today. I was surprised because it was quite emotional, and he's not really that type of person normally. He likes to be one of the lads and laughs things off. He does not like to talk about feelings, but the letter was really honest and touched me. I hadn't realised what he was going through. I guess sometimes he has it hard too.

10 April

Noah surprised me with a bunch of roses at work today. I wasn't quite sure what to do. After that letter… I felt like he needed some support. Of course, I couldn't turn him away in front of Heather and Sadie and a client, so I had to smile and accept the flowers. Then he really pushed his luck by inviting me out for dinner. With everyone watching us with goofy smiles, I felt like I had to say yes. So now we're meeting at our old favourite restaurant, the Italian in Covent Garden. Sometimes I think I should stop fighting it and just go with the flow. Maybe Noah is the one for me. The only person who didn't look too happy at work today was Sadie. I don't think she trusts Noah. It's strange because she hardly knows him.

28 April

I've not been feeling well lately. I feel so tired all the time and my muscles ache. I went to the doctors, and they said they'd run a few tests. I'm worried, to be honest. I'm too young to be feeling like this. I'm scared that something really serious is wrong.

10 May

Work was a nightmare today. I had a big bust up with Sadie. Luckily Heather wasn't there to hear it. She'd popped out to meet a friend for lunch. I never realised Sadie could be so vicious. She called me all sorts of names then swore at me. I don't know what I've done to upset her. She's clearly unhappy about something. I'm starting to suspect she might be jealous of me.

13 May

Things are still awkward at work. Sadie is very tense and standoffish and refuses to talk to me. She says it's because I lied to her when I said things were over with Noah, but I don't think that's true. I think she's actually keen on Noah herself. I can't believe I didn't see it before. She doesn't really have any friends, and I've never seen her go out on a date. Things are going quite well with Noah this time, so I'm not going to let Sadie spoil things.

14 May

I don't have anyone to talk to. I'm feeling really alone right now. I don't want to go out or do anything. I just want to sleep. My results came back from the GP. He said everything is fine apart from my CRP levels being a little raised. He doesn't seem to be worried, but of course, he wouldn't be. It's not him who's feeling ill.

30 May

Noah went out with his friends last night. I was staying at his flat, and when he got home, he was in a really strange mood. He grabbed my arm when I tried to walk away from him and it hurt. This morning I've got a row of little bruises where his fingers gripped my shoulder. I showed him, and of course, he was full of apologies. I don't like it when he's drunk. It's like he has a whole different personality.

2 June

Well, it's happening again. Inevitable really. Last night, I went to Noah's. We were supposed to be having a quiet night in and I planned to cook. I made a lasagne. When I was about to put it in the oven, he texted to say that he was going out for a few drinks after work.

I was a bit cheesed off, but figured we'd still eat together later. He didn't come home until ten p.m.! And surprise, surprise he was drunk again. History is repeating itself. I should never have taken him back.

4 June

My GP clearly thinks I'm a hysterical woman who should be ignored. When I went back today to tell him I still felt ill, he tried to give me antidepressants. I mean, seriously? I'm not depressed. I'm ill!

5 June

I joined a forum yesterday. It's a little bit weird, but it's full of people like me. People who have been feeling unwell and have been let down by doctors. In fact, some of them have it a lot worse than me. Some people can't even work or manage to shower every day. I've been absolutely shattered recently and had some really weird symptoms. It's strange, but it feels nice to know I'm not alone in this. At least now I have some people I can talk to.

10 June

I had a big argument with Noah last night. He was moaning about the fact I'm always on my laptop. He doesn't seem to get the fact that I'm on the computer because there are people I can talk to who understand me. I've told him how bad I've been feeling, but he says if it was something serious the doctors would have found something with their tests. Then he said it's probably a virus. Don't you just love the way people become medical experts as soon as you tell them you've not been feeling well?

15 June

It's funny. I'm close to my mum and dad, and I still live at home, but I don't feel like I can talk to them about this. I suppose I don't want to worry them. And I know they do worry about me. I should be able to talk to my boyfriend, but well, Noah is Noah. I had a nice chat with Melissa last night. It was really good to get together. We haven't seen much of each other recently and I miss her.

18 June

I've made a couple of friends online from the forum. It's strange that I don't know what they look like, and I've never met them in person, but despite that, I feel like I really know them. One of the girls from the forum lives in America, so I doubt we'll ever meet in person, but a couple of others are in London so maybe one day we could meet up.

20 June

Noah and I had a massive row last night. He came back to his flat drunk again and something in me snapped. I was really tearful. My muscles were aching so much. I'd taken paracetamol and had a hot water bottle but nothing was helping. Then he came home tripping over his own feet and singing some stupid football song.

So I picked up my laptop and tried to leave. He got really angry.

But I wasn't going to let him push me around any more. I told him it was over. He was livid. I was scared he might do something really awful. But he didn't. He stood aside and screamed at me to get out of his flat. I ran out and managed to get a taxi home. This is it this time. It's over for good. I'm not taking him back.

25 June

I can't believe it. I just found out Noah had been cheating on me. I shouldn't care now because I want him out of my life, but I have to admit, it really hurts. Especially her. Why? How could he do that when he said he loved me?

That was the last entry. Mackinnon put down the notes. It was uncomfortable reading.

Thorne said he took Ashley's laptop because he suspected her of seeing someone else, yet he was the one who'd been cheating according to Ashley's diary. The information about Sadie was a surprise, too. Mackinnon made a mental note to look into that further.

Noah Thorne was their main suspect, but they really

needed to identify the people Ashley had been communicating with on the forum.

Mackinnon put the notes down and stood up, stretching. He needed to get some sleep. With luck, tomorrow, they'd have some answers from Ashley's laptop.

CHAPTER TWENTY-NINE

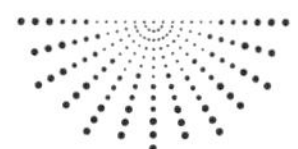

EARLY THE NEXT MORNING, Evie Charlesworth rushed along the corridor to the tech department. She'd noticed something odd about Ashley Burrows's diary and wanted a second opinion. She'd asked her friend, Joan Cuthbert, to take a look at it if she could find a gap in her schedule, and when she woke up she'd seen a missed message from Joan, asking Evie to come to the tech department.

Did Joan want to rake her over the coals for wasting her time? That wasn't really like Joan at all. So that must mean Joan had found something unusual about the diary too.

Joan looked up as Evie burst into the room. She was sitting at a long white bench, a bright lamp illuminating the diary.

"Did you find something?" Evie asked breathlessly.

"I think you were right. The diary is missing pages. It's been done very carefully. Both sides of the paper have been removed, but there are tiny scraps of paper still left in the binding. I'm impressed you noticed. I had to look through the microscope."

"Which pages were missing? And how many?"

Joan slid the diary towards Evie so she could see it clearly. "Three pages, and they are missing from this section."

Evie scanned the prior entry. The missing pages came directly after the mention of Noah's relationship with another woman. Had he torn the pages out so the woman couldn't be identified?

Evie wasn't sure but she knew she had to tell someone about this. It could be very important evidence in the investigation.

Mackinnon had arrived for work at seven thirty, intending to go over the case notes as he waited for DI Tyler to arrive. He was surprised to see Evie waiting at his desk. Unusually flustered, she filled him in about the missing pages in Ashley's diary.

"Good work," Mackinnon said. "It looks like the evidence is starting to pile up at Noah Thorne's door."

Tyler walked through the doors at seven forty-five, and they went straight to the tech unit to talk to the new head of the department, Araminta Dupris.

Araminta was in her late thirties, a short curvy woman with wavy brown hair and bright blue eyes.

"Hello, gentlemen. I take it you're not here on a social call."

"Not this time," Tyler said. "We're hoping you've got a report for us on Ashley Burrows's laptop."

"We have a preliminary report. Todd worked on it last

night." She walked to the long table set against the wall and plucked a file from a stack beside one of the computers.

"Was it wiped?" Mackinnon asked. Evie found pages had been ripped from Ashley Burrow's diary, so it looked like someone was trying to cover something up. He was expecting that same someone to have attempted to erase any evidence from the laptop, too. Right now, Thorne seemed the most likely culprit.

Araminta looked surprised. "No, everything seemed to be intact."

"We interviewed her ex-boyfriend last night. He was the one who had the laptop and told us he'd wiped it accidentally."

A puzzled frown puckered Araminta's forehead. "Perhaps he's not very computer savvy, or not used to Macs. I suspect he tried to log on as a guest. Once he managed to gain access, it would have looked like there was no personal information on the computer. But all the personal files are under Ashley's username."

"Excellent," Tyler said. "Did anything stand out as unusual?"

"Todd went through her browser history and reported on that as well as a list of applications installed on the machine. We can go into further detail if you need us to. Particularly social media."

"Thanks." Tyler took the file from Araminta and leafed through the pages. "She visited a lot of sites."

Araminta nodded. "She did. Todd noticed a bit of a trend too. She visited a lot of health sites if that's relevant?"

"It could well be important. We are looking for a particular forum she visited a lot. Probably a health forum."

"I see. Well, let's take a look on the computer here. I have a digital copy and it's easier to search on the computer than it is to scan through the paper copy." Araminta sat in front of one of the large monitors and opened up a file. "As you can see, we can sort by the names of the websites and also the number of hits. This is the most common site she visited in the last six months. It's called *cureityourself,* and she visited that site over two thousand times."

"Two thousand times?" Tyler let out a low whistle.

Araminta nodded and quickly tapped on the keyboard bringing up the website. "Here it is. It's a health forum. There are a lot of posts about alternative medicine and it's open to the general public."

"Can we look at the posts she made on that forum?"

"Yes, luckily, her parents gave us the password for the laptop, and Ashley used Keychain on her Mac. That means all her passwords are remembered, so we can log in to pretty much everything she used. It certainly makes our job easier."

"This is very helpful," Mackinnon said.

"She's made eighteen hundred posts on the forum," Araminta said, studying the screen.

"Can you make a copy of them and print them out for us?" Tyler asked.

"Absolutely. She's also sent quite a few PMs."

"PMs?" Tyler asked as he distractedly looked through the rest of the file.

"Personal messages," Araminta explained.

"Oh, yes, of course. I've heard of those. This is really great work, Araminta. Please give our thanks to Todd."

"I'll email you the information and send the printout up to your office when it's done," Araminta said.

"Thank you Araminta," Mackinnon said as they left the tech department.

She smiled brightly. "Not a problem. And call me Minty!"

* * *

DI Tyler arranged a briefing for nine a.m. They often held briefings informally in the open-plan office area, but today Tyler had booked a large meeting room to accommodate the extra officers who'd been brought in to help with the investigation.

Mackinnon glanced at the whiteboard standing at the front of the room. Noah Thorne's name and photograph were in the upper left-hand corner. Ashley's photograph was in the centre. He guessed DC Webb had written up the board because he recognised the thin, slanted handwriting.

Mackinnon slipped into a seat near the front next to Charlotte. "Morning."

"Morning. I hear Noah Thorne's interview didn't go well yesterday."

"It could have gone better."

"Is he still our top suspect?"

"So far. I'm hopeful the information we get from Ashley's laptop will give us more to go on."

DI Tyler called the room to order. "Okay, settle down. We've got a lot to get through this morning."

He held his notes in front of him for a moment then set them down on the table beside him. Though everyone else in the room was sitting down, Tyler remained standing.

"You may have heard we made an arrest last night. Noah Thorne was taken into custody after we found Ashley

Burrows's laptop at his flat. He was released late last night after questioning. That doesn't mean he's in the clear. We need to know everything about Noah Thorne. I want us to go over every inch of Thorne's life with a fine-tooth comb. But that doesn't mean we should ignore other lines of enquiry."

Tyler turned to Evie Charlesworth. "Evie. Could you give us a quick update on the details you found in Ashley's diary please?"

Evie gave a nervous nod and stood up. She was thorough and conscientious, but she didn't enjoy talking in front of a large group of people.

She cleared her throat. "I've transcribed sections of the diary I feel could be relevant to the investigation. I've made copies. You'll find them in your briefing notes. My interpretation of the diary is that Noah Thorne and Ashley Burrows didn't have a healthy relationship. There wasn't overt physical violence, but Ashley recorded incidents in her diary where she felt threatened." She paused to take a deep breath. "Another thing of interest is that she mentions visiting her GP, and feeling let down by the support he gave her, she joined an Internet forum. She had made friends with certain individuals on the forum. We'd like to know who those friends were. Even if they weren't involved in Ashley's death, they could provide further information that could help the investigation. One further thing that stood out to me was the fact she recorded Noah Thorne had been cheating on her. She didn't mention the woman by name, but it's my interpretation that Ashley knew her. Three pages had been removed from the diary. It's possible they could have been ripped out by Ashley herself, but more likely they were taken by someone with something to hide."

Evie gave a brief nod to the room and then sat down.

"Thank you Evie," Tyler said.

Before Tyler could move on, DC Webb spoke up, "We should be careful about assuming he was having an affair with a woman. Could have been a man."

"Not in this case," Evie said. "If you look at the notes I've made, you'll see Ashley describes the person Noah was having an affair with as *her*."

Tyler added, "For the record, Thorne denied having an affair. We haven't told him about the diary. Identifying the woman Ashley believed had a relationship with Thorne is one of our top priorities. Sadie Griffith is a possibility. Those pages were removed by someone. We need to find out who.

"From Ashley's laptop we've already managed to get a great deal of information thanks to Todd and Araminta from tech. The forum Ashley joined was called *cureityourself*. She'd visited regularly. Very regularly. There are two thousand forum posts as well as some PM's to go through." He looked directly at Charlotte. "Any volunteers?"

Charlotte accepted her fate with a smile. "Sure. I'll do it."

"Thank you, and DC Webb, I'd like you to go through Ashley's social media messages and contacts."

"Not a problem," DC Webb said making a note. "Do we have her passwords?"

Tyler nodded. "We do." He flipped through his notes. "We initiated a search of Noah Thorne's flat last night. It's a difficult situation. We know Ashley had been there in the past so forensics aren't going to be much help on this occasion. Plus, looking for DNA evidence at the scene probably won't help us much either —we won't be expecting to find blood. We have no evidence Thorne kept Ashley at his flat against her will. In fact, because he invited her parents to his flat during the days Ashley was missing, it's unlikely he held her there."

"Plus the bedbug bites. She had to get them from somewhere," Mackinnon said.

Tyler nodded. "Right. How far have you got with that?"

"There were no reports of bedbugs in Noah Thorne's block of flats within the last six months. No reports anywhere near the Burrows's home in Limehouse, either. Her work address had no history of an infestation. Working on the premise Ashley was bitten while she was being held in the days before she died, I've tracked a few addresses along the number twenty-two bus route."

"We're assuming the man on the number twenty-two bus dumped Ashley's body?" DC Webb asked.

"Yes, it's an assumption, but a logical one. That said, I don't have a definitive list. According to the pest control expert I spoke with, some people don't report incidents of bedbugs."

Charlotte shivered.

"How many addresses?" DI Tyler asked.

"Only three close to the bus route. All three are residential buildings."

Tyler nodded. "That's a manageable number. Look into those addresses and speak to the owners."

Mackinnon nodded.

Tyler turned to Collins with a frown. "Any further news on the CCTV?"

Collins flushed red. "Unfortunately not. The files are still scrambled. At this point, it's not looking hopeful."

Tyler gave an exasperated sigh and moved on. "I'll speak to Kate Squires, the family liaison officer. I need her help to get

Maxine and Tim Burrows to identify the clothing and other items found at Noah Thorne's residence. No doubt, he'll say they were left there when Ashley used to stay at his place. But we need to be thorough."

Tyler assigned more tasks, gave a final summary of the status of the investigation and then called an end to the briefing.

Mackinnon took his notes and went straight to the coffee machine. He needed caffeine before he started contacting the owners of the bedbug addresses.

He called the first two addresses, making an appointment for later that day. He reassured the residents that it was an enquiry and nothing more. People tended to panic when they were contacted by the police out of the blue. They assumed someone they knew was in trouble or hurt.

He sipped his coffee then picked the phone up again to call the owner of the third property on Pine Avenue. His search had brought up both landline and mobile numbers, but no one answered either, and unusually, there was no voicemail available.

He hung up and decided to try again after calling Melissa West.

There was no answer from her mobile. He'd expected her to be feeling pretty rough after the amount of alcohol she'd consumed, but he needed to speak to her as soon as she was feeling up to it.

If she suspected Noah Thorne was responsible for Ashley's death, he wanted to know why.

CHAPTER THIRTY

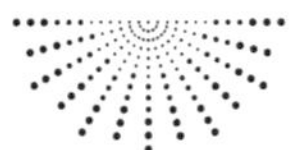

DC Collins walked miserably back to his desk after the briefing. He had really messed up. He wasn't a newbie. He was an experienced officer who had plenty of investigations under his belt. He wasn't a novice at using CCTV systems either. He couldn't even count the number of times he'd downloaded files from different systems and transferred them back to the station, which is why his screwup made no sense.

It was unfortunate the files got scrambled when they were downloaded. That part wasn't his fault. But the fact the files had been scrambled *and* he'd mistakenly deleted the originals, meant he had set this investigation back by days. Maybe weeks.

It was possible they'd never find Ashley Burrows's killer, and if they didn't, he would have to accept responsibility.

He sank down into the chair opposite his computer and stared at the dark screen. They *had* to find her killer. He wasn't sure he could live with himself if they didn't.

"There you go." Someone put a mug of coffee on his desk.

He looked up, surprised and saw Charlotte smiling at him.

"Are you all right?"

"Yeah, fine," he said, trying to talk normally despite the lump in his throat. Then he shook his head. "Actually, no. I'm not all right. Not really. I've really messed this up, haven't I?"

Charlotte pulled a chair from another desk and sat down beside him. "It was a mistake. We all make them. But we're still going to get whoever did this to Ashley Burrows."

She sounded so certain. Collins wished he had her confidence.

"I really hope you're right," he said.

"Of course I am." She nodded at the mug of steaming coffee. "Drink that. Coffee always makes you feel better. I'm going to make a start on the forum posts now. There are a lot of them if you fancy giving me a hand."

Collins managed a smile. She was trying to keep him busy, to keep his mind off his failure. "Sure, where do you want me to start?"

They sat in companionable silence going through the forum posts carefully, highlighting anything that could be of interest.

At eleven o'clock Collins's stomach rumbled loudly. He pushed aside his copy of the printouts, rolled his shoulders and stretched. "My stomach is demanding a bacon sandwich. Can I get you anything?"

Charlotte shook her head. "No thanks. I'm fine."

"Won't be long," Collins said, standing up and grabbing his wallet.

There was a café just around the corner from Wood Street station. Working in the centre of London meant most types of food were available within a five-minute stroll. That was the plus side of working in the middle of the city. The downside was lack of parking and traffic.

It was his and Debra's anniversary tonight. They were supposed to be going for a meal. He wasn't really in the mood to celebrate, but he wouldn't let her down. He'd let enough people down recently.

He sent his wife a quick text.

Looking forward to tonight. x

He stepped inside the café and was greeted by the smells of frying bacon, sizzling sausages and freshly brewed coffee. Pleased to see there was only one person in the queue, he stepped up to the counter. He'd known this place to be queueing out the door. They did lovely bacon rolls—the bacon extra crispy, the bread rolls crunchy but light and fluffy inside, and they used real butter.

Not exactly good for his waistline, but he needed something to cheer him up today.

After he paid for his bacon roll, he headed back to the station, eating as he walked. He'd finished by the time he got back and carefully wiped the grease from his mouth with a paper napkin.

As he walked into the main entrance, he paused to pat down his pockets for his security swipe card and overheard part of a conversation between the desk sergeant and an agitated young woman standing at the counter.

"Look, I know you must have lots of these types of cases, but my sister isn't the type to just disappear. She met someone on the cureityourself forum, and I haven't seen her since."

The desk sergeant mumbled some sympathetic words and scrawled something on the paperwork in front of him.

The cureityourself forum? The same forum Ashley had been using? That couldn't be a coincidence.

Collins approached the desk.

"Sorry, I couldn't help overhearing as I was coming in. I'm Detective Constable Collins. You said your sister is missing?"

The woman turned to face him. She was younger than he'd first thought. Maybe nineteen or twenty. She wasn't wearing any make-up, and her light brown hair had been pulled back off her face and tied with an elastic band. She wore casual clothes, the type you'd wear to the gym.

"Yes, my sister, Tammy Holt. She told me she was meeting a man called Brendan, whom she'd met on a forum called cureityourself. But she didn't come home."

The desk sergeant intervened. "Miss Holt reported her sister missing yesterday. It's being handled by DC Black. They are putting in a missing person's report."

"I see," Collins said. "I'll speak to DC Black. Miss Holt, I'd like to help. Would you come upstairs with me and tell me more about Tammy's disappearance?"

He didn't mention the fact they were investigating another woman's murder that could be linked to the forum. Her young face was already tense with fear.

He didn't want to scare Miss Holt, but he needed to speak to her. He'd been in this job long enough to know, coincidences like this were very rare.

He'd messed up the CCTV, but he'd make things right. If luck was on his side, not only would they find Ashley's killer, but they'd also save Tammy Holt at the same time.

* * *

Melissa West felt awful. The sun was beating down on the back of her head and she wished she was still tucked up in bed. But that wasn't an option today. She was on a mission. The sunglasses were helping a bit. She'd bought the oversized, Jackie O shades from Dubai airport.

Rubbing the middle of her forehead, trying to massage away the pain, she walked briskly to her destination, sidestepping a woman carrying a large takeaway coffee. The smell was very appealing, but Melissa didn't dare drink anything yet, let alone coffee. She'd had enough trouble with water this morning. As soon as she'd woken up, she'd gulped down a whole bottle of mineral water from the fridge, and then promptly thrown it back up again.

It didn't matter. She'd have time to drink later when she was feeling better.

She paused outside Flyaway Travel Agents and peered in through the tinted windows in between the posters listing bargain flights. It was quiet inside. Good.

Taking a deep breath she pushed open the door and walked in.

Heather, Ashley's boss wasn't around and there were no clients. Perfect.

Melissa walked up to Sadie's desk and sat down.

Sadie attempted a smile, her usual downturned mouth, curving up at the edges but only slightly. They'd met once before, briefly when Ashley had introduced them when they'd run into each other on a night out. That night Melissa had thought Sadie was shy, a bit mousey, but she hadn't known the half of it.

"How can I help?" Sadie asked.

Melissa reached up and took off her sunglasses and was pleased to see Sadie pale when she recognised her.

Sadie licked her lips nervously and looked over her shoulder, but they were still alone. "You're Ashley's friend, aren't you?"

"That's right. I wanted to talk to you."

"I'm really sorry about Ashley, but I'm kind of busy right now. Can we do this later?"

"No, we can't."

Spots of colour appeared in Sadie's pale cheeks, and her eyes narrowed beneath her long, flat fringe. "Well, it's not convenient for me right now."

"I don't care."

Sadie put her hands on the desk and linked her fingers tightly together. "Perhaps I should go and get my manager and ask her to remove you from the premises."

Melissa felt a cold rush of rage. "I wouldn't do that if I were you."

Sadie leaned back in her seat, a sulky expression on her face. "Why shouldn't I?"

"Because I know your sordid secret, Sadie. Ashley told me everything."

* * *

Sadie Griffith crouched over the metal wastebasket and tried for the fifth time to light the match. Her hands were shaking. With a grunt of annoyance, she threw the unlit match in the bin and tried again with a fresh one.

This time a small yellow flame appeared at the end of the match, and she chucked it into the bin, watching eagerly as a small, flickering fire took hold. The paper curled inwards and grew black at the corners before turning to ash.

Relieved, she stood up and put her hands on her hips. That got rid of the evidence, but it didn't help with the problem of Melissa West. Sadie had begged her not to go to the police, but deep down she knew she hadn't convinced Ashley's friend not to talk.

She flicked her fringe back from her eyes. There was no way out of this. How had things gone so far?

Sure, she'd argued with Ashley over Noah. It wasn't fair. Ashley was pretty and outgoing. She could have her pick of any man she wanted, and she'd told Sadie things were over between her and Noah.

After Heather had caught them arguing at work, and given them a dressing down, Ashley had invited Sadie to her house for a pizza and movie night to clear the air.

Of course, like a sad hanger-on, Sadie had gone. A lack of friends, meant she spent most evenings alone. Ashley was fun, lively and lived an exciting life. Sadie wanted to be part of that. Falling out with her only friend had been devastating.

The memory of that evening still hurt. They'd eaten the pizza, a garden vegan-style one for Ashley and a spicy pepperoni for Sadie. Chatting didn't come easily and things were stilted, but Sadie really made an effort, then after Ashley had put on the film, she'd fallen asleep. It was like a slap in the face. That made it clear how stimulating she found Sadie's company. *Humiliating*.

She wasn't proud of what she did next. But really, was it her fault? If Ashley hadn't been so rude and fallen asleep, Sadie would never have done it.

The movie was boring, and so Sadie, feeling angry and

hurt, had decided to poke around Ashley's bedroom. She'd spritzed herself with Ashley's favourite perfume – Dolce & Gabbana, Light Blue. And rifled through her make-up drawer, making mental notes about which foundation and what colour lip glosses she used.

Then she'd stumbled across Ashley's diary.

Her mother always said nothing good came out of poking your nose into other people's business. But Sadie couldn't resist opening the pages and started to read.

She was horrified when she got to the section about her. It was completely biased and unfair. When Ashley woke up, Sadie stuffed the diary back beneath the bed where she'd found it and said she had a headache and needed to go straight home.

Reading Ashley's description of her had hurt so much.

Then, when Ashley went missing, Sadie realised Ashley's words could be seen in the wrong light. She'd panicked. The last thing she wanted was someone to go rifling around in Ashley's diary, trying to find clues to her whereabouts, so she'd gone to Ashley's house and told her parents she was very sorry but she needed to get the curling irons she'd lent Ashley last week.

They were very trusting, which made Sadie feel even more guilty. They even let her go to Ashley's room alone, where she quickly shut the door behind her, grabbed the diary and as carefully as she could removed the offending pages.

Looking back now, she could see it had all been a waste of time.

She wafted away the curling grey smoke from the bin. It was strange that a few pieces of paper could create so much smoke.

How could she have been so stupid? Now she was completely out of her depth. She'd burned the pages she'd taken but she wasn't safe. She should have removed every single page with a mention of her name, but she hadn't had time with Ashley's parents just upstairs.

And after all that stress and worry, it turned out Melissa West knew her secret after all.

Sadie was running out of options. The way she saw it, there was only one possible way forward.

CHAPTER THIRTY-ONE

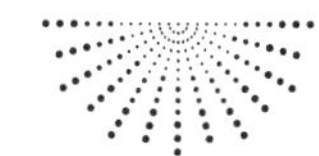

TAMMY ROLLED onto her side and a wave of dizziness hit her suddenly. She closed her eyes.

He'd drugged her again.

Biting down on her bottom lip, she tried not to cry. She was never going to get out of there. He'd brought her a fresh bottle of water a little while ago, and like a fool, she'd gulped it down. The heat in the loft was overwhelming, and she'd been so thirsty.

The metallic taste should have tipped her off, but she hadn't been able to resist swallowing the water.

She slowly opened her eyes and tried to sit up, but it was no use. Her muscles felt like jelly. Exhausted, she flopped back down against the wooden boards and focused on her breathing.

"It's going to be okay," she muttered to herself.

Once the drugs wear off, I'll escape. Nothing's changed. I still have a plan.

She tried to ignore the terror pushing its way into her thoughts. Her mind was going places she didn't want it to go. She had to be strong. Imagining the worst wouldn't help.

But she couldn't stop. Why was Brendan drugging her again? What was he going to do to her?

The room was moving now. At least, that's how it felt. The floor shifted beneath her as though she was on a life raft rocked by waves. She held a shaky hand up in front of her face, trying to focus on something other than the fear.

She stifled a sob. There was no point feeling sorry for herself.

She'd thought up a good plan, but the sedative running through her system made it impossible to act on. What if this time the drugs didn't wear off? He might keep giving them to her. Then it would be impossible to escape. What if this was it? The end?

She'd read somewhere that if she created a rapport with her abductor, it would make it harder for him to hurt her. If Brendan felt like they had a connection, he wouldn't kill her, would he?

She wouldn't be able to make a run for it in this state, but maybe she could still talk to him, try to get his sympathy and tell him he could let her go and she'd tell no one.

He kept going on about this grand plan of his and how he needed her to help him. Well, maybe she should just go along with it, pretend to be really keen to help and then once she'd gained his trust… Then she could escape.

But it was hard to create a rapport with a monster. And that's what Brendan was. He was convinced he was doing nothing wrong, as though abducting someone, tying them up and keeping them in your loft was the most natural thing in the world.

Trying to reason with him would be pointless. How did you create a bond with a madman?

She had no idea what the time was. Sleepiness crept over her. Was that because it was nighttime, or simply the drugs? Back home, her mum might be cooking tea, whistling away to the radio. But, no, by now she'd be panicking because Tammy hadn't come home yet. How long had she been missing? It felt like weeks but as far as she knew it might have only been hours.

Would Julie have given Brendan's name to the police? Even if she did, would it help the officers find her? How many people in the City of London were called Brendan? Maybe not too many. It was more of an American name. Tammy's thoughts were becoming fuzzy.

She wondered if she should try calling out for help again, but she suspected Brendan was still at home and didn't want to anger him, especially while she was still under the influence of the sedative and couldn't fight back.

Taking three long breaths, she tried to calm her racing pulse. Was that the side effects of the drugs or fear?

She heard the now familiar sound of the loft hatch scratching across the boards. She froze before slowly turning her head and looking at the dark opening.

Brendan appeared. His eyes were cold and watchful.

"Hello, Tammy. How are you feeling?" He set a clear box on the boards and hauled himself up.

How was she feeling? How did he think she was feeling? Not only had he kept her up here against her will, but he'd also drugged her again. She felt terrible.

She turned away from him, staring at the rafters and the dark material between them. She'd realised now that material was a type of soundproofing and that's why nobody came when she screamed.

"You're ignoring me, are you?" Brendan said. "Well, that's very mature. I have to say I'm very disappointed with you, Tammy. I really thought you were the one. I thought you would help me."

Tammy forgot all about creating a rapport. "Why would I help you? You've tied me up!"

"I didn't want to," Brendan said, grabbing the box and walking awkwardly towards her. He cradled the rectangular box in his arms. It looked empty.

"Then let me go. I could come back and help you, but you don't need to keep me tied up here."

"I wish we could do it that way, Tammy. But it wouldn't work. This is the only way. Believe me I didn't want to do this."

"You've given me that sedative stuff again. I feel sick."

"You gave me no choice. He pointed at the bruise high on his cheekbone. This is what you did to me last time. So now for my safety, I've given you a sedative. If you start to work with me instead of against me, perhaps that won't be necessary in the future."

Tammy felt a rush of rage and if her hands had been free… She swallowed her anger, remembering her plan. Get him onside. Create a relationship.

"When are you going to tell me about this scheme of yours?"

Brendan pulled a face. "I don't really like the word scheme. It's too close to scam for my liking. This is my research. One day, people are going to remember what I did."

"I'm sure they will," Tammy said. *But not for the reasons you think.*

Brendan pulled a Stanley Knife from his back pocket, and Tammy held her breath. He eased the sharp blade through the cable ties that bound her wrists.

"Have you been chewing these?" he demanded, inspecting the teeth marks on the plastic.

Of course, I have. I'm going to get out of here, and then you'll wish you'd never crossed me.

Tammy shook her head. "So you really are a scientist. You didn't lie about that?"

"Of course not. I mean, I have a day job, but science is how I spend my spare time."

He must have seen the scepticism on her face because he continued, "All the most famous scientists started out with science as a hobby, a passion. I don't work in a commercial lab. A company doesn't pay me a salary and dictate my research. No, I choose my own research subjects."

Her muscles were weak and her limbs flopped uselessly at her sides as the sedative took hold, but her mind was still active.

She wasn't sure how long she could remain conscious, but she didn't want to pass out with Brendan so close.

"And what are you researching?"

A thin smile spread across Brendan's face. "I'm glad you asked."

Tammy's skin prickled, and her stomach rolled in disgust as Brendan shuffled closer. He pulled the rectangular box towards him until it sat between them.

"What's that?"

"Some of my research subjects." He tapped the side of the box.

Tammy watched, horrified as tiny insects scurried about at the bottom of the glass box.

"What are they?" Tammy asked, unable to keep the panic from her voice.

Brendan angled the case so she could see there was a circular rubber seal on one side of the box.

Tammy's heart thundered. What was he going to do?

"Now, this won't really hurt. You'll hardly feel it. So don't give me any trouble, okay?" His eyes narrowed. "Otherwise you'll find out I'm not always such a nice guy."

Tammy could have laughed. Nice guy? He really was delusional.

He grabbed her wrist, and Tammy instinctively tried to pull away, but her limbs wouldn't cooperate. She was completely at his mercy, and the thought terrified her.

"What are you doing?" Tammy screamed as he forced her hand into the rubber seal, pushing until her whole forearm was enclosed in the glass case with the insects.

She wanted the darkness to claim her now. She wished she could pass out so she didn't have to remember any of this. Her breathing was fast, too fast, and her heart was beating so hard she felt a pain in her shoulder and wondered if her heart would give up.

When he'd first shoved her arm into the box, the bugs had scurried away, but now they were tentatively making their way back towards Tammy's skin.

"What are they going to do to me? Get them off!" She

could feel their tiny feet as two of the bugs crawled onto her hand.

"They need to feed," Brendan said. "Don't worry. It doesn't hurt. Most people are asleep when they bite, and it doesn't wake them up. They secrete anaesthetic and anti-coagulant when they bite. They're fascinating little things really."

"Then you put *your* arm in the box and you get bitten. Get this off me right now!"

Brendan looked at her coldly. "I'm very disappointed, Tammy. As I told you, this is research. These little bugs contain parasites. When they bite, the parasites will be delivered into your blood and I'll be able to study them using my microscope downstairs."

"You're giving me parasites?" Tammy was shaking and her voice came out slurred. It wouldn't be long now until she was completely out of it.

"Yes, but I've got the cure. I told you. Don't worry. You can trust me."

Trust?

Tammy's eyes flickered closed as the welcome blackness finally enveloped her.

* * *

Brendan carefully carried his precious bugs downstairs.

When Tammy had kicked off, he was scared she was going to squash them. Of course, he could always get more, but that wasn't really the point. Tammy was severely testing his patience.

Still, she would be an adequate incubator for the parasites, and whether he had to drug her for the whole time was neither here nor there. He would do what was required.

He put the case down in the kitchen and studied the insects. Most of them had taken the opportunity to feed and were swollen and engorged with blood.

He hadn't been completely honest with Tammy. So far he'd been unable to see the parasites under the microscope, using his own blood. But he knew they were there.

He'd picked Tammy because of her symptoms. He believed she was already infected and after the bugs had fed on her blood they would become carriers. He strongly suspected he'd see the parasite when he examined the bugs under the microscope, and he'd finally get the result he'd been searching for.

He poured himself a glass of water. As he put the glass on the counter, he noticed his hands were shaking. That was Tammy's fault. She made him nervous and doubt himself. Typical woman. Nothing was ever good enough.

He raised the glass to his mouth, took a sip, then heard a voice behind him.

"You, dirty boy. What have you brought into my kitchen?"

Brendan coughed, spluttering water all over the counter.

He turned around and stared at his mother with wide eyes. "N…n…nothing," he stammered. "I just… I'm doing an experiment."

"An experiment? You? Don't make me laugh. Good for nothing, you are. You're always bringing dirty things back into my home, you disgusting boy."

Brendan's whole body began to shake. "No, this isn't real. You're not real. You're dead."

"Dead, am I?" His mother cackled. "If I was dead, could I

do this?" She thrust her face an inch from his and screeched in his face, smacking and pinching him at the same time.

Brendan sunk to the floor, pushing himself back against the kitchen cupboards and cradling his head from the blows.

This isn't happening. This isn't happening. It's not real.

But the abuse continued. She screamed at him over and over, kicking and shouting. Telling him he was worthless, a waste of space and sick in the head.

Dirty. Dirty. Dirty.

Brendan remained crouched on the floor for a long time after his mother's voice faded. When he finally dared to look up, the kitchen looked normal and there was no sign of his mother.

It had been a hallucination. Another one. They were getting more and more frequent.

Trembling, he pushed himself up from the floor, leaning on the counter for support. She wouldn't leave him alone.

He wiped tears from his cheeks. Would he ever be rid of her?

CHAPTER THIRTY-TWO

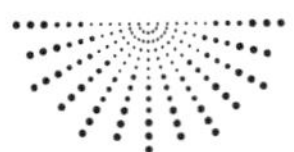

COLLINS TOOK Julie Holt to the open-plan office area so he could call the office manager to book an interview room.

He stopped by his desk and picked up the phone. "This won't take long. Do you want to sit down?"

But Julie remained standing, moving constantly. Nervous energy, Collins guessed.

While he was on the phone, Julie stood beside him. Her hands tightly gripped the strap of her handbag, and she chewed on a thumbnail.

"Thanks very much." Collins said to the office manager when she'd assigned the interview room.

He hung up and smiled at Julie, trying to put her at ease. "Right, we've got interview room two. Ready?"

It wasn't the nicest of the interview rooms, but it was a fair size and the chairs were comfortable.

Julie nodded.

"Can I get you a drink? Coffee?"

She pushed a few loose strands of hair back from her face. "Just some water, please. It's really hot up here."

"Sure. There'll be bottles of water in the room. And sorry about the heat. Our air-conditioning system isn't exactly state-of-the-art. We're not really used to hot weather in the UK, are we?" Collins said. "It never lasts very long anyway, so we make do with box air-conditioning units that make a lot of noise but never seem to cool anything down."

Julie nodded absently.

She was extremely tense, which was understandable. Collins wanted her to see him as someone she could trust and talk to. Someone to confide in. He'd dealt with cases in the past when the police hadn't had the whole story because the family were ashamed or embarrassed to tell them. Sometimes that meant it was too late to make a difference.

Collins opened the door and let Julie enter the room first. He was pleased to see a fan in the corner of the room. Bottles of water and stationery had been set out on the table. He pulled out a chair for Julie.

He switched on the fan and angled it towards her. "Is that any better?"

She nodded. "Yes, thank you."

Collins sat in the seat opposite her, grabbed a notepad and picked up a pen. "Now, I know you've already spoken to DC Black about your sister's disappearance, but I want you to tell me about the last time you saw her or spoke to her and what you think might have happened to prevent her coming home."

Julie nodded. "Okay. My sister hasn't been well recently. She's been ill for the past year or so. Fibromyalgia. It really gets her down. And I suppose it makes her vulnerable. I worry about her.

"I got a text message to say she was meeting somebody from a forum because they could help with her recovery. She said his name was Brendan."

Julie paused and her lower lip wobbled. She covered her face with her hands. "I should have told her not to go. I can't believe I just let her meet somebody off the Internet on her own. It's my fault."

"How old is your sister?"

"She's twenty-three."

"Then she is responsible for her own decisions. It's not your fault."

Julie shrugged miserably. "It feels like it is. I'm sure my mum thinks it is, too. She was horrified when I told her Tammy had texted me her plans and I hadn't tried to stop her."

"Do you know the name of the forum?"

Julie nodded. "It's called cureityourself. Tammy had been spending a lot of time on there recently. She said people understood her there in a way others couldn't—meaning Mum and me, of course. She had a point. I wasn't always as sympathetic as I could have been. I thought if she got some fresh air, ate better food and did some exercise regularly, she'd build up her immune system and start to feel better. But I think Tammy took it as a criticism when I suggested that. She probably just wanted me to listen and I didn't."

Julie's shoulders slumped.

"When was the last time you saw her?"

"The last time was at home last Tuesday. We had dinner together with Mum. Tammy still lives at home, but I've got a place in Ealing."

Collins made a quick note on the pad in front of him. "And

the last time you communicated with her via text was this message saying she was going to see Brendan?"

"That's right."

"Did she tell you where they were meeting?"

"Yes, in a Costa Coffee near Whitechapel station. In fact, I've got my phone. The messages are on there if you want to see them."

Collins said that he did and waited while Julie rummaged around in her bag. After unlocking it, she pushed her white iPhone across the table towards him.

Collins read the messages.

"I should have told her not to go, shouldn't I?" Julie said miserably.

"It's easy to think of things you could have done differently in hindsight. You can't blame yourself."

"I can't help it."

Collins paused. There wasn't anything he could say to make her feel better. The only thing that would help was finding Tammy and getting her home safely.

"You said Tammy lives at home with your mum?"

"Yes, that's right. Mum came to the station with me yesterday to report Tammy missing, but she didn't want to come here today. She wanted to stay at home in case Tammy comes back."

"And what about your dad?"

Julie shrugged. "He's not on the scene. I haven't seen him since I was two."

"And you and Tammy share the same father?"

Julie nodded.

"You've tried to call Tammy?"

"Of course, loads of times. I phoned all the friends I could think of and posted on social media, but there's been no sign of her. No one's seen her since she met that man, Brendan."

"Okay. Do you know how Tammy accessed the forum? Was it on her phone or on her computer?"

Julie thought for a moment. "Both, I think."

"And Tammy didn't leave her phone at home?"

Julie shook her head. No she must have taken it with her. That's another reason I know something is very wrong. She's got a popular account on Instagram. She posts every day at the same time. She's got loads of followers, and she wouldn't let them down. Plus there's all this stuff about demographics and the best time of day to post. She is pretty obsessive about it."

"Okay. So it's likely Tammy can't access her phone. Do you know what mobile network she uses?"

"O2, I think."

"And the number?"

Julie reeled it off and Collins made a note.

"What about her laptop?"

"I think that's still at home."

"Then it would be really helpful if we could take a look at that. If she met Brendan on the forum, then we may be able to see their messages and find out who Tammy met at the coffee shop."

"Do you think Brendan was a fake name?"

"It's possible. But even if it isn't, a first name doesn't give us much to go on. If we can get more information we might be able to find out where he lives and then we can question him."

Julie nodded slowly and gave Collins a tearful smile. "Thank you. Thanks for taking it all seriously. I didn't feel like they really wanted to do much about it when we first reported her missing."

"We'll do our best to find her, Julie. I've just got a few more questions. It won't take long. Afterwards, could you go back to your mum's place and explain the situation? I'll send some officers round to pick up the laptop, and if you and your mum agree, they'll take a look around Tammy's room to see if they can find anything to help us discover where she's gone."

Julie agreed and looked at him full of gratitude. Collins really hoped he didn't let her down.

Mackinnon stood up and looked at his grey suit jacket on the back of the chair. It was too hot to even contemplate wearing it today. He usually wore a tie and a suit when he was working. But today, he would have to lose the jacket.

The case seemed like it was slipping away from them, and he was pinning his hopes on the addresses where the bedbugs had been recorded. They needed to make progress. He had two appointments lined up for the residential addresses but still hadn't been able to get in touch with the owner of the empty three-storey building. He'd have to try them again later.

He picked up his wallet and mobile and was heading out of the office when the phone on his desk rang.

He walked back and picked up the handset. "DS Mackinnon."

"Jack, it's Bob down in reception. I've got someone here at the front desk asking for you."

"Did they give a name?" Mackinnon glanced at his watch, a gift from Chloe on his last birthday. He still had some time to spare before he needed to be at the first address on his list.

"She says her name is Sarah," Bob said. "Shall I tell her you're coming down?"

"Yes, thanks, Bob."

Sarah. So she'd turned up? At least he guessed it was Chloe's Sarah. He wasn't expecting anyone else. He considered texting Chloe to let her know Sarah was safe but decided to wait until he'd seen her for himself.

Mackinnon headed down the stairs, taking them two at a time. He checked his watch. He didn't know how long this was going to take, and he had those appointments to keep.

When he walked into the reception area, he saw Sarah straightaway. She stood by the desk, scowling and looking miserable.

He couldn't remember the last time he'd seen her smile, and he softened a bit. It was easy to focus on how the situation with Sarah and her mother was affecting his life and making things uncomfortable for him. There had to be a reason for her bad temper and moods. Perhaps if he tried to be a little more understanding…

"Hi," Mackinnon said, fighting the urge to demand to know where she'd been and why she'd put her mother through so much worry. "This is a surprise."

Sarah folded her arms over her chest and looked at him stonily. "Yes, I had nowhere else to go."

"Is something wrong?"

"I need money."

Mackinnon's heart sank.

He pulled out his mobile phone. "Have you spoken to your mother?"

Sarah shook her head. "No, and I don't intend to. She's being completely unreasonable."

"Well, I know she's worried, so I'm just going to send a quick text message to tell her you're safe and you're here."

Sarah's features tightened. She looked irritated, but she didn't try to stop him sending the message.

"Now, what do you need the money for?"

"I just owe somebody some money and I haven't got any."

"How much do you need?" Mackinnon asked, trying to remember how much he had in his wallet. He was pretty sure he had forty quid and change, but knowing Sarah, that wouldn't be enough.

"A thousand."

He'd expected it to be more than forty, but still, a thousand pounds? What could she possibly need that for? She'd been living at home rent-free, and Chloe paid for all her food and day-to-day necessities.

"That's too much, Sarah. I can't get my hands on that kind of money quickly, and even if I could, I'm not sure it's a good idea to give you the money."

"Not a good idea?"

Mackinnon sighed. "Why do you need so much money?"

"I told you. I owe a friend."

"A friend?"

"Yes, they bailed me out a few times and now I need to pay them back."

"But borrowing from someone else to pay off another loan isn't helping. You need to get a job, earn some money and then pay your friend back."

Sarah rolled her eyes as though he was being completely unreasonable.

"Are you going to help me or not?"

"Tell me, are you in any trouble? If you are, you can tell me."

"No, I'm fine. I'm not a child."

"Right." Mackinnon was very tempted to say she might not be a child but she was definitely acting like one.

"So I guess that's a no then?"

"I can't get that much money in a day."

"Then get two hundred and fifty from the cashpoint. I'll wait."

Mackinnon reached for his wallet and then stopped. "No, Sarah. This is your debt, and you need to pay it off yourself. If you're scared of the person who lent you the money then you need to tell me."

"I don't need to do anything. I told you I'm not scared of them. They're just a friend."

"Then the answer is no."

She stared at him with such animosity he was at a loss. Did she really expect him to just hand over a thousand pounds?

Then without a word, she spun around and stalked out of the station.

Mackinnon walked after her but paused on the stone steps as Sarah crossed the road. She got into a red Corsa that had seen better days. Two of the hubcaps had fallen off and there was a large dent in the bodywork on the passenger side.

He couldn't make out the driver, but he made a mental note of the licence plate before they drove off.

He turned around and walked back into the station and caught the eye of Bob behind the desk.

Bob whistled through his teeth. "Kids, eh? Who'd have 'em?"

CHAPTER THIRTY-THREE

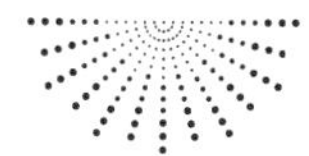

MACKINNON WENT BACK UPSTAIRS FEELING VERY uneasy. He would have to tell Chloe that Sarah was asking for money again, but perhaps that was a conversation they should have in person. Sarah said she wasn't afraid and didn't appear to be in immediate trouble.

He sat down at his computer and searched for the licence plate number of the red Corsa. According to the DVLA's records it was owned by a man called Robin Courtney, of 17, Marigold Plaza, Hackney. Date of birth, the twenty-seventh of May, 1980. That made him a lot older than Sarah.

Had Courtney been driving the car? Mackinnon hadn't been able to get a good look at the driver.

The image they had on file for Robin Courtney showed a man with a long, narrow face, messy brown hair and a squint that made it look as though he distrusted the photographer.

If it had been Courtney driving, how did Sarah know him? From university? Was he a mature student?

Mackinnon paused only for a moment before opening a new screen and searching the police database for Robin Courtney.

What he saw made his stomach churn.

Courtney had been arrested and charged for an assault four years ago.

Mackinnon scanned the details. It had been an incident outside a nightclub, and Robin had been given a suspended sentence.

As he scrolled down the screen his worst fears were realised. Courtney had been arrested for drug dealing three times. Once in 1999 and twice in 2009.

Was that how he knew Sarah? Was it possible she was taking drugs? That would certainly explain her mood swings *and* her need for money.

For a long moment Mackinnon just stared at the computer screen. He was going to have to talk to Chloe about this. Would he get a chance to get back to Oxford tonight? This couldn't wait until tomorrow. He'd have to make time.

He glanced at his watch. He only had a few more minutes before he needed to leave the station and head to Mile End to talk to the owners of the properties that had been infested with bedbugs. Perhaps he'd be able to get away late tonight and then come back to London early tomorrow morning.

If he drove, he could leave at five a.m. and even if the traffic was terrible, he'd still be back for work at a reasonable time.

"Everything okay, Jack?"

Mackinnon turned to see Charlotte looking at him from her desk. "You look lost in thought."

Mackinnon sighed. So they wouldn't be overheard, he got up and walked over to her desk.

He sat down. "It's Sarah. She just visited the station to ask me for money."

"Oh?" Charlotte didn't say any more, but she didn't need to. Mackinnon was well aware Charlotte thought Sarah could be selfish and self-centred at times.

"I said no, but when she left, she got into a car. I checked and it's owned by a man called Robin Courtney, a known drug dealer."

"That's not good. Have you told Chloe?"

"Not yet. I'll go back to Oxford tonight and talk to her. It's not something I want to tell her over the phone."

"I can understand that. Do you have any reason to believe Sarah's taking drugs?"

"I haven't seen her that much recently, but when I do, she is miserable, lashes out for no reason and is difficult to live with. Now she's asking for money."

Charlotte frowned. "I don't know, Jack. I know Sarah has been difficult in the past, but why would she take drugs after what happened to her friend?"

Charlotte was referring to an incident a few years ago when Sarah's friend had overdosed on contaminated heroin. She'd been distraught.

"I don't know for sure. The only thing I am sure of is that Chloe should know about it."

Charlotte nodded. "You're right. She should."

Charlotte's computer pinged with an incoming email. She turned to look at the screen. "Sorry, that's the digital copy of the private messages and posts from the forum. There are loads of them, so I'd better make a start. But if you need anything, just ask."

Mackinnon smiled. "Thanks. Hopefully it'll turn out to be a false alarm."

Mackinnon got to his feet as Tyler and Collins walked into the office area.

"Before you go, Jack," DI Tyler said. "We've had a development."

Tyler and Collins wheeled over chairs, and Mackinnon sat down again.

"Julie Holt came to the station to report this disappearance of her sister yesterday," Tyler said. "The missing woman's name is Tammy Holt. Collins has done a tremendous job finding out that Tammy was using the same forum as Ashley – *cureityourself*. Julie also told him her sister was going to meet a man she'd met on the forum called Brendan. This could be it. This could be the same person who took Ashley. If so, Tammy's life could be in danger and we need to act fast."

Mackinnon felt a jolt of adrenaline. Tyler was right. This could be the breakthrough they needed. "Do we know anything else about Brendan yet?"

"Not much," Collins said. "I'm going to speak with Tammy and Julie's mother. The dad isn't on the scene. Julie hasn't seen him since she was a kid. I'm taking a search team with me to go over Tammy's bedroom and bring back her laptop for analysis."

"So this helps me narrow things down," Charlotte said. "I need to look through the forum messages to see if Ashley communicated with somebody called Brendan."

"Exactly," Tyler said. "We need to get on this quickly."

"What do you need me to do?" Mackinnon asked. "I was going to follow up on the bedbug cases today."

"I still think you could be onto something there," Tyler said. "You go ahead with that this afternoon. Collins will follow up with Tammy's family, and Charlotte can search the forum posts. DC Webb will be looking at social media to see if we can find a link between Tammy, Ashley and a man called Brendan. Of course, we can't get carried away. Brendan may not be his real name. But if we can find the messages and link him to a Facebook profile or IP address, I think we have a good chance of nailing him."

Mackinnon nodded. "I hope so."

"Right," DI Tyler said getting to his feet and loosening his tie. "I'm going to speak to Kate Squires and see if the Burrowses know anyone called Brendan." He smiled. "I have a good feeling about this." He slapped Collins on the back. "Good job, mate. You've redeemed yourself after the CCTV disaster."

Collins winced and flushed red. DI Tyler was never subtle.

* * *

Mackinnon was preparing to leave when he got another call from the Desk Sergeant telling him he had a visitor. This time, it was Sadie Griffith.

He asked for her to be shown upstairs to interview room two.

Fidgeting nervously, she shifted in her seat as Mackinnon entered the room.

"I understand you have something to tell me, Sadie," Mackinnon said, taking the seat opposite her.

Her eyes were wide as she nodded. "That's right. I've come to confess."

"Okay." Mackinnon found it hard to hide his surprise. Surely she wasn't going to confess to Ashley's murder? He'd suspected they were rivals because he knew from Ashley's diary that she suspected Sadie of having a crush on Noah.

"I've done something really stupid, but you have to believe me. I didn't harm Ashley. We were friends, but everything has grown so complicated." She put her head in her hands.

"Let's start at the beginning," Mackinnon said. "If you haven't done anything wrong, Sadie, you don't have anything to worry about."

"But that's just it. I have done something wrong." She began to cry.

"Tell me about it, I might be able to help."

She wiped her eyes with the back of her hand. Sniffing, she said, "I took some pages from Ashley's diary because I didn't want anyone finding out that I had a relationship with Noah Thorne."

"I see." He paused, not wanting to ask more questions until he was sure she had nothing more to tell him.

"I'm sorry, I panicked and burnt the pages so I can't show you them. The thing is, Ashley was angry with me for getting together with Noah. I thought things were completely over between them, but she told me I was going against some kind of girl code. She was probably right, but I really fell for him. And Ashley… she was gorgeous, you know. She never had any problems attracting blokes, so I couldn't understand why she wasn't happy for me. Her constant warnings about Noah being controlling were really over the top, and I'm sure she was saying it just to break us up." She looked up at Mackinnon through wet eyelashes. "I love him."

"Does Noah feel the same?"

She hesitated, then said, "Yes, I'm sure he does. I mean, with everything going on he hasn't been in touch, but that's understandable, isn't it? He's probably trying to protect me."

As Mackinnon asked more questions, the whole story came out. Sadie and Noah had a fling, and when Ashley discovered their relationship, she'd tried to warn Sadie. Whether that was through jealousy, or genuine concern for her friend, it was hard to say.

The only thing Mackinnon knew for sure was that Noah hadn't wanted this to come to light during the investigation. To his irritation, he realised they'd been following the wrong trail.

Ashley already knew about the affair, so there was no reason for either of them to kill her. Sadie or Noah could have wanted her out of the way, perhaps. But the likelihood of either of them abducting Ashley and keeping her captive over this was low.

"Noah didn't mention your relationship to us when we questioned him," Mackinnon said.

Sadie blinked and then her lower lip wobbled. "No, I thought he was looking out for me, but now I'm starting to realise he didn't really care about me, at all. He hasn't answered any of my phone calls."

Her face crumpled. "I've been such an idiot, and Ashley was really kind to me. I just got swept away by the whole idea, but she was right. He was just using me to make her jealous. I'm such an idiot."

"I don't think you're an idiot, Sadie, but you have made

some bad choices. Perhaps Ashley was right. Maybe you're better off steering clear of Noah Thorne."

Sadie nodded and dabbed her eyes with a tissue.

He felt sorry for her but also irritated in equal measure that this hidden relationship had acted as a smokescreen to cover the real motive for Ashley's murder.

His gut instinct told him Noah Thorne had been hiding something, but if he'd only been concealing his secret relationship with Sadie, then they'd been wasting their time on the wrong suspect.

CHAPTER THIRTY-FOUR

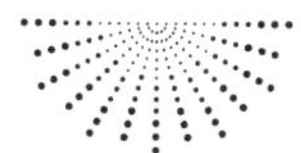

MACKINNON MADE his way to Mansion House underground station, keeping to the shaded side of the road.

He walked swiftly past groups of tourists, who strolled slowly, dawdling along, wearing lightweight T-shirts and flip-flops. Mackinnon hoped they'd brought raincoats and proper footwear too. They'd probably need warmer clothes in a few days, knowing the English weather.

The traffic was normally slow-moving in the area, but today it was worse than usual. Things had been brought to a standstill by a red double-decker bus struggling to pass a section of road that had been narrowed by roadworks. The driver of a black cab sounded his horn in frustration.

As he approached the entrance to the station, Mackinnon's mobile rang. Standing aside so as not to block the stairway, Mackinnon pulled out his phone.

It was DI Tyler.

"You just caught me," Mackinnon said. I was about to head

down into the sweaty misery that is the London Underground."

Normally, he found the underground convenient, but in this weather, it was close to unbearable.

"Sorry, Jack. There's been a change of plan. I need you to call into the Costa Coffee shop in Whitechapel first. They still have CCTV from the day Tammy Holt went missing. If we can get an image of Tammy and Brendan together…well, I don't need to tell you how important that could be."

Mackinnon glanced at his watch. He hated being late for appointments. He'd never make it to Whitechapel and then back in time for his appointment with each of the bedbug cases.

But Tyler was right. This was their chance to get an image of their main suspect. Everything else would have to take a back seat.

"Okay, I can do that. I'll phone ahead and tell the Mackenzies and the Saddlers, that I'll be late."

"Thanks, Jack. Appreciate it. Collins was going to go himself, but he's gone to speak to Tammy's mother."

"Not a problem. Do we know for sure the coffee shop kept the CCTV?" Mackinnon asked. He'd been stung in the past when vital evidence had been wiped or recorded over.

"Yes, it's their internal system. I've checked with them, and they keep the footage for fourteen days. There's a camera set up right behind the counter, which should give a good view. I've already spoken to the manager. His name is Victor. He knows the date and time you need, so I hope he'll have it all set up ready for you when you get there."

"All right. I'll head there now and let you know how I get on."

"Thanks. I'm emailing you a couple of shots of Tammy we got from her sister, so you'll recognise her on the CCTV. Let me know as soon as you get an image of Brendan."

"Will do." Mackinnon hung up.

Before heading down the steps, Mackinnon waited for his email to refresh. He wouldn't have a signal on the Underground and wanted to get the images of Tammy before he walked down into the subterranean oven.

When the emails came through, he put the phone back in his pocket and headed down out of the bright sunshine and into the hot, stale air.

Once he was on the Upminster-bound District Line train, he opened the images of Tammy. They were clear, close-up pictures. Some looked like selfies. She appeared younger than twenty-three. Her long, light brown hair softly waved around her face. She had soft hazel eyes and dimples when she smiled.

Staring down at Tammy's smiling face, Mackinnon could only hope they weren't too late to save her.

It took him fifteen minutes to get to Whitechapel. And he was glad to leave the underground system and get back into the fresh air.

The coffee shop was very close to the station. He stood aside as two young girls came out holding iced drinks and squabbling, followed by their harassed-looking mother.

She thanked him for holding the door. "I can't wait for the summer holidays to be over," she said and rolled her eyes.

Mackinnon smiled and headed inside.

The cool air was a welcome relief. The coffee shop was busy, but surprisingly, there was no one waiting to be served.

Two members of staff were working behind the counter. A

blond-haired man stood beside the till and a short pink-haired woman cleaned the metal milk frothing spout on the coffee machine.

Mackinnon discreetly showed his ID. "I'm looking for Victor," he said to the blond man.

"That's me."

He had a subtle accent Mackinnon couldn't immediately place. Swedish? Or maybe Finnish? His eyelashes and eyebrows were pale, and he had startlingly blue eyes.

"I spoke to your colleague," Victor said. "If you'd like to follow me, I'll take you to the computer so you can view the footage."

"Great." Mackinnon followed him, impressed with his efficiency.

As they walked into a small admin room, he saw Victor had already paused the CCTV on the screen. Very organised.

"I've already got to the right day and approximately the right time for you," Victor said. "We can go through it together if you'd like. Teresa will hold the fort. Here is the fast forward and this is the rewind button," he said, pointing to the arrow keys on the keyboard.

But Mackinnon didn't need to use the keys yet. There, in the middle of the screen, was Tammy, sitting at a table with a man who had to be Brendan.

Mackinnon thanked Victor and slid into the chair behind the computer. It was a side-on view. Both Tammy and Brendan were in profile, so it wasn't the best angle for identification purposes.

At some point Brendan must have faced the counter, which meant he'd look directly at the camera.

"We are interested in these two individuals here," Mackinnon said pointing out Tammy and Brendan. "This is a good start, but if we can find an image of him looking at the camera, that would be a great help."

Mackinnon noticed Brendan had a cup in front of him. "Can we go back to the point where he buys his drink?"

"Sure," Victor said and pressed the back arrow to rewind the footage. It took a while but then Brendan got to his feet and appeared to walk backwards towards the counter.

Mackinnon held his breath as Brendan turned, giving an excellent view of his face.

Got him!

"Can we zoom in?"

Victor obliged, enlarging the image.

Brendan didn't have the type of face that stood out from a crowd.

He was pretty average. Maybe a little taller than most, but he wasn't overweight or particularly skinny. His hair was a common shade of brown. It was hard to tell his eye colour from the CCTV freeze frame, but Mackinnon guessed his eyes were probably brown too. His skin tone was Caucasian but was neither very pale, nor tanned, and he wore casual clothes —a navy hoodie and a pair of blue jeans.

Very unremarkable. Mr Average.

Mackinnon guessed his age to be mid to late twenties. He looked older than Tammy, but appearances could be deceptive.

He asked Victor to press play so he could get a real-time view and see how Brendan moved and interacted with his surroundings. Mackinnon was looking for any standout characteristics, maybe a limp or a nervous tic perhaps. But there was nothing.

There were no signs to indicate Brendan was unlike any of the other men in the coffee shop. No anxiety. No signs of stress.

Mackinnon watched disconcerted as Brendan smiled shyly at the woman beside him in the queue.

He'd thought their suspect would be a loner. A man who distanced himself from normal society. But he seemed perfectly at ease in the busy coffee shop, interacting with people normally.

Mackinnon rewound the footage and made a note of the time stamp on the screen when Brendan entered the coffee shop and then fast forwarded the CCTV, noting the time Brendan and Tammy had left together. Then he went back to the head-on shot of Brendan and paused the footage.

"Is that a good enough image?" Victor asked.

Mackinnon had forgotten he was standing there.

"Yes, sorry, Victor. This is fantastic. Thank you for getting it all set up ready. It's saved me a lot of time."

Victor smiled. "Of course, you're very welcome.

"I'd like to take a couple of screenshots and email them to my address. I'd also like to take a copy of the CCTV with me."

They could go through the rigmarole of getting a warrant, but they wouldn't need to if the manager gave his permission.

"Sure thing," Victor said. He tapped a few buttons and slid a DVD into a separate drive beside the computer. "It will probably take a few minutes to copy across."

"Thanks." Mackinnon wished all CCTV footage was as easy to get hold of.

"If you get the images you want on the screen, I'll take the screenshots and email them over to you."

Mackinnon lined up the images of both Tammy and Brendan, then made sure to get a couple of clear shots of Brendan facing the camera.

"What's your email address?"

Mackinnon dug out a business card that contained his contact details and gave it to Victor.

Victor attached the images to an email, then clicked on the paper airplane icon. "Okay. Sent."

Mackinnon thanked him and checked the time. He was going to be at least half an hour late for his first appointment. But it couldn't be helped. He had a hunch that the bedbugs would be important to this case somehow, but a hunch didn't beat out sensible police work, and in this case, an image of Tammy and Brendan together was very important. Getting hold of it before the CCTV was wiped was crucial if they wanted a successful prosecution at the end of this case.

The computer beeped an alert, signalling the copying was complete.

Victor removed the disc, slid it into a case and then handed it to Mackinnon. "There," he said. "Is that everything?"

"It is. Thank you. You've been a great help, Victor."

Mackinnon made his way out of the coffee shop. Before going down to the Underground, he forwarded the emails to Tyler so he'd have a copy of the screenshots of Brendan.

Now they had a face for the man they were looking for.

Mackinnon put his phone in his pocket and jogged down the steps towards the ticket barriers, feeling hopeful. Things were heading in the right direction.

CHAPTER THIRTY-FIVE

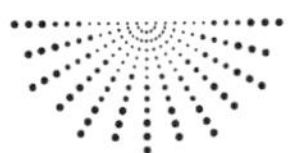

DC Charlotte Brown knocked on the door of Araminta's office in the tech department.

"Come in," her cheerful voice called out.

Charlotte entered. "I hear you have Tammy Holt's computer?"

Araminta nodded. She was sitting at a long bench, with a grey, bulky Lenovo laptop in front of her.

"I just got my hands on it five minutes ago. I'm running some primary tests and doing a backup." She nodded to the hard drive beside the computer.

"Great," Charlotte said, looking at the laptop and hoping it provided the answers they needed. "I'm not sure how much you know about the case, but we now think another young woman is at risk."

Araminta nodded to the laptop. "Tammy Holt. The owner of this laptop. She's disappeared, right?"

Charlotte nodded. "Yes. We believe she met a man calling himself Brendan at a Costa Coffee shop in Whitechapel. No one saw her after that point, so he is our main suspect."

"Understood," Araminta said.

"We think she met Brendan on the cureityourself forum, and that could be where Ashley met him too. We want to find a link between Tammy Holt, Ashley Burrows and Brendan."

Araminta opened the browser and navigated to the cureityourself forum. "It's our lucky day, Tammy has given the browser permission to store her login information. We can search through her PM's but it might take a while."

Charlotte frowned. "How many has she got?"

"She's had private conversations with forty-five people." She clicked on one at random. "Some of the conversations go on for pages."

"It's probably the most recent PM."

Araminta focused on the screen and her fingers zipped across the keyboard. "All right. Here we go." She pointed at a section of text on the screen.

Charlotte moved closer to read the message.

It was the arrangements they'd made to meet. He called himself Brendan, but the username he used was @lookingforacure.

Charlotte smiled. "Okay, I think the net is closing around Brendan. We need to go back to Ashley's personal messages and see if she communicated with the same individual."

Araminta pushed away from the laptop and spun on her wheeled chair to face the screen of a large desktop computer.

"I can do it myself if you've not got time," Charlotte said. "I have a copy of Ashley's PM's and forum posts."

"That would be helpful," Araminta said. "DC Collins has asked me to focus on Tammy's laptop and see if I can trace Brendan's IP address or track down his web footprint. I'll try to get an ID."

"Great. You do that, and I'll go back through Ashley's communications. Thanks Minty!"

"No problem," Araminta said as Charlotte left the office.

Charlotte was buzzing as she walked upstairs. They were *so* close. If she found evidence of communication between Brendan and Ashley then they'd have a concrete link between both cases.

Her copper's instinct told her the cases were linked. But a jury wouldn't convict anyone based on her instinct. They needed concrete evidence, and Charlotte was going to give it to them.

She used the digital copy of the forum posts and personal messages from Ashley's computer and performed a search for Brendan's username.

She groaned when she saw how many forum posts he'd made. It would take ages to go through them all. But she was most interested in the personal messages because that's most likely how he'd have arranged to meet Ashley just like he had Tammy.

She scanned the recent PMs, and like Tammy, Brendan was the last person Ashley had communicated with via personal message. That in itself was damning.

Charlotte opened up the PM and began to read. She'd only scanned a few lines down when a knot formed in her stomach. It was hard to read and witness the grooming and the growing trust Ashley had for this guy she'd met on the Internet, knowing how things turned out.

Charlotte's anger grew as she continued to read. It was too late for Ashley. But it wasn't yet too late for Tammy. They still had a chance to save her.

CHAPTER THIRTY-SIX

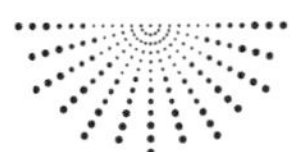

MACKINNON GOT to the Carson house half an hour later than originally planned. The Carsons lived in a small terrace on Mullett Avenue. The house was in the middle of a long row, built in the eighties. Each property along the road had a thin strip of front garden, which was only just large enough to store the bins and maybe a couple of flowerpots.

Before knocking on the door, he scanned the immediate vicinity, looking for anything unusual about the area. Nothing stood out, or struck him as odd.

This property had reported the bedbugs and had been treated by A1 pest control, but the bugs could also be in any of the properties nearby. There was a chance, however small, that this was where Brendan had kept Ashley and was now keeping Tammy.

Most of the houses were well-kept and the gardens well-maintained. One directly opposite the Carsons's home, looked more rundown than the other houses in the neighbourhood. A collection of rubbish was piled up in the front garden, just beneath one of the dirty windows. The paint on the door – green – was peeling, revealing the original white beneath.

Squeals of joy and laughter rang out, and Mackinnon watched as two kids, he judged to be seven or eight, exploded out of the front door, shouting and shooting each other with water pistols. The two small boys, who looked like they were taking advantage of the summer holidays by not bothering to comb their hair, both wore blue shorts and no T-shirts. Mackinnon couldn't blame them in the current heatwave.

He turned away and knocked on the Carsons's front door. The door had been painted in a shiny black, and the brass lion's head knocker and matching letterbox gave it a smart appearance. He noticed they'd also had new uPVC windows installed recently, the bright white a startling contrast against the red brick.

Around the doormat, someone had sprinkled white powder. Mackinnon wondered if they'd had a problem with ants. The hot summer had led to an explosion in the ant population in Oxford and probably by the looks of it here too.

The door was opened by a woman in her mid-thirties.

She wore a white T-shirt, beige cargo trousers and a pair of pink flip-flops. Her red, curly hair was pinned up. She patted it self-consciously.

"Sorry I'm late," Mackinnon said, showing his ID.

"It's fine. I was off work today anyway, catching up on the cleaning." She stepped back. "Would you like to come in?"

He followed her inside. From his first impressions, the place looked immaculate. In the hallway, there was pale wood flooring and no carpet on the stairs. Ivory walls and bright white woodwork made the area look spacious and clean.

She led him through the hall into a long, narrow sitting room and then into the small kitchen at the front of the house.

"Can I get you a coffee? A tea? Or maybe you'd prefer something cold in this heat?"

She gestured for him to sit down at the kitchen table, and Mackinnon did so. "A glass of water would be great, thanks, Mrs Carson."

"Call me Daphne, please." She gave him a nervous smile and took a glass out of the cupboard. "You want to know about the bedbugs we found a few months ago?"

"That's right."

"I'm not sure what it is exactly you want to know about those horrible things. To be honest, I'm surprised you even wanted to come into our house. I'm still looking for them everywhere. I can't relax. I have to admit, the whole thing has made me paranoid."

"I can imagine."

"It was a real shock to the system." She put a glass of water on the table in front of him and then sank into the seat opposite. "We'd only recently moved here. We'd been here less than two weeks, when I realised I was getting bitten. At first, I put it down to the fact I'd been spending a lot of time in the garden, doing weeding and general tidying up. I thought I'd been bitten by midges or something like that, but when I showed my mother the bites, she suggested getting someone from pest control to take a look. I'm so glad I did. He found them straightaway. I was horrified. The couple who owned the house before us had three cats and two dogs, so I wondered if I was getting bitten by fleas."

"But it wasn't fleas?" Mackinnon asked.

Daphne shook her head. "Sadly, no. Apparently, fleas are

much easier to get rid of, and they only tend to bite you when their natural host isn't around. We had a chap from A1 pest control take a look and he was the one who told us about the bedbug infestation. He found them living beneath the wallpaper in our upstairs bedroom." She shivered. "He was fantastic. He sprayed the walls and the carpets, and I haven't been bitten since, so I'm pretty sure we've got rid of them." She looked around as though expecting to see insects crawling along the carpet and scratched her arm.

"How long ago was the treatment?"

"It was the beginning of May."

"Do you remember the name of the man who sprayed the house?"

She bit her lip. "I'm sorry, I don't. Is it important?"

"Probably not. Don't worry. How many people live here?"

"It's just my husband and me." She frowned. "Can I ask you a question?"

Mackinnon nodded.

"Well, you said you were from the police, not the council?"

"That's right."

"So why are you interested in an infestation of bedbugs. It's not usually a police matter, is it?"

"Not usually, no. But in this case, we are interested in properties in the area known to have a recent infestation. It's related to a case I'm working."

Mackinnon didn't really want to elaborate any further.

"I see," Daphne said, though she still looked confused.

"Do you know if any of your neighbours have had similar problems with the bugs?"

She pursed her lips. "Well, I know it's wrong of me to judge on outward appearances." She got up from her seat and pointed out of the kitchen window towards the house across the street.

Mackinnon stood too and looked out.

"They are not exactly the tidiest and cleanest residents on the street. Just yesterday I saw their youngest boy standing by the front door and scratching his legs for ages." She caught the look on Mackinnon's face and flushed. "Sorry, like I said, I shouldn't judge."

"Have you noticed anything unusual around here over the past few weeks?"

"With the neighbours you mean?"

Mackinnon nodded.

"Not really. It's a pleasant place to live, people mind their own business. I mean, the Dawsons over the road are a bit rowdy, and their kids run wild, but apart from them, it's a pretty quiet street.

"Any men living alone on this road?"

She thought for a moment and then shook her head. "No, it's all couples or families as far as I know."

Mackinnon nodded. He didn't like asking leading questions. It was better when the person interviewed volunteered information without being guided, but in this case, they could be running out of time to save Tammy Holt. The last thing Mackinnon wanted was for Mrs Carson to say at a later date, *Oh, yes there was that odd man living at the end of the road, but you didn't ask me about him."*

"Do you know anyone called Brendan?"

"Brendan?" She repeated the name thoughtfully and hesitated.

Just when Mackinnon thought he might be getting somewhere, she shook her head firmly. "No, sorry. I don't know anyone called Brendan."

Mackinnon hid his disappointment. It was a long shot. They didn't even know if Brendan was his real name or just a pseudonym he used online.

After he'd asked a few more questions, Daphne offered to show Mackinnon around the house, including the bedroom where they'd found the bedbugs. The walls were bare, having been stripped of wallpaper.

"I couldn't keep it on there once I knew they'd been living beneath. We left it for a few weeks as the pest control guy suggested. He sprayed both bedrooms upstairs and the hallway, and then came back to spray again two weeks later. As soon as the treatment was over, I stripped everything off and washed everything down." She scratched her arm and gave Mackinnon a sheepish smile.

"The worst thing is, I'm a bit of a clean freak. I hate mess or dirt. But we weren't allowed to vacuum or wipe down any surfaces after they'd sprayed. Can you believe it? It already felt like the place was really dirty and then I wasn't allowed to vacuum." She shook her head. "Hopefully we've seen the last of the horrible things now. I have to say I was really shocked. I thought in this day and age we would have got rid of them."

"They seem to be making quite a comeback," Mackinnon said.

Daphne gave a more violent shiver this time. "Well, I just hope they don't come back here."

* * *

Tom Bradley was running behind again. This job would be the

death of him. He broke hard, swung his hire van into a narrow space at the side of the road and yanked on the handbrake. After tugging off his seatbelt, he jumped down from the driver's seat and left the engine running as he fumbled with his clunky scanning device, trying to open the back doors of the van at the same time.

He swore under his breath when he saw his carefully stacked piles of parcels had fallen over. He'd spent ages getting them sorted in order of delivery address. Now he'd have to search through the whole lot for the parcel for number twenty-one.

He clambered inside the van, tempted to chuck all the parcels onto the side of the road and drive off. He was sick of this job.

He flipped the scanner over only to find the screen was blank. Again. The third time today. It had to be faulty. Either that or it hated him. He shook it violently and the screen flickered into life. *Finally.*

According to the handheld device, there were two parcels for this address. He found the first one quickly enough, but the second was a tiny square box he eventually found wedged underneath one of the bigger parcels at the back of the van.

If he didn't make it before the cut-off final delivery time of eight p.m., he'd have to give the company a penalty payment.

He'd had to do that twice in the last month. On days like today, it barely made it worthwhile getting out of bed and going to work in the first place.

What with the cost of the van hire, plus the diesel, he wasn't exactly raking it in on good days either.

Working as a delivery driver had appealed to him. He liked the idea of being on the road on his own for most of the day. He figured he could listen to podcasts and a couple of his favourite radio shows. But he hadn't factored in the horrendous London traffic and those stupid penalty payments.

Maybe being a delivery driver outside London would be better. But for now, he was reconsidering his career choice. He grabbed the two parcels, jumped out of the van and jogged across the road to number twenty-one.

He rang the doorbell and clenched his teeth in annoyance as the chimes played a stupid nursery rhyme. Didn't the owners find that annoying? He did, and he'd only listened to it for five seconds.

He scanned the parcels and saw to his annoyance that they needed a signature. He couldn't just leave them on the doorstep.

"Come on, come on," he mumbled under his breath. Why did they always take so long to answer the door when he was in a rush?

Running late again. It was the story of his life.

He muffled a sigh as the homeowner finally opened the door.

"Delivery for you, love," he said holding the machine for her so she could sign digitally. As soon as she'd scrawled something on the screen, he whipped it away and thrust the parcels at her, turning away before she had a chance to reply.

He jogged back over to the van. He had no time for niceties today. He briefly considered rearranging the parcels in the back again so they were in delivery order, but what was the point if they all toppled over again when he took a corner too fast?

He climbed up into the cab and pulled out into the traffic,

causing the driver of the bus he drove in front of to sound their horn.

"They think they own the road. Bloody buses," Tom grumbled to himself.

He looked at his satnav. His next stop was only a short distance away. He flicked his indicator and then cursed as the traffic lights changed in front of him. He broke hard and heard the parcels shift about in the back. *Typical.* At least he hadn't wasted his time trying to put them in order again.

A woman with an annoying nasal voice was talking on the radio. A member of the public had called in to chat about her experiences shopping locally rather than at major supermarkets.

"Who cares?" Tom yelled at the radio as the lights turned green.

He stamped on the accelerator. Why did the producers of radio shows think people wanted to listen to members of the public? If he'd wanted to listen to that sort of rubbish he'd go down to Sainsbury's and strike up a conversation with some numbskull, or head down to the local pub and ask for someone's opinion on supermarket dominance.

They were getting paid to put on the shows, but filled it with free content by having people call in and talk about rubbish.

He flicked off the radio with a grunt of annoyance and slid a CD into the slot. Amy Winehouse. One of his favourites.

He sang along, trying to put the ticking clock out of his mind.

Who would have thought being a delivery driver could be so stressful? He'd left his job in local government, thinking he'd have more time at home to spend with his wife and kids. He'd expected the salary cut but hadn't expected the stress.

He really didn't get paid enough for this amount of trouble, he thought, as he pulled up outside his next destination. If he didn't have a better day tomorrow, he'd jack it in. Life was too short.

CHAPTER THIRTY-SEVEN

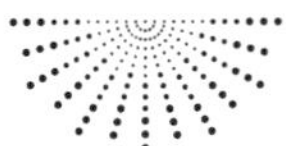

TAMMY TOOK a deep breath and struggled to push herself into a sitting position. Her arms were stinging. She wasn't sure what those insects had been. Fire ants? Whatever they were, they'd bitten her and left bumps all over her arms.

She scratched the raised lumps. Did those little bugs really carry a parasite? Fear twisted her stomach.

She shook her head, refusing to admit the possibility of a parasite living in her blood. No. She'd been taken in because she was so desperate for someone to help her. His whole theory was nonsense. They were just insect bites. Pure and simple. She'd be absolutely fine when she got out of there and got hold of some antihistamine.

Brendan had put a rag in her mouth and topped it with duct tape over her lips. She slowly peeled back the edges of the tape. Although her hands were bound in front of her, she could still remove the tape now that she was conscious. She felt a surge of anger. Covering her mouth like that after he'd given her so many drugs was stupid and reckless. She could have choked on her own vomit and died.

Not that he'd care. He wasn't normal. He was a complete and utter maniac.

He actually thought she would go along with his plan, whatever that was. Tammy remembered the look of shock on his face when she'd slammed her elbow against his cheekbone. She'd learnt that move in first defence class before she got too ill to go. Her elbow had connected with a satisfying thud and he'd screamed in pain, then shuffled off, leaving her alone for a while at least.

She'd been aiming at his nose, so the blow hadn't been on target, but she'd managed to inflict some damage, and that was the important thing.

Tammy ran a hand over her forearm. She needed to stop scratching the bites, but they were *so* itchy.

She planned to do more than put her elbow in his face the next time he came back up to the loft. She had to face facts. This wasn't all some big mistake. He wasn't suddenly going to feel bad about what he'd done and release her. There were only two likely ways this could end.

He'd kill her, or she'd kill him. Acknowledging the fact made her feel dizzy. She wasn't stupid. She knew the first outcome was more likely.

Bile rose at the back of Tammy's throat as she thought what he might do to her.

She linked her fingers and squeezed her palms together. The effects of the drugs were wearing off now. She didn't feel so out of it, so the next time he came up here… that was her chance. She'd throw everything she had at him.

A little voice at the back of her mind told her to just go

along with what he wanted. *Don't rock the boat. Don't make him angry.*

But he wasn't going to let her go. He was going to kill her.

She'd found the other woman's clothes up here, hadn't she? He'd kept another woman up here before Tammy, and who knew if there had been only one other woman? He could have been doing this for years, preying on young women who joined the forum for help. Poor, stupid women like her, who really believed he could help after Western medicine had failed them.

Angrily, Tammy raked her skin with her fingernails.

If she was going to die up here, she was going to do as much damage to him as possible. If she managed to take him by surprise, she might have a chance. All she had to do was momentarily disable him and give herself enough time to access the loft hatch, climb down the ladder, then down the stairs and to the front door.

If the front door was locked, she knew there was a window in the kitchen big enough to crawl through. That was plan B.

All she had to do now was wait.

It was hot in the loft, and the warmth made her drowsy, despite the adrenaline running through her system. Exhaustion made her limbs feel heavy and her eyelids droop.

She wondered how her mum was getting on and her sister. They'd be so worried by now. Then she thought about Instagram. Surely her followers on there would be sending concerned messages. She'd be missed.

Tammy sniffed. She wasn't going to give up without a fight. By this time tomorrow, she could be safely back in her own bed. She imagined getting back home and giving her mum the biggest hug…

Tammy jerked awake and blinked. How had she fallen asleep sitting up? She was so tempted to lie down and go back to sleep but didn't want to be groggy and only half awake when he next came up to the loft. She needed to be fully alert.

She smothered a yawn and then froze at the sound of the loft hatch scratching against wood as Brendan pried it open.

This was it.

Tammy lowered her head, so her hair fell forward, blocking her face from his view. She peered through the strands of hair and saw his head and shoulders appear through the hatch. A wave of repulsion rippled through her body, making her shudder.

Her first plan had been to find something heavy to use as a weapon, but she hadn't found anything suitable. Shame. She could have hit him as soon as he stuck his head through the hole and clobbered him over and over again until he was unconscious.

Tammy was resourceful, though. Her weapon of choice was tucked in close to her feet. She just needed him to come closer to be able to use it.

"Tammy, I hope you're in a better frame of mind now. If you play up again, I'll be forced to give you more drugs. I don't want to do that. I'd prefer it if we could work together as a team."

Tammy said nothing, but kept her eyes trained on Brendan. He hauled the glass box into the loft, and Tammy's heart began to race.

Not again.

She couldn't stand the idea of those insects scurrying across her skin for a second time.

He lifted himself into the loft slowly, keeping his eyes on her warily.

Her skin prickled.

Talk to him. You need to get his trust. Get him to let his guard down.

Words froze in her throat as he carried the glass case closer.

After he set the box on the board beside her, Tammy got a closer look at the bugs. She didn't know what they were, but they didn't look like ants. The reddish-brown insects scurried across the glass. Maybe they were some kind of beetle, but they had flat bodies, as though they'd been trodden on.

"Do we have to do this again now?" Tammy asked, her voice trembling. My arms are still incredibly itchy."

"Sorry about that. It's a common side effect although some people can get bitten and not react at all, did you know that?"

Tammy shook her head.

"Oh yes, it's all to do with body chemistry. Take me, for example, I react, but only a little." He smiled at the bugs. "They're my little pets. I can feed them, and I barely notice the bites."

He reached out and grabbed her hand. Tammy tried to yank away, but his fingers tightened around her wrist.

"I thought we were going to try to get along," he snapped.

It took a lot of willpower for Tammy to relax and let him inspect her arm.

"They do look a bit sore. I've got some cream downstairs. But you really have to try not to scratch. You don't want the bites to get infected."

"I can't stop. It's so itchy."

"I'll get you some cream. And I've got some gloves you can use, too. That should stop you scratching when you sleep."

He stood up and turned his back, preparing to go back to the hatch.

This was it. Her chance.

For a moment, the feeling was so overwhelming she did nothing. She'd had a whole plan worked out of how she'd get him to turn around and face the other way. She'd been going to say a bird was trapped in the rafters, but now she didn't need to.

He'd turned his back on her.

If she didn't act now, she'd lose her chance. He was walking away, towards the hatch.

Tammy grabbed the handbag beside her and stood up. Her legs shook, but somehow she managed to stay upright. She flung herself at Brendan.

He heard her moving, of course, but his reaction was too slow. He didn't turn in time.

Tammy looped the strap of the pink handbag over his neck, twisted it and then jumped on his back.

He fell forward heavily against the wooden boards. The breath left his lungs in a hiss as she coiled the strap around both hands and pulled back with all her strength.

It wasn't easy. Even sitting on his back, her weight wasn't enough to keep him pinned to the floor. He writhed and bucked, but Tammy just kept pulling the strap.

She couldn't keep him still. He was so much taller and bigger than her, but all she had to do was keep her grip on the bag and not let go. She pulled tighter and tighter, praying the leather strap didn't snap under the stress.

He tried to push her off his back, then to punch her, but the angle of his arms, weakened his blows. He couldn't get enough purchase to knock her off.

Then he put his hands flat on the floor, pushing up, attempting to tip her off his back, but Tammy kicked his arms out from under him until he collapsed back on the floor.

He was weakening. Gasping for breath. His fingers scratched and pulled at the strap constricting his airway.

Tammy leaned back, pulling harder. A scream echoed in her ears, and tears were running down her cheeks, but she kept pulling.

It felt like hours passed. Her arms ached with the effort, but she kept the strap pulled taut until Brendan finally went limp.

Was it a trick? Or was he really unconscious? She didn't trust him and kept the strap tight around his neck for another thirty seconds.

The screaming was still echoing around the loft and it took a moment for her to realise the scream was coming from her. She closed her mouth then everything was silent and still.

She sat there, still on his back, holding the straps, not wanting to let go. Was Brendan acting? Maybe he'd gone limp intending to attack her as soon as she let go of the straps.

But she couldn't stay there. She willed herself to get moving. She had to get out of there.

Tammy whimpered with fear as she lowered the bag and let the strap loosen.

Brendan didn't move.

She slowly lifted herself from Brendan's back and stood up, but didn't let go of the bag just in case.

But he lay motionless on the wooden floorboards. He looked odd. Pale. Was he unconscious or had she killed him?

She turned slowly, daring to look over her shoulder at the open loft hatch.

So close.

She could do it.

Slowly she lowered the bag to the floor, leaving the strap looped around Brendan's throat, and then in a mad rush, flung herself at the loft hatch.

Panic and the fact her hands were still tied together, didn't make her descent easy and she slid down the last three steps of the ladder, landing on her backside.

But she didn't stop. She was straight back on her feet, lunging towards the stairs, taking them two at a time until she was in the hallway, and there, in front of her was the front door.

She was nearly there. Almost safe. She turned back. Was that a noise? Was he coming after her?

She fumbled with the keys.

Quick, quick.

She managed to turn the key and yanked open the door. Sobs racked her body as she flung herself out into the daylight and ran.

The uneven pavement scratched her bare feet as thoughts flooded her mind. She needed to get to a phone. She needed to call her mum. She needed to talk to the police.

But the overwhelming physical need to flee overrode everything else. She ran, despite the fact her brain was telling her she should stop at a neighbour's and ask for help, her legs wouldn't stop moving. She wanted to put as much distance between her and Brendan as possible.

She ran along the residential street in her underwear, scratching her arms. The thought running through her mind on a loop was that she had to get away.

* * *

Tom Bradley was in a slightly better mood now. The last two stops had been very quick, and he'd managed to catch up a little. Maybe he wouldn't end the day with a penalty payment, after all.

If he could put his foot down and make the next two deliveries in good time…

Then, at the worst possible moment, he saw a long line of traffic in front of him. He groaned and slapped his palm against the steering wheel.

Why could he never catch a break? Everything was always stacked against him. That was it, he decided. If he got a penalty payment today, then he was looking for a new job in the morning.

As he came to a stop behind a grey Hyundai, Tom pressed a few buttons on his satnav. Maybe there was a shortcut, a cut through he could use to avoid this traffic.

Growing angrier by the minute, he enlarged the screen and tried to work out the different routes available. The satnav was *supposed* to help him avoid traffic. The gadget was a waste of space. He had a sneaking feeling it enjoyed making his life a misery.

But Tom worked out if he took the next left he could cut the corner, and that would certainly save some time.

Impatiently, he drummed his fingers against the wheel as he edged the van through the traffic until finally he spotted the turning. He indicated and accelerated hard, misjudging the size of the gap available, which earned him an angry glare from a black-haired woman in a VW Passat.

Tom held up a hand in apology.

Then he pulled around the parked cars and accelerated. He had to get to his next delivery point in five minutes or that was it. He'd have to admit defeat.

He turned right into the next road and stopped at a pedestrian crossing as a young woman and a small boy, both eating ice-creams, strolled across the road.

"Come on," Tom grumbled. "I haven't got all day."

Oblivious, the woman and the boy took their time. The little boy, smiling through a smear of melted ice-cream, held up a hand and waved at him.

With a grunt of impatience, Tom waved back. Yes, he was running late and people dawdling across the road were annoying, but he wasn't a heartless monster.

Once they were safely across, he accelerated hard again, glancing down at the satnav to check he was going the right way.

When he looked up, he couldn't understand what he saw. The message his eyes sent his brain didn't make sense.

A young woman sprinted across the road. She was almost naked, and her long hair streaked out behind her as she suddenly changed direction and veered in front of him.

Tom slammed on his brakes and the van's wheels screeched on the tarmac as it skidded towards her.

He'd known then, in that fraction of a second, that he wasn't going to stop in time.

It was the worst moment of his life. There was nothing he could do.

He was going to hit her. It was inevitable.

She turned at the last moment, her eyes wide as the van slid towards her.

Then he winced at the dull thud.

"No, no, no," Tom mumbled desperately as he fumbled with his seatbelt and tumbled out of the van.

Was she underneath? Had he driven over her?

He didn't want to look, but he had no choice. He patted his pockets, looking for his mobile phone.

She lay motionless on the tarmac. A single trickle of blood snaked its way along her forehead.

He hadn't driven over her, thank goodness. She'd hit the bonnet and been knocked further along the road. But it didn't look good. She wasn't moving.

He leaned closer. She had a head injury, and they were really bad, weren't they?

He fumbled with the phone, cursing the screen lock on his phone. His fingers felt like sausages as he tried to dial 999.

"Ambulance, I need an ambulance," Tom shouted down the phone as soon as the call was answered.

CHAPTER THIRTY-EIGHT

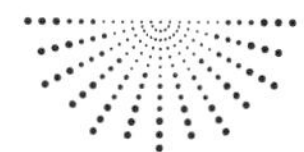

Mr and Mrs Pohl and their two children occupied the second address on Mackinnon's list of residences that were close to the bus route and had reported a recent bedbug infestation. They lived in a ground floor flat in a converted Georgian house.

Mackinnon pressed on the intercom, and after a dull buzz, a male voice tinnily echoed out of the small speaker.

"Yes?"

"Mr Pohl? This is DS Mackinnon. We spoke earlier."

"Of course, come in."

The dull buzz sounded again and the lock clicked. Mackinnon pulled open the door and stepped inside.

The entrance was large and spacious, and the floor was covered with an intricate black-and-white tile. Against the wall were old-fashioned mailboxes for the tenants. A sweeping ornate staircase led up to the next floor.

It had to cost a packet to rent a place like this. Proof

bedbugs could live anywhere. They didn't care how much money you had.

Daphne Carson had been a disappointment. There was no link between the Carsons and the missing women. He was hoping to get more out of Mr and Mrs Pohl. Although he hadn't spoken to her husband, Daphne Carson was a very unlikely suspect. Of course, it was bad policing to rule them out completely, but Mackinnon thought it unlikely Daphne or her husband were involved in Ashley Burrows's death and Tammy Holt's disappearance.

Directly ahead, a tall thin man with a shaved head stepped out of the ground floor flat and moved into the hall.

He stood by the open door, smiling as he waited for Mackinnon to approach.

"I hope you didn't have any trouble finding the place," he said.

"Not at all. It's a lovely building."

Mr Pohl nodded. "Yes, we've been here three years. Now the children are getting bigger we really should think about a larger apartment or even a house, but we'd hate to leave this place."

"How old are your children?"

"Kelly has just turned six, and Samuel is eight next month."

He stood aside so Mackinnon could enter the flat. Tinted lighting had been installed in the coving, reflecting on the sleek, highly-polished wooden floor and bright white walls.

Mr Pohl led Mackinnon into the kitchen, which was filled with every kind of gadget imaginable. There were *three* coffee machines, an electric pressure cooker, some kind of huge multipurpose food processor as well as a bread machine.

"Can I get you a drink? Coffee perhaps?"

"A coffee would be great, thank you."

The air was cool, thanks to the air-conditioning. There was a barely perceptible hum in the background. Nothing like the units they had back at the station.

Mr Pohl busied himself with one of the coffee machines, putting a bright purple capsule into the opening at the top and pressing a flashing button as the machine gurgled into life.

He grabbed the milk from the fridge and then turned to Mackinnon. "How exactly can I help you?"

"We're interested in cases of bedbugs in the area. It's related to a crime we're investigating."

Mr Pohl's eyebrows crept up his forehead. "Really? I can't imagine how they'd be involved in a crime." He chuckled. Then grew serious. "I hope it's nothing too terrible."

"Horrible things," Mr Pohl said, walking back to the coffee machine. "Do you take milk or sugar.?"

"No thanks."

"Are you happy sitting here?" he asked, nodding at the kitchen table, "or we could go through into the living room?"

"Whatever is easier."

"In here then," he said putting the two coffee mugs on the table and sitting down. "Don't tell my wife, but I'm terrified of messing up the living room. The cream carpet cost a small fortune, and the furniture is all cream too. Not a very practical colour." He chuckled.

"Is your wife at work?"

He nodded. "Yes, Claire works at the hospital. Shift work. Not an easy job. But luckily I work from home, so I can pick the kids up from school."

"Mr Pohl, could you tell me when you first noticed the bedbugs?"

"Please, call me Nigel. It was about a week after we got back from holiday. We'd been to Italy, had a great time, but we all returned to find we had been bitten. I thought it was just a delayed reaction to mosquito bites we'd had on holiday. But after a week or so, we realised we were still getting bitten. Poor Samuel had the worst of it. He was absolutely covered in bites. The school even called us in to ask what was wrong with him. They thought it might be chickenpox."

"Why were Samuel's bites so bad? Were they in his room?"

"Yes. The pest control chap who dealt with the problem said that's where most of the little critters were hiding out. He found most of them nestled between the wooden slats on Samuel's bed. He thinks we brought them back in our suitcases. We'd never been bitten *before* going on holiday, you see. So it makes sense."

Mackinnon nodded. "And when was this?"

"Beginning of June."

Mackinnon made a note. "And they are gone now?"

"Thankfully, yes. The pest control company did a fantastic job. They were really thorough with everything. We did get a bit paranoid. I washed every item of clothing we owned at sixty degrees! Horrible business. I scared myself witless by reading about the bugs on the Internet. I learnt far more than I wanted to about bedbug resistance to chemicals and pesticides and how they're increasing rapidly." He grimaced. "But we're one of the lucky ones. We got the apartment treated really quickly after we noticed getting bitten, and we let our neighbours know, and they haven't had any bites at all, so we think we're in the clear now."

"I'm glad they got rid of them so quickly. From what I've learned, it's quite a problem in the city."

"That's what I read, too. Not just London but all over the world. In fact, it's much worse in New York."

Mackinnon ran through his list of questions, and Nigel Pohl answered them readily. Nigel was the type who made interviews easy. He had nothing to hide, and he'd had no previous bad experience with police to colour his attitude, so he was open and transparent. Either that, or he was a very good actor.

Again, Mackinnon couldn't help feeling that this was another dead end. He'd been so sure that the bedbug bites on Ashley's arms were an important clue, but so far chasing up reported incidents had been a waste of time.

"Do you mind if I ask about your neighbours? Are they families, couples?"

"There's a family on the floor above us. They've got a new baby. Seven weeks old and a bit of a crier." He pulled a face. "Poor things. I think it's been a shock to the system. I saw Paul the other day, and he looked like a zombie. I don't think he's getting much sleep. Above them, is an elderly couple. They're Swedish, but they've been settled over here for years. Magnus and Tilda. Lovely people."

"And there's no one else in the building? No men living alone?"

Nigel hesitated. "I don't like the sound of that, to be honest. You'd tell me if we had something to worry about, wouldn't you?"

"We have to ask these questions to be thorough, but no, I don't think you have anything to worry about."

Nigel nodded slowly but didn't look convinced. "They're

our only neighbours and we know them pretty well. No single men in the building."

"What about in the houses next door?

"Well, I can't say I know them too well, to be honest. I think they're rented out, and the tenants change pretty regularly."

"Do you know anyone who lives in the area called Brendan?"

Nigel templed his fingers beneath his chin and looked thoughtful. "No, I can't say I do. Sorry."

Mackinnon finished up with a few more questions and then drained his coffee.

"Right, I think I've taken up enough of your time. Thank you for being so helpful and thank you for the coffee."

"You're welcome. I hope you solve the case soon." Nigel Pohl got to his feet and led Mackinnon out of the kitchen.

They walked past a closed door and Nigel nodded at it. "It was nice to take a break. I'll have to get back to work now." He didn't look happy about it at all.

"And what do you do for a living?" Mackinnon asked.

"I'm a copywriter. Adverts mostly." He brightened. "In fact, you might have heard one of my ads on the radio. Have you heard: *For nappies, get Dr Sprinkles', no more night-time tinkle tinkles*?"

Mackinnon was not so much surprised by the words of the jingle but the fact Nigel Pohl had sung them.

"Um, no, I don't think I've heard that one."

Nigel shrugged. "Oh, well. It was only on regional radio stations," he said, opening the door to his office.

It was a small room with a desk facing the window and one tall bookcase. A laptop sat in the middle of the desk.

Nigel Pohl pressed a key on the keyboard and the laptop screen illuminated. A word document was open but it was blank.

"I'm working on something new now," he said.

Mackinnon raised an eyebrow.

"Yes," he nodded sadly, "I know it's blank. It's the story of my life. I'm waiting for inspiration to strike."

* * *

Tom knelt beside the young woman lying on the road. He'd taken her hand in his and was praying.

He hadn't prayed since he'd left school, but it seemed the right thing to do.

Why was the ambulance taking so long?

People were so selfish these days. He'd seen vehicles barely move an inch when an ambulance came up behind them with its blue lights flashing and siren blaring. He'd even seen other cars try to slip in behind an ambulance, trying to get to wherever they were going faster.

Society was falling apart.

Tom sniffed and ran a hand through his hair.

"You're going to be all right," he told the woman for the fiftieth time. "The ambulance is nearly here. I just need you to hold on, okay?"

He felt a slight pressure on his fingers and stared down at his hand. "Was she responding? Could she hear him?

"My name is Tom," he said. "I'm going to stay with you until the paramedics get here. Is there anybody you want me to call? What's your name?"

She didn't move her head, but her lips parted, and a

bubble of blood appeared at the corner of her mouth. "Tammy," she said softly.

Was that Tammy? Or did she say Lammy? No, it definitely sounded like Tammy.

"Listen to me, Tammy. You're going to be just fine. I promise. Try not to move."

He'd seen that on TV shows. After someone had been in an accident, it was a bad idea to move them in case they'd suffered a spinal injury. "I just need you to keep nice and still for me, okay, Tammy?"

"Yes," she breathed. "Don't leave me."

Her fingers tightened around his. Her grip was getting stronger. That was good, wasn't it?

"Don't you worry. I'm not going anywhere. I promise."

A crowd had gathered at the side of the road, and a woman in flip-flops ran over to them. "Oh, no! What happened?"

Tom glared at her, feeling irrationally angry.

As if he was going to tell her the gruesome details with the poor woman lying on the floor in front of them. Besides, wasn't it obvious what had happened?

Tom ignored her question. "I've called an ambulance. We are waiting for it to arrive."

The woman shot him a worried look and then said in a loud whisper, "Why is she only in her underwear?"

That was a more astute question. Tom had to give her that, but Tammy was conscious, and it was rude to talk about her as though she wasn't there.

"That's not the most important thing right now," Tom said. "We're just concentrating on…"

Sirens sounded in the distance.

"It won't be much longer, Tammy. I can hear the ambulance. It must be just around the corner."

Tammy didn't speak but clutched his hand tighter.

She didn't have any clothes on her, so she certainly wouldn't have any ID. He was sure the paramedics would ask for her details when they got there.

"Can you tell me your last name, Tammy?" he asked, ignoring the growing crowd around them.

Tammy took a couple of shallow breaths and then said something like, *Hole* or *Halt*. He couldn't quite work it out.

"All right, I'll tell the paramedics your name as soon as they get here. You'll probably want to get in touch with your family. Do you want me to call anyone for you? You don't seem to have a phone on you," Tom said, stating the obvious.

He was babbling, but he wanted to keep her talking. He wanted her to stay conscious. He *needed* her to be okay.

Tammy whimpered. "It hurts."

"I know, love. As soon as the paramedics get here, I'm sure they'll give you something for the pain."

Tom looked over his shoulder. Why was the ambulance taking so long?

CHAPTER THIRTY-NINE

CHARLOTTE STARED at her computer screen and a smile slowly spread over her face.

It was him. She was sure of it.

The search had taken far too long but finally she'd found a match for their suspect. She navigated to the print screen button on the database page and selected the closest printer. She was ninety-nine point nine percent certain Brendan Maynard was their man, but before announcing it to the rest of the station, she needed to double check all her details.

As the printer hummed into action, she re-read the file.

Brendan Maynard, twenty-eight, of seventeen, North Quay Road.

Thanks to the centralised system pulling data from sources all over the city, they even had a photo of Brendan Maynard. He had no driver's licence, but in this case a City of London bus pass provided the picture. These days everything was digitalised or moving that way. She was glad. It made her job easier.

Charlotte stared at Brendan's picture.

He had brown hair, brown eyes and a neutral Caucasian skin tone.

Was this the man responsible for Ashley Burrows's death and the abduction of Tammy Holt? There was nothing about the image that suggested Brendan was anything other than an ordinary man, but Charlotte was probably staring into the eyes of a killer.

She shuffled through the papers on her desk, looking for the CCTV still she'd printed out earlier. The image Mackinnon had taken from the CCTV at the coffee shop was pretty good as security footage went.

She held it up to the screen, comparing it to her picture of Brendan Maynard. It was definitely the right guy.

She stood up and walked towards DI Tyler's office, only to see when she was halfway across the open-plan area that he wasn't at his desk.

She turned around, headed back to her own desk and picked up the phone, dialling DCI Brookbank's extension.

Janice answered.

"Hi, Janice, it's DC Brown. Could I be put through to the DCI please?"

"He's in a meeting with DI Tyler at the moment. The door is closed, but if it's important, I can interrupt him."

Charlotte hesitated, looking down at the papers on her desk.

"It is important, Janice, but don't worry. I'll come up there and tell them the news in person."

Charlotte hung up and pressed print on the screen to

produce more copies of Brendan Maynard's details. She collected them from the printer on her way to the DCI's office.

Janice gave her a nervous smile as Charlotte entered the small room where DCI Brookbank's assistant was stationed.

"Is everything all right?" Janice asked.

Charlotte nodded. "Yes, things are finally moving on this case, and I need to give the DCI an update."

Janice got to her feet, rapped on the DCI's door and then pushed it open. "Sorry to interrupt, DC Brown would like to have a word."

"Come in," Brookbank said in his usual deep, gruff voice.

Brookbank looked the same as he always did. A solid man, hunched over, reminding her of a grumpy bulldog. Tyler looked tired and stressed. As SIO, he had a lot on his plate. Hopefully her news would ease some of his worries. Now they finally had a breakthrough, things would start moving in a more positive direction.

Charlotte walked in and handed out the paperwork. "We've got him," she said. "We have his address."

Both men looked down, skimming the details on the printout.

Then a grin spread across DI Tyler's face. "Excellent work, detective. We'll arrange a little visit to 17, North Quay Rd."

A smile even tugged the corners of DCI Brookbank's lips. "Yes, very good work indeed, DC Brown."

* * *

Brendan woke up, coughing and spluttering. What had that nasty cow done to him? He felt shaky, too unsure of the strength in his legs to stand up, so he flopped over onto his back and stared up at the roof.

He bit down on his lip. Why were his assistants always so ungrateful? He'd worked hard for them. Look at all the modifications he'd done on the loft. He'd added extra insulation to keep them warm, and installed the soundproofing so they could scream to their heart's content without disturbing the neighbours.

He'd even put extra wooden boards down on the floor so they'd have more room to move about. Had they been grateful? Appreciated his kindness? No.

He'd been very considerate, taking into account their needs. And he'd even been understanding when they lashed out. He'd expected a period of adjustment would be required and knew it would take a while for them to come round to his point of view and understand the importance of his work, but the violence… He'd never expected that.

He reached up, gingerly touching the welts around his neck. She could have killed him. *So irresponsible.*

He took a shallow breath and sat up. It hurt to swallow.

His neck ached and felt stiff. Trying to loosen things up, he moved his neck from side to side, but that only made it worse.

He clenched his teeth.

How had he been so taken in? She'd seemed so genuine, like someone really in need of help. He'd been prepared to give his help freely, but the first time things got a little difficult, she'd lashed out. It wasn't as though he *wanted* to tie them up. He didn't have a choice. No one understood. He'd worked so hard on this.

Brendan shuffled over to the loft hatch feeling sorry for himself. At least she hadn't bolted the hatch behind her. She must have left it open in her rush to get out when she left him there to die.

He felt a twinge of sympathy. He supposed it must be hard for them to understand at first. The truth always was, so perhaps he couldn't really blame Tammy or Ashley for falling apart. They'd been destined to fail from the start. People like them didn't have the tenacity and the intelligence to see this through. They were just normal young women. He scowled. Even so, there was no excuse for Tammy's violence. First she'd given him a bruise on his face and now she'd almost choked him to death.

He made his way down the ladder and into the hall. Legs trembling, he steadied himself against the banister as he made his way to the bathroom.

When he looked in the mirror he let out a sharp gasp. He had bright pink welts around his neck caused by the strap on the bag Tammy had used to strangle him.

He reached up to touch the raised pink skin and winced. Staring forlornly at his reflection, he shook his head, hardly recognising himself. Gaunt cheekbones, bruises, even his eyes looked hollow. He looked lost.

Tears pricked the corner of his eyes. Why was everything going wrong?

"Because you're a failure. You're just a dirty boy who always ruins everything."

Brendan closed his eyes and tried to tune out his mother's voice. "You're not really here," he said. "You're dead."

"I'll never die, not really. Not while you're still alive, Brendan."

He shook his head and ran out of the bathroom.

"You won't get rid of me that easily."

She cackled, and Brendan slapped his hands over his ears, trying to block out the noise.

He ran towards the stairs, wanting to get away from the haunting laughter, only to stub his toe on the corner of the banister.

He howled in anger and frustration and leaned down to check his toes for blood. There was none, but it hurt so much. Why did something as simple as stubbing a toe cause so much pain?

He limped away from the echoing laugh and then froze at the sound of another noise.

The new noise led to fear creeping around him, like a serpent constricting his chest.

Sirens.

Ashley hadn't been able to talk. As fate would have it, when she'd finished her role in the project, she'd been silenced. Nothing to do with him, of course. He couldn't be held responsible for that unfortunate incident, but Tammy? Would she go to the police?

He stood in the hallway shaking as the sirens got louder. No, surely she wouldn't report him to the authorities. She'd be the one to get in trouble. She'd stayed with him for a couple of days, sure, but he hadn't tried to *murder* her. He was the one with the wound around his neck from where she'd tried to throttle him.

He held his breath, ears straining. But eventually the sound of sirens faded. Thankfully, those sirens weren't for him. At least not today.

He breathed a sigh of relief, but it had been a good reminder. He needed to protect himself. Tammy was out there now and could tell anyone about his project.

He tried to remember just how much he'd told her. Not much. Confiding in her hadn't been possible in the hours they'd shared. Thanks to her prickly, difficult nature and violent tendencies, they hadn't really had much opportunity to talk. Now he looked back and realised that was a good thing.

But he should protect himself from future problems. In time, the mark around his neck would fade, and it would be his word against Tammy's. He needed evidence. He fumbled his way downstairs, looking for his mobile and eventually found it beneath a sofa cushion. He took it back to the bathroom and used the mirror to try to get a shot of his injury in the reflection. It wasn't easy to get both his face and his neck in the photograph. He took a few pictures, one from the front and two from the side.

That was something at least, but photographs could be manipulated. Perhaps the police wouldn't take them as evidence. He needed someone else to see his injury so they could confirm his story. Who could he trust? He needed to think about that.

First, a drink was in order.

He made his way downstairs, thankful that his mother disappeared quickly this time, and poured himself a large glass of whiskey.

His head was banging so alcohol probably wasn't the wisest choice, but he needed it to calm his nerves. He lifted the glass of whiskey with a trembling hand.

Yet again his project had been wound back to zero. Why did things keep messing up? Although it might not be all his fault, he had to take some responsibility. He had picked the assistants after all.

He took another mouthful of whiskey and contemplated his failure.

He'd have a lot to write about in his journal tonight. Brendan's usual daydream of someone discovering his journal in a few years from now and realising what a scientific genius he was, failed to comfort him today.

Tammy's behaviour had really shaken him, mainly because he hadn't expected it. It had come out of the blue and taken him completely off guard.

She'd seemed so nice.

He swallowed painfully and gritted his teeth. It was all so unfair. He hadn't hurt her, had he? So why had she behaved so badly?

He sat down in his mother's faded old chair, the one that looked like a normal armchair but moved like a rocker.

He rocked himself slowly, cradling his glass of whiskey and staring down into the amber liquid.

Then suddenly he smiled. It was obvious where he'd been going wrong.

He'd been dealing with amateurs, and he needed a professional.

CHAPTER FORTY

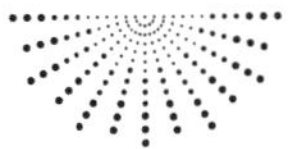

Dr Wendy Willson, got up from her desk with a sigh. She'd been sitting in the same position all day, and her back was killing her.

She walked around her small room, thinking of the lectures she gave her patients on the dangers of a sedentary lifestyle. Being a GP, she didn't find it easy to reach ten thousand steps in a day though she still tried.

A few months ago she'd taken to walking through to the waiting room and calling the next patient's name in person, rather than using the intercom, but these days there didn't seem to be time for that. Extra patients had been squeezed onto her list after one of the practice doctors had left to go and work in Australia.

Wendy had to say she was tempted to move abroad, too. The practice had been advertising for a replacement GP for six months without success. There simply weren't enough GPs to go around.

She picked up her can of Diet Pepsi and looked at it miserably. This was another addiction she would have to quit. But the mid-afternoon caffeine fix helped her get through the afternoon appointments.

And she definitely needed it today. She was the GP working the late shift tonight.

A couple of years ago, the surgery had started opening earlier and closing later to accommodate people who had to work during the day and found it hard to get time off work, which was a high proportion of their patients.

The practice manager had also come up with some ridiculous ideas to increase efficiency. Now if patients wanted a doctor's appointment, they had to call the surgery first thing on Monday morning. That was for both urgent and non-urgent appointments, so the amount of time they had to wait to get through on the phone was absurd.

That was the most common complaint she heard from patients these days. Most appointments started with patients grumbling about the time they'd spent on the phone trying to get a slot with the doctor. After apologising, Wendy would try to steer the conversation around to what was actually wrong with them.

Wendy had a lot of sympathy for their complaints. They were right. It *was* ridiculous. It meant people with urgent concerns had to wait on the phone line with those who just wanted to book a standard appointment for some point in the next two weeks.

Standard of care and efficiency had declined in GP practices— not just hers, but those all over the country. And it was devastating to be in the middle of it but not able to do anything about it. Doctors like Wendy wanted to spend time with their patients, get to know them and help them. That's why she'd become a GP and not a registrar or surgeon.

When she'd first started medical school, Wendy had a romantic idea of living somewhere in the countryside, where everyone in the village knew her by name.

But now here she was, working in the City of London, with a comfortable salary, but a ridiculous number of patients, and she'd probably only recognise ten of them if she saw them in the street.

Patients rarely got an appointment with their named doctor. They were allocated to whoever was available. And as today was Dr Farquhar's day off, it meant every other doctor had to pitch in and take a few more patients.

The extra patients made the GP surgery more profitable of course, which some patients didn't realise. They assumed GPs were paid a standard salary by the NHS, but it wasn't that simple.

GPs surgeries were independent contractors, and the NHS paid the practice a set amount per patient. So the more patients, the more profits for the practice. But with over forty appointments every day plus paperwork, Wendy had grown tired of the system. She didn't see any of the extra profits but was expected to work longer hours. The partners benefited of course.

She'd never considered herself political, but had a sneaking respect for the senior oncologist who had voiced his opinion that the GP system was broken. He was coming from the other side of it, as the doctor GPs referred patients to, but she very much admired the man for having the bravery to come out and speak publicly on the subject, despite the backlash he'd received. He'd been due a lifetime achievement award, but that had been retracted. Wendy took a sip of her Pepsi and shook her head. Awful really. Just for voicing an opinion in a country where, supposedly, people could speak their mind freely as long as it didn't hurt others.

Dr Farquhar was not someone she would socialise with after work, but he wasn't bad as bosses went. For a while shortly after her son, Davey, was born, she'd worked as a locum and that had been a horrendous experience. The doctor in charge had managed multiple practices, and rumour had it he was one of the few GPs in the country earning over two hundred thousand pounds a year. He'd wanted her to use a five-minute timer to make sure she didn't spend too long on each patient.

She hadn't known quite what to say when he proudly presented the timer to her on her first day of work.

It was a large object, which looked very much like an over-sized egg timer—with coloured sand that trickled away as the seconds passed, but it lasted for five minutes rather than three.

She'd hardly ever met her five minute target. Mainly because you were supposed to review the notes and the patient details in the consulting time as well as ask questions and perform examinations. It was no wonder things got missed and the patients felt they weren't getting the time and focus they deserved from their GPs when surgeries acted like that.

She was better now at multi-tasking, reading while talking to patients, and was quicker at dealing with them, but was that a good thing? In her heart of hearts, she didn't believe so.

It wasn't easy. There wasn't the time to give everyone the standard of care they deserved, and it broke her heart when she allowed herself time to think about it.

Wealthy residents living in the City of London could afford to see private GPs. But poorer residents didn't have a choice, they had to put up with the long waiting times if they wanted a non-urgent appointment, and people in other areas of the country didn't even have the opportunity to go private unless they wanted to travel miles and miles. The whole country's medical care had been set up to flow through the GP referral system, and in Wendy's opinion, it was at breaking point. Something had to give. She wasn't sure throwing more money at the matter would really solve the problem. Mismanagement was probably responsible for some of the issues, but not all.

She believed something needed to change, but didn't know what. It was easy to point out problems, not so easy to find solutions. Some of her colleagues supported the idea of super practices. If they had centres with x-ray facilities and minor injury units, that would ease some of the pressure on accident and emergency departments in hospitals.

There may be cracks and problems with the NHS system, but when she'd taken Davey to A&E a year ago when she feared he had meningitis, she couldn't fault the system. The doctors and nurses had been wonderful.

There was a knock at the door, which made Wendy jump.

"Come in."

The new receptionist entered tentatively. "I'm ever so sorry to bother you doctor."

Anne had only been working at the practice for six weeks. She was quite unlike the other two receptionists they employed on a part-time basis. Timid, quiet and very polite, she had a kind nature when dealing with patients. Wendy liked her.

"Not at all. I've nearly finished my break. I'm just slurping down the rest of this. And before you say anything, yes, I'm a doctor, and yes, I should know better," Wendy joked, holding up her half-finished Pepsi.

Anne didn't smile. "The thing is, there's a patient causing a terrible nuisance in the waiting room. I've asked him to sit down and he won't. He hasn't been violent, but he is scaring the other patients."

Wendy set the can on her desk. "What's his name? Does he have an appointment?"

"It's Brendan Maynard. I saw there is a note on his file…"

Wendy felt a chill at the mention of Brendan's name. She wasn't normally like that. She'd seen all sorts in her time as a GP and had always managed to be compassionate rather than fearful, but for some reason, she found it hard with Brendan. There was something about him that made her want to run away and hide.

"I would have gone to Dr Farquhar, but he's not here today," Anne continued.

Wendy nodded slowly. "It's okay. I'll deal with him. What is he asking for?"

"He just wants an appointment. I told him he'd have to phone on Monday morning because we're all booked up this week, but then he got very angry. So I said I'd ask one of the doctors if he would just sit down, but he refused and went on a rant about GPs."

Wendy checked her watch. "Okay, I'll tell you what. Send him in here now. It's not really fair on the other patients, now they'll have to wait longer, but at least they won't have to put up with him in the waiting room."

"Oh, that would be wonderful," Anne said. "Thank you so much." She turned to leave the room and then hesitated. "Are you sure you'll be all right with him on your own. I saw the note on his file that said he has mental health issues."

Wendy tried to sound more confident than she felt. "Yes, I'll be fine. I've dealt with him before."

When Anne left the room and the door closed with a click, Wendy shivered.

She'd be fine. She just had to deal with him for ten minutes and get through the rest of the day. Her husband would be picking up Davey from school soon. In a few hours she could go home, kiss Davey good night and read him a bedtime story.

Glancing at the small photograph of Davey on her desk, she smiled. She was biased, but he was the sweetest, best-looking child she'd ever seen. He'd inherited the best from her and her husband. He had her jet black curls and dark brown eyes and his dad's smile and happy demeanour. Wendy had always been a serious child, a worrier, so she was glad Davey hadn't inherited that. Her son's skin was just a shade or two lighter than hers.

She tried to focus on Davey to get herself to relax, but it wasn't working. As soon as she sat down behind the desk, her back started to ache.

Less than a minute later, the door opened again, and this time Brendan Maynard walked in.

She could tell from the lines etched on his face and the tense way he held himself that he was angry. He had a nasty bruise just below his eye. Had he been in a fight? He looked flushed, but that could be the heat. He wore a polo neck jumper, a very unusual choice for such a hot day.

"Hello, Brendan, how can I help you today?"

He smiled but didn't sit down, instead leaning on the back of the chair.

Wendy took a deep breath, trying to calm her nerves.

"I've got a special job for you today, Doctor."

Wendy tried to keep her tone light. "Really? And what might that be?"

"I need you to come back home with me. Then I'll tell you all about it."

"I can't do that," Wendy said. "I've got other patients to see this afternoon and you know I don't do home visits. You've asked before."

Brendan's expression darkened.

"I can help you though, Brendan. I know things are tough at the moment. So, I thought I could book you into Trevelyan house for a few days. It would be good for you to have a nice rest, and they'll be able to assess you and determine what the best course of treatment is going forward." She smiled at him hopefully.

His smile widened and he chuckled. "I know you think I'm mad, but I think I'm the only sane person around here. And I don't have time to go to Trevelyan house I'm afraid, Doctor. I'm in the middle of a very important experiment and I need your help."

"Brendan, that's simply not possible," Wendy said, trying to hold back her irritation. "You saw I have a waiting room full of patients. I can't let them down."

"It's a shame, but you'll have to let them down I'm afraid. The experiment comes first."

He was being ridiculous. She went to reach for the phone, and as she did so, he turned his head, and the polo neck shifted, revealing bright red marks on his neck.

She forgot about the phone and got to her feet, moving closer to him.

"Brendan, what are these marks on your neck? Have you tried to hurt yourself?"

He hesitated, seemingly at a loss for words, and his confidence evaporated. "I… I… No, I didn't do it. It wasn't me."

"Oh, Brendan. You have to let me help you. I want to help you feel better. I need you to trust me, okay?"

He didn't seem so scary now, Wendy thought. He looked more like a little boy as he hunched over and then flopped into the seat.

"It's going to be okay. We'll get you through this," Wendy said, sitting down at her desk and tapping on the keyboard to look up the number to make a referral.

Brendan cowered in his chair, stooping lower and lower.

"Brendan are you feeling faint?" Wendy asked.

He shook his head. "Can't you hear her?" He grimaced.

"Hear who?"

Wendy looked at where he was pointing over his shoulder. There was nobody there. He was hallucinating. Things were progressing fast.

"Listen to me, Brendan. I know this is very scary, but your mind is playing tricks on you. Focus on me, okay. We're going to make this stop. We're going to make you feel better."

Brendan sniffed, and as Wendy turned back to her computer, he pulled something from a messenger bag that made Wendy freeze.

It was a knife.

A knife, with a long, shiny steel blade.

It's said your life flashes before your eyes when you're about to die, but Wendy didn't think about *her* life. All she thought about was Davey. Davey asking where his mummy was when she didn't come home to read him a story tonight. Davey crying at her grave. Davey growing up without her.

"Brendan, that's not going to help."

"Listen to me, you're not the one in charge. If you do exactly what I say, no one will get hurt. Now, get up. You're coming with me."

Did he really expect they could walk out through the waiting room and nobody would stop them or call the police? He really was crazy.

Wendy shakily got to her feet as Brendan walked around the desk and opened the window. He released the safety catches, so it opened fully, creating a gap large enough for them to climb out.

So he didn't intend to walk out through the waiting room after all. How long would it be before someone noticed she was missing? Anne was sensible. She'd call the police as soon as she realised something was wrong. But would it be too late?

While he was distracted, Wendy reached for her mobile, but he noticed.

Grinning, shaking his head and tapping the knife on the desk, he said, "I think you should leave that here. And before you decide to do anything stupid like call for help, I should let you know that I have your son. Davey. Cute kid."

Blood roared around Wendy's system. Davey? No. It wasn't possible. Her husband would be heading to the school to pick him up in—she glanced at her watch—five minutes. How would Brendan have taken Davey from school? How could this be happening?

Brendan nodded at the open window. "So, now we understand each other, let's move."

CHAPTER FORTY-ONE

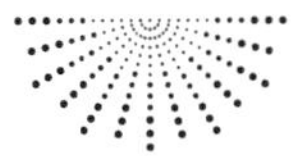

ANNE GLANCED at the clock behind the reception counter. Dr Willson had been seeing Brendan Maynard for over fifteen minutes now. The usual appointment lasted about ten minutes, give or take, but she understood a patient with Brendan's needs might require more attention.

He had mental health problems and was definitely very upset today. Though Anne was new to the surgery, she was well aware of the undercurrent of tension between Dr Willson and Dr Farquhar. She'd also paid close attention to patient files and had seen Brendan had been transferred to Dr Farquhar. There had to be a reason for that, and if Anne was a betting woman, she'd put money on the transfer being due to Dr Willson feeling uncomfortable treating Brendan alone, which was understandable.

Anne had studied nursing for a couple of years when she was in her twenties. She liked the idea of helping people and nursing seemed like such a noble profession. Trouble was,

Anne was not good with blood, or any bodily fluids really. She learned quickly that she was too squeamish for nursing. So she'd signed up for special training to become a consultant's secretary, and she'd been very good at it, too, before she'd taken a career break to raise her children.

Now both her sons were in primary school, she'd decided the time was right to come back to part-time employment and had been pleased to take up a job at Dr Farquhar's practice. The surgery was within walking distance of their flat and the money certainly helped out with two growing boys to look after. They seemed to need a new pair of shoes every two months recently.

It was just her luck for them both to be going through a growth spurt at the same time.

Anne got to her feet and rushed into the waiting area as she saw Mrs McCafferty struggling to her feet after the practice nurse called her name over the intercom.

The elderly woman dropped her walking stick. Anne collected the stick, handed it back to Mrs McCafferty with a smile and then helped the elderly lady to the practice nurse's room.

"Thank you, dear," Mrs McCafferty said.

"Not at all."

Anne walked briskly back to reception. Seventeen minutes had passed now. Perhaps she should go and check on Dr Willson?

It was almost the end of her shift. In fact, she thought with a frown, her shift should have ended five minutes ago, but as usual, Viv, one of the other receptionists, was late. Viv had worked at Dr Farquhar's practice for over five years and saw herself as the boss. She liked to lord it over everyone, even though she was employed under the exact same terms as Anne. She was condescending, rude and always late, despite that, Anne tried to keep the peace. She certainly didn't need to create an enemy at work.

As another minute ticked by, Anne began to get increasingly concerned. Of course, the appointment would run longer than usual if Dr Willson had to arrange a referral, but Anne had felt uneasy since the moment Brendan Maynard had walked into the doctor's surgery.

Finally Viv bustled into the waiting area.

She was a large woman, with dyed red hair and the type of trowelled-on make-up that made you wonder what she really looked like underneath. Anne thought if she ever saw Viv barefaced, she wouldn't recognise her.

"I'm glad you're here," Anne said, preparing to explain her worries about Dr Willson.

"For goodness sake, Anne. I'm only five minutes late. I'm sure that's not inconvenienced you too much."

Viv turned her back and shrugged off her cardigan then stashed her handbag beneath the desk. The air was thick with Viv's floral perfume.

Anne tried again. "The thing is, we had a very agitated patient come into the surgery and demand to see one of the GPs. He is in with Dr Willson now and has been in there for almost twenty minutes. I'm a bit concerned."

Viv rolled her eyes. "I'm sure Dr Willson is fine. She's dealt with plenty of difficult patients in her time. When you get a little more experience, you'll understand."

Anne felt a flare of anger. "I've plenty of experience, Viv," she said, trying to keep the irritation from her voice. "I've worked with patients for most of my career."

"Yes, but you've had a lot of time off, haven't you?"

"I took a career break when I had my children," Anne said. "That doesn't wipe my memory, or make me inexperienced."

"Seven years is a very long time to take off work," Viv said with a sniff.

"Anyway," Anne said, determined to get back on topic. "I'm concerned about Dr Willson. The patient's name is Brendan Maynard," she added in a whisper so Viv could hear but not the rest of the waiting room.

"Oh, him, the *hypochondriac*. That's what all the doctors call him. I think he's harmless."

"Harmless? But his file said he had mental health problems, and Dr Willson wanted to refer him, and then he was transferred to Dr Farquhar's list."

"What's your point?" Viv said sitting down heavily on the chair beside Anne.

Anne thought it was very clear what her point was.

"My point is that Dr Willson could be in trouble. I think one of us should check on her."

"And by 'one of us,' you mean me because it's my shift now?" Viv said raising a carefully drawn eyebrow.

Anne pursed her lips. Yes, actually she did think Viv should get off her backside and go and check on Dr Willson.

"That might be a good idea," Anne said pointedly.

Viv gave a little huff under her breath. "You can check on her if you like, but I've got work to do."

She reached over and picked up the box of patient samples. The samples weren't due to be collected until tomorrow. Viv was just being difficult.

"Fine," Anne said. "I'll check on her before I go."

"Knock yourself out," Viv said.

Anne grabbed her handbag, looped the strap over her shoulder and walked around the reception desk towards the back of the surgery.

Viv was impossible, luckily Anne didn't have to spend much time with her and only saw her during handovers. It seemed Viv saw herself as Queen bee and wanted to mark her territory like a dog peeing over everything.

Anne knocked on Dr Willson's closed door.

She might receive a sharp reprimand from Dr Willson for interrupting when she was seeing a patient, but it was better to be safe than sorry.

There was no response to her knock, so she tried again, banging on the door a little harder.

Still nothing.

Anxiety trickled through Anne's body.

She reached for the doorknob, turning it and then pushing the door open slowly.

"I'm very sorry to interrupt," she called from the hallway not wanting to walk inside and interrupt an examination.

But there was still no response. Swallowing hard, Anne stepped inside Dr Willson's room. She wasn't behind the desk. Anne turned to the small curtained area where patients could undress to get ready for an examination, but the curtains were wide open and there was nobody there.

She walked inside, turning a slow circle, taking in every corner, but the room was empty.

Where were they?

Then her gaze fell on the open window.

Anne's stomach clenched with fear.

* * *

Mackinnon pulled his mobile out of his pocket and answered the call from DI Tyler.

"I've got some news, Jack. We have a full name and address for our suspect. Brendan Maynard, 17 North Quay Road. I'm sending his details over to you now."

"Great news. What's the next step?"

"We're heading to his flat now to arrest him and search the property.

"Do you need me?"

"No, we've got plenty of officers as well as a search team ready to go over his flat with a fine-tooth comb as soon as we've arrested him. Have you had any luck on the bedbug addresses?"

"No," Mackinnon said with a sigh. "It looks like the bugs and Noah Thorne were both false leads."

"You can't win them all, Jack. You followed the correct procedure to chase down all logical leads. That's all anyone can expect."

"I know," Mackinnon said, but he couldn't help feeling he'd rather be on the scene when they arrested Brendan Maynard rather than traipsing around London talking to people about bedbugs. "I don't suppose 17 North Quay Road was on the list of bedbug addresses?"

"No, it wasn't on the list. I checked myself before leaving the station, but it is within walking distance of the No 22 bus route."

"I guess the bedbug theory was a waste of time then."

"I don't know about that. I think you were on the right track. Charlotte found out something very interesting regarding Brendan Maynard's job. He's a self-employed pest controller."

Mackinnon paused to digest the information. He guessed that could make sense. If he'd had an infestation at his property, he would have treated the problem himself, and perhaps introduced the bedbugs into his flat from his work."

The pieces of the puzzle were slowly fitting together.

"That's an interesting connection," Mackinnon said. "Good luck with the raid. Do you know if he is on the premises?"

"We've had someone watching the flat while we waited for the paperwork, and no one has seen him leave. But no, we don't know for sure if he's there. I'm keeping my fingers crossed that even if he isn't home, Tammy Holt will be at the address."

After Mackinnon hung up, he put his phone back in his pocket and walked along Fir Street.

He'd been distracted by the unrelated strands in this case. Ashley's ex, the bedbugs… they'd all been diversions, leading him in the wrong direction.

If Brendan Maynard was responsible, then it looked as though there was no connection to Noah Thorne, Ashley's ex-boyfriend.

But Mackinnon had been very sure the man was hiding something. Of course, it could have been a secret completely unrelated to Ashley Burrows's death. And he had to admit they had found no link between Noah Thorne and Tammy Holt.

So his hunch about Noah Thorne had led him away from the real culprit. Noah had been hiding something all right. His affair with Ashley's work colleague, but that didn't make him a killer.

After that, Mackinnon had focused on the bedbug angle, wrongly believing it would lead them to the location where

Ashley had been held and potentially where Tammy was still being kept against her will.

The two addresses he'd visited today had proved fruitless. Appearances suggested they were normal families, very unlikely to be involved in either woman's disappearance, and he still couldn't get an answer from anyone at the third address. Perhaps the listed number was wrong.

He should go back to the station and start on his paperwork. He had plenty of forms to fill in for this investigation as well as outstanding reports on the Aleena case. It wasn't as though he didn't have plenty to do, but he couldn't help wishing he was heading to 17 North Quay Road as the net tightened around Brendan Maynard.

He reached the corner of the road and contemplated whether to turn right and head to the underground station or turn left and go to the third address on his list. He was close. Even if no one was home, perhaps he could talk to one of the neighbours and ask around.

DI Tyler already had his suspect's location, so it was probably a waste of time, but a nagging feeling wouldn't leave Mackinnon. His instinct was telling him to check it out. If he didn't, he'd spend the rest of the day wondering what he could have found at the property.

He checked the map app on his phone and then headed left, away from the underground station. The paperwork could wait a little longer.

A quick visit to Pine Avenue wouldn't take long, and he'd be able to cross it off his list. One thing he'd learned being a police officer was that it paid to be thorough.

CHAPTER FORTY-TWO

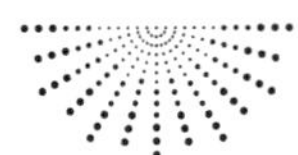

TYLER CLENCHED his fists as DC Charlotte Brown reported the last room in the flat was empty. Neither Brendan nor Tammy was here. All the rooms were clear.

"And there's no sign that Tammy and Ashley were ever kept here?" Tyler asked.

"I haven't seen anything to indicate they were, sir," DC Brown said. "Perhaps the search team will uncover something."

Tyler nodded slowly as the search team filed in ready to methodically take everything apart. There was still a chance, but in his gut Tyler felt this was a dead end.

Just when he thought they had the culprit cornered, things shifted.

Tyler cursed and walked away from DC Brown to look out of the large windows above the sofa. He stared out, trying to come up with a strategy. The sky was no longer an unbroken blue. Grey clouds were gathering above them, the sign of the storm to come.

He turned away from the window, facing DC Brown again. "We need to talk to every member of his family and all his friends. We have to track him down. Does he have business premises?"

DC Brown shook her head. "He lists this address on his tax returns."

"Any other properties in his name?"

"None on record, sir."

Tyler let out a sigh that sounded more like a hiss. "Right, get back to the station, DC Brown. We are going to turn over every rock and look in every nook and cranny until we find this man."

"Yes, sir," she said and turned to leave.

DC Collins passed her in the doorway.

"Did you speak to the neighbours?" Tyler asked him.

Collins nodded. "Yes, and according to his neighbour directly opposite, he hasn't been around for weeks. He thinks Brendan might be staying at his mother's place."

"And I don't suppose he has an address for Brendan's mother?"

Collins shook his head. "Sadly not. Though he said he thought it was within walking distance from what Brendan told him."

"Right, then get back to the station. You need to look up every other Maynard living in the area. Let's hope she shares the same surname as her son."

Collins nodded and started to head out but turned before he got to the door. "I was so sure they were going to be here," he said. "We have to catch him, sir."

Tyler recognised the desperation in Collins's eyes and knew he was feeling guilty for his previous screwup with the CCTV. Officers were only human and mistakes happened, but that wasn't going to make Collins feel any better right now.

Tyler put a hand on his shoulder. "Oh, we'll find him. Believe me, Collins. We'll not stop until we do."

As they walked across the yellowing, dry grass towards the red front door, Wendy turned back to Brendan in desperation. Underneath the hoodie casually draped over his arm, was his knife. The pointed edge pressed against her skin, a warning in case she dared to run. But she would never try to escape, not when he had her son.

"Where is Davey?" she asked, desperation making her voice sharp.

"Inside," Brendan said, reaching for his keys and moving to unlock the door.

"Please, just let him go. You have me now."

"I can't just let him go," Brendan said, shaking his head. "He's a little boy. He'll get lost or some nasty person will pick him up. What kind of mother are you?"

"I could call my husband to collect him. I won't mention you and I'll stay here—"

"Don't be ridiculous." He pushed open the door and shoved Wendy inside.

The door slammed behind them, and Wendy screamed out, "Davey! Davey, where are you?"

Brendan gave her another shove, pushing her from the

hallway into the living room. "Are you trying to annoy me? Keep your voice down."

Wendy rushed around the living room, checking for any places a little boy could hide and then tried to make her way to the stairs.

Brendan roughly pulled her back. "Stop. If you want to see him again, you need to do what I tell you."

Wendy was beside herself. She wrapped her arms around her stomach as tears rolled down her cheeks. "Okay. I will. Anything you want."

"Sit there." He nodded at an old-fashioned armchair.

Wendy did as she was told and he walked through the archway at the end of the living room that led into the kitchen. She couldn't see him from her seat, though she could hear him moving about. Was this her chance to rush upstairs to get Davey while he was occupied?

But she couldn't afford to make him angry, not when there was a chance he would hurt her son.

She sat in the chair and rocked back and forth. How had it come to this? She'd known Brendan needed help. She'd suspected delusional parasitosis for some time, but not this. She'd never expected this.

Brendan walked back into the living room holding a scrap of material, cable ties and a glass of clear liquid. She knew without being told that it wasn't water.

He handed her the glass. "Drink this, then I'm going to tie your hands together with these." He held up the cable ties. "It's for your own safety. As long as you cooperate, you won't get hurt and neither will your son."

Although her brain was screaming not to trust him, she

had no choice. She couldn't call his bluff, not when Davey's life could be at stake.

She took the glass from him and began to drink. It was bitter but she gulped the liquid down.

"Very good," he said when she passed the glass back to him. "Now put your wrists together."

She did as she was told, and he fastened her arms together with two cable ties, then he held up the scrap of black fabric. "I was going to use this as a gag, but if I can trust you to not make a noise, then I won't use it."

Wendy nodded frantically. "You can trust me. I won't make a noise."

He nodded slowly. "Okay, let's get you upstairs."

Wendy got to her feet too quickly. She swayed a little and reached out her bound hands to steady herself on the chair.

Brendan grasped her elbow, and she shuddered at his touch as he pulled her towards the stairs. She had more trouble with the steps than she'd expected. Her arms were tied together but that shouldn't affect her balance. Whatever drugs he'd put in that drink were working quickly. She drank the stuff down willingly like a trusting fool, eager to see her son, but she was likely to be out of it within minutes. Fresh tears rolled down her cheeks.

"Is he up here?" she asked after stumbling on the top step.

"Just up there," Brendan said. He nodded to an aluminium ladder leading up to the loft.

Slowly, feeling like her limbs weren't obeying her brain, Wendy climbed the ladder with Brendan behind her. The hatch was open and she crawled out onto the wooden boards, whipping her head around, looking for Davey.

"Davey, where are you? It's Mummy." Her words were slurred.

There was no answer.

Brendan climbed through the loft hatch behind her and then slid the cover over the opening. Wendy, still on her hands and knees, scrambled away from him. Her head was swimming and she didn't think she could stand.

"Where is he? What have you done with my son?"

Brendan rolled his eyes. "I assume he's safe at home with his father. You really don't know me at all. I'd never hurt or involve a child in this. What kind of monster do you think I am?"

Deep down, Wendy had known this was coming, but as the truth hit her and she couldn't deny it any longer, she began to cry great heaving sobs. He'd tricked her. But at least Davey was safe.

"Look, you don't have to cry. I'm really not going to hurt you. I just need your help," Brendan said. "I'm a scientist, practically a doctor like you. We've got a lot in common."

Wendy stared at him with hatred. She wanted to scream at him that they had nothing in common, that he was a sick, twisted individual who thought he could mess with other people's lives, but she wouldn't say that aloud. Her only chance depended on her ability to create a bond with Brendan. She needed to be more cunning and more intelligent than him. She'd allowed herself to be manipulated as he'd played on her greatest fear – the loss of her son. Now she needed to play him at his own game, press his buttons and bend his will to hers.

"All right," she said, through her tears. "I can work with you."

She blinked, looking at Brendan and realised he wasn't

standing as confidently as before. He hunched over, facing the wall. Then he flinched, curling further over inward, as though he was trying to hide.

"What's wrong, Brendan?"

He was shaking. "She's back? Can you see her?"

Wendy looked around the dim corners of the loft. There was only one lightbulb, hanging in the centre of the large space, which made it hard to see. The ceiling was covered with some kind of black material – probably soundproofing. A few black rubbish bags were piled in one corner, but other than that, the loft was empty.

"I can't see anyone, Brendan. Who's there?"

He shook his head, still trembling. "She's not really here. She's dead."

He was hallucinating. This wasn't good.

"Talk to me, Brendan. She can't hurt you if she is dead."

He screwed his eyes shut. "I'm not dirty. It's not my fault." He dropped to his knees.

Wendy tried to move towards him, but the floor seemed to shift beneath her. The drugs were making her woozy. "Who is it, Brendan? Who's talking to you?"

He kept his eyes shut, and his lip wobbled as he spoke. "It's my mother. She won't leave me alone. I only ever wanted to help her, but I was never good enough."

"Maybe she loved you but found it hard to tell you that."

"No, she hates me. She thinks I'm dirty and good for nothing. She told me she never wanted to see me again. She said I made her skin crawl."

"Brendan, she was probably very angry at the time and said things she didn't mean. We all get angry sometimes and lose our tempers. Take some deep breaths and look at me, Brendan."

The drugs were affecting her vision now, it seemed like she was looking at Brendan through a long, dark tunnel.

"I tried so hard. After she said she never wanted to see me again, I thought up an idea. It was stupid, but I hoped it would work. I put the bugs in her house. I thought she would call me for help. She knew it was my job, but she didn't ask for my help. She called another company. I was never good enough."

He flinched as though someone had hit him and curled up in a ball on the floor. "I'm sorry. I only tried to help. Please, go away. Please."

Mackinnon approached the third address on his list. It was a small terrace, owned by Mrs Penny Crumb.

The house looked ordinary enough, a two up, two down. The windows were old and had aluminium frames but were clean. The property itself appeared to be well-maintained. The garden was another matter. Long yellow, dry grass covered the small, square section of lawn at the front of the house. Weeds covered the narrow flowerbeds. Mackinnon paused by the gate.

The curtains were open. No lights were on, but then they wouldn't be at this time of day. Though the sky was now dark with heavy clouds, threatening to burst. Close to the front door was an outdoor tap that dripped onto the concrete.

Next door a man, who looked to be in his sixties was busy

weeding. He looked up and nodded when he noticed Mackinnon standing at the gate, but didn't speak.

Mackinnon walked up the path and knocked on the front door and waited. As he'd expected there was no answer.

"Do you know your neighbours well?" Mackinnon asked the man next door.

The man set down his hoe. "I used to get on with Penny. But I don't know the lad well. He tends to keep to himself. Doesn't look like he's home."

"So Penny Crumb doesn't live here any more?"

"No, sadly she passed away. About six months ago, I think it was. Her son lives here now. Penny used to keep the garden well," he said, nodding at the yellowing patch of grass. "But young'uns don't take the same sort of care, do they? Can't really blame them. I sometimes think it's a thankless task. My back is aching from all the weeding, and I've still got to spray the roses today."

"Do you know Penny's son's name?"

The man sucked in air through his teeth and looked up at the sky. "I should know it. But it escapes me at the moment. Sorry. Were you a friend of Penny's?"

Mackinnon shook his head and discretely held out his warrant card. "I'm from the City of London police. DS Jack Mackinnon."

The man's eyes widened. "Oh, is the boy in trouble? He didn't really seem the type to do anything illegal. Drugs, is it?" He sighed. "Neighbourhood is going to the dogs."

"What's your name?"

"Trevor, Trevor Cranson."

"Have you seen him bring any women back here, Trevor?" Mackinnon asked.

"Funny you should ask, he came home not long ago, maybe half an hour, with a woman. I don't like to pry, but I paid a bit more attention than I normally would because she seemed upset."

Was he referring to Tammy? "What did she look like?"

"Um, short, brown hair, quite a tall lady. Mixed race, I think."

That didn't sound like Tammy.

Mackinnon pulled out his mobile and opened up a photograph of Brendan.

"Is this him?" Mackinnon asked.

The old man looked at the picture and nodded. "Yeah, that's him.

"Brendan?"

"Oh, yes that's it! Of course, sorry. I'm terrible with names, but now that you've said it, I remember. His name is definitely Brendan."

"Thanks, you've been really helpful."

"No problem. Happy to help. Well, if you don't need anything else, I'd better make a start on my roses. Although it looks like we're about to get a downpour."

"Actually," Mackinnon said, "I think it's probably better if you head inside for a while."

"Oh, don't worry about me. I'm not afraid of a few drops of rain." Trevor chuckled, misinterpreting Mackinnon's warning.

"I'm not referring to the rain."

The old man paled. "So Brendan has done something wrong then."

Mackinnon nodded. "Possibly. It's probably safer if you stay inside for the next few hours."

As the man scurried inside, Mackinnon scanned the windows. There was no sign that someone inside was watching him, but he didn't want to tip Brendan off. If he was watching, Mackinnon wanted him to think he'd given up.

He walked away but stopped at the end of the street and pulled out his phone to call DI Tyler. He still had a view of the address. Maybe Tyler had already made an arrest and found Tammy Holt, but if he hadn't, Mackinnon thought this could well be where Brendan Maynard was hiding out.

CHAPTER FORTY-THREE

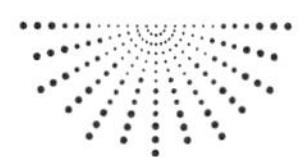

TYLER TOOK a while to answer Mackinnon's call. When he finally picked up, he said, "Bad news, I'm afraid, Jack. There was no sign of Brendan Maynard at the flat. According to the bloke who lives opposite, he hasn't been there for a few weeks."

Tyler's update convinced Mackinnon he'd discovered where Brendan Maynard had been staying.

"I think I might have something. I'm at the third address on my list—Penny Crumb's property, 9, Pine Avenue. There was no answer, so I spoke to her neighbour. He said she died a few months ago and her son is living there now. And get this, the son's name is *Brendan*."

"Wait a minute? Did you say Penny Crumb?"

"Yes."

He heard Tyler shouting at someone in the background and the muffled, scratchy sound of a hand covering the phone.

"We've been trying to track down his family, and I've got a

copy of his birth certificate here somewhere. His last name is Maynard—from his father. But Brendan's parents never married. His mother's surname is Crumb. I'm sure of it. Ah yes, here it is. Penny Crumb."

"So it's got to be where he's been keeping Ashley and Tammy."

"It looks that way, but don't do anything stupid, Jack. I'm sending an urgent response unit there now, and I'm getting in the car myself."

It sounded like Tyler was walking while talking on the phone. Every so often, his conversation was punctuated with orders to officers at the station.

"I showed the neighbour the CCTV still," Mackinnon said, "and he identified him as Penny Crumb's son, Brendan."

"All right, it sounds like we've got him. DC Brown, you're coming with me."

Charlotte's response was too quiet for Mackinnon to hear.

"Do you think he's there now?" Tyler asked.

"I don't know if he's at home. He's not answering the door if he is. All the curtains are open and everything looks normal. There's a garage block to the left of the property. That might be worth a look, too."

"All right. Understood." Tyler then barked an order at DC Webb before returning to his conversation with Mackinnon. "Your job is to sit tight and watch the property until we get there. We don't want him slipping out, but we don't want any heroics either, okay Jack?"

"Okay, but–"

"No buts!"

"I understand, but–"

"But what, Jack?" Tyler shouted, exasperated.

"Brendan's neighbour said he had a woman with him when he returned to the property about half an hour ago."

"Tammy?"

"The description didn't sound like her. He said the woman was tall, shorthaired and mixed-race. He also mentioned she seemed upset."

Tyler groaned. "Things don't look good for Tammy if he's got himself another one, do they?"

Mackinnon heard a car door and an engine rev. He was silent for a moment and then he said, "No, they don't."

Tyler sat in the front passenger seat, tapping his mobile phone impatiently against his thigh. The traffic was not on their side today. They hit jams as soon as they left the station. DC Charlotte Brown sat in the back seat, a look of grim determination on her face.

PC Connor was driving. She switched on the blues and twos and then put her foot down.

Tyler held his breath as they shot around the corner. He hadn't taken the advanced driving course himself because he preferred driving at a sedate pace, but today that was not an option.

His phone rang.

"DI Tyler."

"Sir, this is DS Bright. I'm calling to give you a heads up. You're looking for a suspect called Brendan Maynard, correct?"

"Yes, that's right. What have you got for me?"

"He's suspected of abducting one of the GPs from Holly

Hill surgery. He turned up there this afternoon in a very agitated condition demanding to see one of the GPs. When the receptionist went to check on the doctor because the appointment was running late, the GP was nowhere to be seen and neither was Brendan Maynard. The GPs name is Dr Wendy Willson."

"Description of the doctor?"

"Forty years old. Five ten, IC4, with short black hair. Apparently, she also has a tattoo of a butterfly on her right shoulder blade."

"Right." It looked like they now had a name for another of Brendan's unfortunate victims. "How long ago was this?"

"It was reported an hour ago. Brendan turned up at the surgery in a very agitated state. According to the receptionist he has medical issues."

Tyler was no doctor, but he could have predicted that one. "Thanks for the update. I appreciate it. Give me a call if there's any more news."

He hung up and gripped the edge of his seat as PC Connor weaved in and out of the stationary traffic, sirens blaring.

Tom paced the hospital corridor like an expectant father. He'd already spoken to the police and been breathalysed. Never in his life had he drunk alcohol and then got behind the wheel, so he didn't have anything to worry about on that account. But he couldn't get the woman sprinting across the road out of his head.

Logically, he knew he could never have stopped in time. It wasn't possible.

He didn't think he'd been going too fast. He'd only just accelerated away from a pedestrian crossing, so that wasn't a factor in the accident.

But he couldn't deny his mind was occupied on other things. If he'd been more focused, would he have been able to stop in time? Or slow down, so the woman's injuries weren't so severe?

A nurse walked towards him. "She's woken up," she said with a gentle smile.

Tom gave a sigh of relief and started to walk around her to go to Tammy's ward, but she put a hand on his shoulder. "Hang on a minute. You said you were family?"

Tom flushed pink. When he'd arrived at the hospital they hadn't wanted to give him any information, and so he'd told a little white lie. He said he was the woman's uncle.

Guilt made him clench his teeth, but he couldn't back out of the lie now. He wanted to see her for himself and make sure she really was on the road to recovery.

"Yeah, that's right."

"You said her name is Tammy Hole?"

"Yep."

"Funny," the nurse said sternly. "When she woke up she told us her name is Tammy Holt."

"Yes, Holt, just as I said."

The nurse frowned. "You wrote down her name for us Mr Bradley. You wrote *Hole*."

"Sorry, I never finished school. I was terrible at spelling."

She weighed him up for a second or two and then said. "All right, I'll take you in to see her, but if Tammy is distressed and you're not her uncle. I'll be reporting you myself."

Tom swallowed nervously, but he couldn't back out now. He needed to make sure the woman he'd hit was okay.

"Did they find out why she was only in her underwear?" Tom asked the nurse as they walked briskly towards the ward.

The nurse hesitated and then shook her head. "Not yet. I'm sure it's something the police will want to ask her, but we're concerned with her medical well-being at the moment. It's probably best to not bring it up unless she does."

"Understood," Tom said as they reached the door to the ward.

Tammy was in the third bed along. When he'd seen the blood coming from her head, Tom had feared the worst, so it had been a relief when he'd learned she hadn't needed to go to ICU.

Tammy was sitting up in bed, her long hair tumbling down her shoulders. She looked pale, but other than that, not too bad. He watched as she reached for a plastic cup of squash and gulped it down.

"Tammy, I have brought your uncle to see you," the nurse said.

A frown of confusion puckered Tammy's forehead, but when she looked up at Tom she smiled. "You're the one who helped me after the accident."

"Are you okay if I leave you two alone?" the nurse asked.

Tammy nodded.

They were hardly alone. They were in the middle of a hospital ward, filled with other patients and nursing staff bustling about.

"Yes, we'll be fine. Thank you," Tammy said.

When the nurse reluctantly turned and walked away, Tom said, shamefaced, "I'm sorry about the uncle thing. They wouldn't tell me anything otherwise, and I just wanted to make sure you were all right."

Tammy nodded. "I will be now. I'm safe." She shivered and wrapped her arms around herself. "They've called my mum and sister. They're on their way here now. I wanted to thank you for staying with me. For holding my hand." Tammy's eyes filled with tears.

The niggling guilt due to his white lie, now multiplied a thousand times. Why was she thanking him? Didn't she know he was the one who'd knocked her down?

"Tammy, I'm so sorry for what happened. It was my van that knocked you down. I couldn't stop in time."

"I know. It wasn't your fault. I was panicking and just running as fast as I could. I didn't even see the van until it was too late. I'm sorry."

Tom realised to his embarrassment he was crying. He'd been so worried about her, and here she was, sitting up in bed talking to him, not only that, she seemed to have forgiven him.

He pulled up a chair and sat down beside her bed and rubbed his face. "Sorry, I'm not normally like this."

"Exceptional circumstances," Tammy said. She looked like she wanted to say more but then simply shrugged and picked up her squash again.

He wanted to know why she was panicking and what she was running from, but he remembered what the nurse had said and kept his curiosity to himself.

Tammy turned and a radiant smile spread across her face. "It's my mum and sister."

Tom turned and saw two petite women rushing onto the ward. The younger one was wearing grey leggings and a sporty black vest top, and the older woman, who had to be

Tammy's mum, was wearing a floral dress. Neither had a scrap of make-up on and they were both crying and smiling at the same time. Something had happened to Tammy before she'd run in front of his van, but it looked like she had people who cared about her and would help her through it.

Amongst all the hugs and tearful kisses, Tom got up and excused himself. He knew there was a lot more to the incident, but all he cared about was the fact Tammy was going to recover.

* * *

Forget about butterflies. Tyler's stomach felt like it had a herd of rhinos jumping around inside. They were almost at the address now. He was tempted to call Mackinnon to make sure he'd stayed in place as he was supposed to. In the past, Mackinnon hadn't always chosen the sensible option, which was funny, because people considered Tyler the unorthodox one.

He tried to focus on the risk assessment he was quickly filling in, but it wasn't easy with PC Connor's driving. Not that he was complaining, she'd get them there a lot faster than if he was behind the wheel. He just hoped they were still in one piece when they arrived.

"Sir?" Charlotte, clutching her phone in her hand, leaned forward to get his attention.

"Yes?"

"I've just had some news, good news really. Tammy Holt's been found. She was knocked down in Cedar Avenue, two hours ago. She was hurt, but her injuries aren't life-threatening. They think she's going to be all right."

"That is good news. Which hospital?"

"The Royal London."

"All right, after we get to this address and the situation is under control, I want you to get down there and talk to her. We need her side of the story quickly."

Charlotte said, "Of course."

"How far is Cedar Close from where we are heading?"

"Pine Avenue is only three streets away from Cedar Close. A four-minute walk according to Google maps."

"Interesting," Tyler said, "Looks like we are finally going to nab him." He turned around in his seat to face Charlotte. "You need to get as much information from Tammy as possible. Because this doctor's life is at risk."

"Yes, sir," Charlotte said a little distractedly as she stared down at her phone. "Um, sir?"

Tyler muffled a sigh. He'd never get this risk assessment done at this rate. "Yes, DC Brown?"

"I've just heard from Evie. She's been chasing down Brendan Maynard's family tree."

"Yes, I know that," Tyler said impatiently.

"Well, she hasn't been able to find a record of Penny Crumb's death."

Tyler frowned. "So Brendan's mother is still alive?"

"Either that, or she's dead but nobody reported it."

PC Connor slammed on the brakes as they approached a turning. Tyler swore. This case was getting more complicated by the minute. It was almost enough to make him wish he'd allowed Mackinnon to continue on as SIO.

* * *

The drugs were starting to take their toll now. Wendy's movements, and even her thoughts, were slow and sluggish.

Brendan had curled up on the floor, shivering and sobbing. Now he was distracted, this could be her chance to get away. If only she didn't feel like she was sleepwalking.

She moved slowly across the boards, wincing as they creaked beneath her feet. But Brendan didn't budge, it was as though he was in another world.

She descended the ladder slowly. Her feet and hands felt numb and wouldn't grip the rungs properly. She was halfway down when she missed her footing and slipped, landing heavily on the floor.

Above her, she heard Brendan give a roar of rage.

Move. Move. Move.

Her brain was screaming at her, but her body was slow to react. Heading for the stairs, she felt as though she was underwater. Taking the steps two at a time, stumbling and bashing into the banister and the wall, she went as fast as she could.

When she reached the front door and found it locked, she screamed with frustration. Where were the keys? Brendan was at the top of the stairs now.

She stumbled into the kitchen and screamed as she banged on the window.

Please, let somebody hear her and call the police. There was no point screaming in the loft, with all the soundproofing, but surely someone would hear her now. They were in a terrace. The houses were close together.

When Wendy saw Brendan's reflection in the window as he appeared behind her, she screamed again.

CHAPTER FORTY-FOUR

MACKINNON STOOD at the end of Pine Avenue, keeping the property in view.

A graffiti-covered bus shelter stood on the opposite side of the road a bit closer to the house. In fact, it was probably a bit nearer than protocol demanded, and Tyler definitely wouldn't have approved. But it would give him a good view and he'd be less conspicuous if it looked like he was waiting for a bus.

The first fat drops of rain started to fall, leaving dark grey splotches on the pavement, and Mackinnon made his decision. Yes, the covered bus stop was a much better idea.

He walked briskly, and shot a glance at 9, Pine Avenue. There was no movement. Nothing to suggest anyone was inside.

A flash of lightning preceded an ominous crack of thunder and then the rain began to bucket down just as he reached the bus stop. The rain formed a wall of water that made it hard to see more than a few feet.

Mackinnon was pretending to look at the timetable when his phone rang.

He glanced at the screen, expecting Tyler to be calling with an ETA, but it was Chloe.

He considered not answering the call. He didn't want to risk the distraction, but Chloe didn't usually call him during the day, so it was probably important.

"Hi, is everything all right?" Mackinnon asked.

"Yes, I've got good news for a change. Sarah's back."

Mackinnon paused. He still hadn't told Chloe about Sarah's request for money, or more importantly, that he'd seen her getting into a car owned by a known drug dealer.

"That's great," he said eventually.

"It is. I know you worry, Jack. But I think we've really turned the corner now. We had a good, long chat this afternoon, and we're planning a girl's evening. Just me, Sarah and Katy. I think it will be really good for us."

"Right. Actually, I wanted to talk to you about something. I was planning to try and get away from here for a few hours tonight, but things are a bit frantic at the moment."

"That sounds serious. Don't tell me, you've got tired of my dysfunctional family?" The tone of her voice told him she was teasing.

"*Our* dysfunctional family. But it was to do with Sarah."

"Go on."

Mackinnon hesitated again. If Chloe had really sorted things out with her daughter, and Sarah was back home, was it worth causing more tension by telling her?

But Chloe had a right to know. Who was he to keep things from her when it concerned her daughter?

"Sarah came to the station to ask me for money."

Chloe groaned. "Yes, she mentioned it. I'm really sorry, Jack. She can be exceedingly difficult at times. I'll get her to apologise when you're home at the weekend."

"It's not just that. The thing is, when she left the station, I saw her getting into the passenger seat of a car. Technically, I'm not supposed to, but I looked up the licence plate and it was owned by a known drug dealer, Robin Courtney."

"Sarah mentioned him. He sounds like a nasty piece of work. She said she got taken in by the wrong crowd, but she's turned her back on them now. She wants to go back to college."

"Do you think the college will allow that after what she did?"

"I think there's a chance. A small one, admittedly. If not, I think I can get her a position in my admin department, so that's an option, too. She just needs some stability. She's not a bad kid deep down."

"All right. Well, I'm glad she's home and safe. Things are really kicking off here, and I couldn't really afford to take any time off, but I didn't want to tell you over the phone."

"It's not nice to find out she's been hanging around with drug dealers. I have to admit I was worried she was on something, but other than her mood swings, I can't see any signs. I'm not proud to admit it...but when she took off, I searched her room. I didn't find anything."

"I'm glad. Perhaps we should just keep a close eye on her over the next few weeks."

"Yes, anyway, I should let you get on. How is everything at work?"

"Pretty good. A breakthrough looks imminent, although I'm currently lurking at a bus stop sheltering from the rain."

"So that's what the noise was! It sounds like someone is playing drums nearby."

"Yes, it's giving the roof quite a pounding. I'm glad I got undercover before the rain got really heavy. I'll call you later tonight. Have a nice time with Sarah and Katy. Where are you going?"

"Just to the local pub. It's steak night tonight."

Above the din of the rain, Mackinnon heard a sound that didn't fit with the quiet neighbourhood.

It sounded like a woman's scream.

"Chloe, I've got to go. I'll call you back."

He hung up and stepped out of the bus shelter to get a clearer view of the house. But the rain was like a sheet of water obscuring his view.

He ran towards the house. It wasn't in line with protocol, but he wouldn't be able to live with himself if something happened to Dr Willson and he didn't try to prevent it.

As he got closer, he saw a woman at the downstairs window. Terror contorted her face. Her mouth moved, and he thought he heard a muffled, "help me."

There was a movement behind her in the shadows, and then she was roughly pulled away from the window.

Mackinnon headed straight for the front door. It was made from uPVC. Red and faded, it was old, but there was little chance he'd be able to smash through the lock. He'd have to kick through the panels instead.

"Police," he called out. "Open the door."

He wasn't really expecting Brendan to comply and when the door didn't open immediately he took a step back.

His first kick was a failure. The rainwater soaked his shoes, making his foot slip and slide rather than smash into the panels.

He cursed and tried again. A better, more direct hit this time, but still not enough force to puncture the panel. On the fourth attempt the first panel gave way, falling more or less intact inside the house.

He heard another scream from inside, and then a male voice ordering him to stand back from the door.

"Brendan Maynard? I need to talk to you."

There was a click as the door unlocked and Brendan pulled it open. He looked at the hole in his door and narrowed his eyes. Only one door panel was missing. The other was hanging off, still attached to the door.

Mackinnon quickly assessed the situation. Brendan held a knife, a long kitchen blade. He was tall, only a couple of inches shorter than Mackinnon and looked athletic. Brendan clutched the arm of the woman beside him, who matched the description of Wendy Willson. Her eyes were unfocused and staring. Had he drugged her?

"Stand back," Brendan ordered. He was trying to hold too many things. Clutching Wendy's arm with his left hand, he held the knife with his right. Under his left arm, he held some kind of clear box.

Within seconds, they were soaked by the heavy rain.

"I said stand back!" Brendan barked as another crash of thunder rang out.

"Brendan, you should put down the knife. This isn't going to have a good outcome. You need to let Dr Willson go."

"No, she is my assistant. I need an assistant."

"Sure, but you don't need the knife. You don't want to hurt anybody, do you, Brendan?"

His eyes darted around, probably looking for the police officers. "I didn't mean to hurt anyone. I haven't hurt you, have I?" He nudged Wendy, and she staggered a little and then swayed on her feet. He'd definitely used something to drug her.

Sirens sounded in the background. Backup was close now. Mackinnon just needed to get Brendan to put down the knife and let go of Wendy.

"Stand back. We're leaving. If you try to follow us, you'll regret it," Brendan warned as the rain began to ease.

"Be sensible, Brendan. You aren't going to get away with this. If you cooperate and put the knife down, things will go a lot easier for you."

He struggled to manoeuvre the glass case. "It's not the knife you have to worry about. It's these."

For the first time, Mackinnon fully focused on the glass box. It was filled with bugs – tiny bedbugs.

"What are you doing with those?" Mackinnon asked.

Brendan's eyes lit up. "They're my research subjects. They carry a parasite. If you don't get away from us, I'm gonna release them and infect everybody in the neighbourhood."

He tried to lift the case higher and lost his grip on the knife. It clattered to the floor, and Mackinnon moved fast, kicking the knife away until it skidded beneath a Fiesta parked outside the house next door.

"Don't come any closer!" Brendan screeched, yanking Wendy's arm and pulling her across the yellow, patchy lawn that was now sodden.

"Let her go," Mackinnon said firmly.

Brendan was now unarmed apart from the weird box of bugs he held tightly against his chest. One-on-one, Mackinnon could take him, but Wendy seemed to be out of it. He didn't want to risk her getting hurt.

Brendan's neighbours were looking down anxiously from upstairs windows, and a group of teenagers were watching from across the street. Great. An audience. Just what they needed.

"If you come any closer I'm gonna release these and infect everybody." Brendan shook the box vigorously.

Gary from the pest control company hadn't mentioned parasites could be spread by bedbugs. In the course of his research, Mackinnon had read the bugs weren't thought to spread disease. But Brendan's conviction gave him pause.

Then suddenly, Wendy elbowed Brendan in the ribs and pulled away from him. He released his hold on her and she ran to Mackinnon.

Standing behind Mackinnon, she shouted, "He's delusional. There are no parasites. I've been trying to get him help for ages."

"That's not true," Brendan said his face flushed and taut with anger. "You'll see. I'll be proved right in the end."

With a harsh yell, he threw the glass box on the floor, and it shattered, the bugs scuttling in every direction.

Mackinnon cursed.

Using the distraction, Brendan tried to make a run for it, but Mackinnon was too quick for him. Within a few feet, he'd grabbed Brendan and forced him to the ground. They both hit the pavement with a thud.

"Don't worry. They're really not infected with a parasite," Wendy said, blinking at Mackinnon as she sat on the wet ground. "I feel so tired."

Even if the bugs weren't infected with a parasite, Mackinnon felt sorry for the neighbours. They would still be a frustrating nuisance.

Mackinnon pulled one of Brendan's arms behind his back and pinned it there. "Brendan Maynard, I'm arresting you for the murder of Ashley Burrows and the abduction of Tammy Holt and Dr Wendy Willson. You do not have to say anything, but anything you do say –"

"I didn't do anything! I didn't kill her!" Brendan screeched, writhing, as Mackinnon struggled to keep him still.

Sirens grew louder, and a police car screeched to a stop just in front of 9, Pine Avenue.

DI Tyler got out and slammed the door behind him.

"Mackinnon, what a surprise."

"I could do with a little help here," Mackinnon replied as Brendan struggled to break free.

It took two PCs to help Mackinnon subdue Brendan Maynard and get the handcuffs fastened.

When they finally put him in the back of the police car, Mackinnon went to find Tyler. The DI stood beside the back doors of an ambulance as they slammed shut. Both men watched the vehicle head off with Wendy Willson inside.

"How is she?" Mackinnon asked.

"The paramedics think he's given her some kind of sedative, so they're taking her into hospital just in case, but she has no physical injuries apart from a sprained ankle. She got the injury falling from the ladder to the loft. She told me he's got delusional parasitosis. It's a mental illness. Sufferers think they have parasites when they don't."

Mackinnon rubbed his hand over his face. "Well, now I suppose we need to get pest control in to get rid of those bugs that are probably burrowing their way into people's houses as we speak.

"Already handled. A1 pest control is on the way," Tyler said. "We need to search the house. You said the neighbour told you Penny Crumb died months ago."

"That's right."

"Well, there's no record of her death, which means she is either still alive or—"

"—Or you suspect her body is around here somewhere?"

"That about sums it up."

Mackinnon and Tyler turned as the rumble of a transit engine alerted them to the crime scene van arriving.

"Time to get suited and booted," Tyler said.

CHAPTER FORTY-FIVE

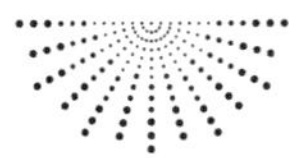

DRESSED IN PROTECTIVE SUITS, Tyler and Mackinnon walked towards the property.

From the house next door, Trevor poked his head out of the downstairs window and said, "Is it safe to come out yet?"

Tyler headed inside number nine, and Mackinnon paused by the wire fence that separated the front gardens of the two houses. From there, he could talk to Trevor without being overheard by the crowd gathering around the police tape. One press van had already turned up, and he was sure there would be more to follow.

"It is, but we're going to be here for a while yet. The streets will be jammed with vehicles and police personnel for a while. Sorry for the inconvenience."

"Don't apologise!" Trevor leaned further out of the window, resting his forearms on the window sill. "I should be thanking you."

Trevor looked down at the bright red dahlias planted

beneath his kitchen window and shivered. "I can't believe he was living next door all this time and we had no idea. Er, what exactly did he do?"

"We don't have all the answers yet," Mackinnon said. "We're still investigating, but I do have a question for you. Which of the garages did Penny and Brendan use?"

Trevor turned his head and squinted in the direction of the garage block. "They had the first one on the right. The one with the white door. I used to have a key. Penny was quite forgetful, and she gave my wife and me spare copies of her front door and garage keys, but after she died, Brendan was adamant we hand them both over." He shrugged. "He was very insistent and said he never lost things. A complete contrast to his mum, who was forever mislaying things. That was Penny," he chuckled. "I lost track of the times she left her keys at work."

"So Brendan took back both keys, for the front door and the garage?" Mackinnon asked, turning to look at the garage with the white door. Interesting. They already knew there was something in the house Brendan wanted to hide from prying eyes – both his odd collection of bugs and the abducted women he'd kept in the loft, but was there something he needed to hide in the garage as well?

"Thanks Trevor. You've been very helpful."

"Not at all. Happy to be of assistance," Trevor called as Mackinnon walked across the lawn.

He passed the beaten up front door and carefully followed the markers on the floor, indicating the correct path to walk into the property, aiming to minimise contamination of the crime scene.

One of the crime scene officers was taking a photograph of a blood smear on the staircase.

"Have you seen any keys?" Mackinnon asked. "I'm looking for the garage key. I want to take a look inside."

The man straightened from his crouched position. "I did see them somewhere. But we'll be moving onto the garage after we've finished here if you don't mind waiting?"

"Actually, I'd like to take a look now," Mackinnon said. "I won't mess anything up. I promise."

There was only a small section of the man's face visible beneath his hooded paper suit. The crime scene officer's eyes narrowed. "I don't know. Hang on a minute."

He called the crime scene manager over.

Mackinnon recognised him from previous cases. "Darren! Good to see you again. I hope you can help me. I want to take a look inside the garage ASAP. Do you have the keys?"

"Probably. Maynard's keys were put in an evidence bag. The garage key will probably be on his keyring."

Darren disappeared into the living room and then came back out holding a box with clear plastic bags inside.

He held one up. "These are the only keys we've found so far."

There were four keys on the ring, along with a plastic picture of a kitten. Mackinnon guessed the larger keys would fit the locks on the front and back doors of 9, Pine Avenue. The third Yale key likely fit the front door of Brendan Maynards's flat in North Quay Road.

The fourth key was smaller than the others and a different shape. That was probably the one for the garage.

"Is it all right if I take these. I just want to take a quick look at the garage before you guys start your search."

"Absolutely," Darren said. "You know the procedure. Don't touch anything unnecessarily, and make sure you're wearing—"

Darren broke off and grinned when Mackinnon held up a gloved hand. "I'm already wearing them."

"Then I'll just sign the form to record the fact you've taken the keys. Bring them back when you're done." Darren handed him the plastic bag.

After walking outside, Mackinnon ripped open the plastic and removed the keyring. The crowd had grown even larger. Neighbours were gossiping among themselves, and a couple of journalists were calling out questions to the PC standing beside the police tape.

As he headed to the garage, he caught sight of PC Connor and called her over. "Would you mind sectioning off the garages for me? We need to make sure none of the residents enters the garage block until we've finished the search."

As PC Connor headed off to find the police tape, Mackinnon took a look at the white garage door. The handle in the middle of the door looked rusty, but the key fitted perfectly and turned easily enough. He eased the lock clockwise and then leaned down, grabbing the base of the metal garage door and lifting it up. It opened with a protesting squeal.

The air was musty. There was no car in the garage or any other vehicles except an old BMX that had definitely seen better days. A metal shelf rack stood on the right, holding two tool boxes, a foot pump and multiple cardboard boxes, containing what looked like photo albums.

None of that caught Mackinnon's attention as firmly as the item right at the back of the garage.

It was dark, but as Mackinnon's eyes adjusted to the

gloom, he spotted a light switch in the corner of the garage. The wires weren't enclosed in any casing. Had the wiring been a DIY job? It looked like Brendan had needed power in the garage.

Bracing himself for what he might find, Mackinnon walked over the dusty concrete floor.

Right at the back, plugged in at the wall, was a large chest freezer.

Its white surface was battered and scratched, and it emitted a constant low hum, probably struggling to keep the internal temperature down in this heat. A padlock had been looped around the chrome handle.

Mackinnon reached for it, testing the lock, but the padlock held firm. There were no other keys on the keyring.

He headed back out of the garage and called PC Connor over. "Would you mind asking one of the crime scene techs if they've got some equipment that could break a padlock?"

When PC Connor hurried off, Mackinnon stood by the freshly hung crime scene tape to make sure nobody came too close. It wasn't long before PC Connor came back with a short, ruddy-faced man carrying a camera and a pair of bolt cutters. He was dressed similarly to Mackinnon, in a white hooded suit. The skin around his eyes crinkled when he smiled.

"So where is the padlock?" he asked.

"In there," Mackinnon said pointing to the freezer at the back.

The crinkles around the man's eyes disappeared as he stopped smiling. "Oh, I see."

Both men entered the garage, leaving PC Connor at the police tape.

"There aren't many reasons a person would lock a freezer,

are there?" the crime scene tech said as he snapped a couple of photographs of the freezer and the padlock.

"No, there aren't."

The bolt cutters made short work of the padlock. Mackinnon braced himself.

When the crime scene tech removed the remains of the broken lock, Mackinnon slowly lifted the freezer lid.

It shouldn't have been a surprise. He'd known what was coming, and yet the sight of it made his stomach churn.

There, curled up at the bottom of the freezer, mouth open in a voiceless scream, was the frozen body of Penny Crumb.

CHAPTER FORTY-SIX

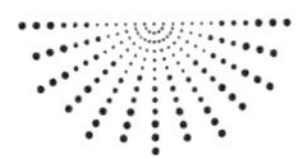

DC Charlotte Brown headed out of Tammy Holt's ward. The young woman was doing well and due to be discharged. Charlotte had found recording her story harrowing, but was impressed by Tammy's resilience.

She'd been pleased to be able to tell Tammy, Brendan Maynard was in custody.

No doubt, the ramifications of what had happened to the young woman would echo for a long time, but it was heart-warming to see the interaction between Tammy, her sister and mother. She had a strong support network, and Charlotte hoped that would help her in the weeks and months ahead.

They'd need to speak to her again, but Charlotte had the preliminary statement, and she felt that covered things for now. It would be enough to make DI Tyler happy.

Charlotte had heard Wendy Willson had been brought to the hospital, and since she was there anyway, decided to look in on the doctor.

A very busy, harassed-looking nurse agreed to let Charlotte make a quick visit. Wendy hadn't yet been admitted to a ward and was currently in one of the cubicles at the rear of the accident and emergency department.

The nurse pulled back the curtains and announced, "Wendy, this is DC Charlotte Brown from the City of London Police. She wanted to have a quick word if you're feeling up to it."

Wendy was sitting on a stretcher bed, wearing a light blue hospital gown and had dark circles under her eyes. "Absolutely," she said. "You did arrest him, didn't you?"

Charlotte nodded. "Yes, he's in custody."

The nurse left them, and Wendy sighed. "That's a relief. He gave me some kind of sedative, and it knocked me for six. I wasn't sure if I'd imagined his arrest."

"Do the doctors know what he gave you?"

"They're still running some more tests, but I had my stomach pumped and am on medication to absorb the rest of the nasty stuff that could be lingering in my stomach. I'm feeling much better, at least, my head is clearer. I still have a little dizziness." She pulled the hospital gown across to cover her legs. "I really didn't want to have my stomach pumped. Believe me, I made a most compelling argument against it, but the doctors ignored me. Good job, too, really. They were right. They do say doctors make the worst patients, don't they?"

Charlotte smiled. "I won't ask you too many questions today. We'll probably follow up tomorrow if that works for you. We can come to you for a formal statement or you can come to the station. It's completely up to you."

"Okay. I should be feeling fine then."

"Do you have a preferred contact number I can take?"

Wendy reeled off her mobile number. "Do you know what Brendan will be charged with?"

"Not yet, we need to do a mental health assessment before we're even allowed to question him."

"I have to admit I feel somewhat responsible. I'd known for a long time that he was struggling with things. If I could have helped him earlier maybe none of this would have happened."

"I'm sure you tried your best. It can't be an easy job."

Wendy shook her head. "No, it isn't. It seems to get harder every day." She looked up at Charlotte. "But I shouldn't complain, your job is probably not a bed of roses either!"

Charlotte grinned. "You could say that. It has its moments."

A man appeared behind Charlotte, and Wendy said, "This is my husband. Pete, this is DC Brown. She's asking me some questions."

Pete put his arm around his wife's shoulders and kissed her forehead.

"I think we can leave the questions for today," Charlotte said. "I'll leave you to recover and be in touch soon."

She left A&E, glad both Tammy and Wendy looked like they would fully recover, but she was just sorry they hadn't been able to save Ashley Burrows. She glanced at her watch. Kate Squires would be telling Ashley's parents they'd made an arrest now. It wouldn't bring their daughter back, but it might give them some closure.

* * *

That night, the team visited The Red Herring Pub.

DI Tyler was in an exceptionally good mood and had even put his hand in his pocket to buy the first round. DCI Brookbank had also graced them with his presence and had thanked every officer individually, praising them for their hard work.

Mackinnon looked down at the plate of chicken wings he'd just demolished. "Do you know, I think I could eat the same again."

"Well, you could order some more. We are celebrating," Charlotte said. "Two successful cases closed in a week. Not bad."

"Pretty good, but don't forget we still have to do all the paperwork," Collins said glumly.

Mackinnon pulled a face. He didn't know one officer who enjoyed the paperwork side of the job.

Collins pushed his plate of unfinished chicken wings in front of Mackinnon. "Fill your boots. I'm stuffed."

As Mackinnon dug in, he noticed DCI Brookbank scratching his shoulder as Tyler filled him in on the bedbugs Brendan Maynard had let loose in Pine Avenue. "We've got pest control in," Tyler said. "They've warned people in the area to be alert, but other than that it's just a case of wait-and-see. The most important thing is tackling the problem early, isn't that right, Jack?"

Mackinnon nodded. "Yes, and we should all be alert too. Just in case we picked up any little hitchhikers."

There was a collective "yuk" from the officers around the table, and Brookbank, not so subtly, moved his chair a little further away from DI Tyler.

Mackinnon picked up his pint of bitter and took a sip as his mobile buzzed in his pocket. He got up and went outside. The smell of rain was still in the air and the heavy grey clouds lingered, but the breeze was much cooler than the past few days. The thunderstorm had broken through the humidity and heat.

He had a text message from Chloe, asking him if everything went okay today. He'd forgotten to call her back after hanging up abruptly earlier.

He replied:

Everything is fine. Just having a quick drink in The Red Herring to celebrate the end of the case. How is your evening going?

He hoped things had gone well with Sarah, but she could be unpredictable.

Having a lovely time xx.

That was a relief. He wasn't sure how long the truce would last, but for now, it seemed peaceful times were on the horizon.

He headed back inside the pub just as Charlotte was walking to the bar.

"Need another drink, Jack?" she asked.

He still had more than half a pint left. "No, but I'll get these. You've already bought a round."

They crossed over to the bar together, and Mackinnon pulled out his wallet, thinking Charlotte seemed preoccupied. Not surprising really. They'd all read extracts from Brendan Maynard's journal before going to the pub.

Although it made uncomfortable reading, it certainly made their life a lot easier. He'd written down all his thoughts and deeds. It was a sad tale. There was no doubt Brendan was deluded. He believed he would be world famous one day for his scientific discoveries.

In his journal, he'd included the sorry tale of how Ashley had died because her bites got infected, and how he'd entrapped both Ashley and Tammy using the forum. The only thing that wasn't recorded in detail was why he targeted Wendy Willson. Though he had included plenty of entries ranting about her and the other GPs he'd come into contact with at the surgery. All in all, the journal made a sad and depressing story.

The sections on Brendan Maynard's mother were especially harrowing. Before she died, Penny Crumb had a difficult relationship with her son. They only had Brendan's side of the story, but Penny appeared to enjoy tormenting him. They had no evidence of physical abuse, but Penny's continual taunts had triggered something in Brendan.

She'd died from blunt force trauma to the left temple. The pathologist had given his initial judgement, though not his full report yet, but they didn't need to wait for the postmortem. Brendan had written up the incident in his journal.

He'd planted bedbugs in her house, hoping she'd call him to help, so he could save the day, and for once, gain his mother's approval. But she hadn't called him for help, instead going to a rival pest control company.

That had been the final straw for Brendan. Furiously angry, he'd argued with his mother and pushed her down the stairs. It was the impact to her head that killed her, but the pathologist suspected she'd suffered other injuries from the fall, including a cracked rib and a broken wrist.

Charlotte recited the drinks order to the barman, and Mackinnon paid just as Kate Squires walked into the pub.

He waved her over. "Kate! We're just getting the drinks in. What are you having?"

Kate asked for a G&T and stood at the bar beside them as Mackinnon placed the order.

"It's been a tough day," she said after taking a sip of her gin.

"How did the Burrowses take the news?" Charlotte asked.

"Okay, I guess. They're glad someone's been caught, but that doesn't heal their grief unfortunately. It's going to take them a long time to get through this."

Tonight was for celebrating a job well done, though it was always bittersweet in these kinds of cases. The outcome was never perfect.

They carried the drinks back over to the tables where the rest of the officers were laughing and joking.

Tyler was sitting beside Janice, looking like he was on top of the world.

Charlotte nudged Mackinnon. "Looks like someone's been forgiven for the food poisoning incident."

Mackinnon was happy for them, but Brookbank didn't look too pleased his new assistant was dating one of his officers. Mackinnon slid into the empty seat beside DI Tyler, putting the tray of drinks on the table.

Then he handed Tyler his pint and Janice a glass of red wine. "You two look like you're back on friendly terms again."

Tyler beamed. "We are."

Janice nodded. "Yes, although it might be a while before I let him cook for me again!"

DC Webb, who was sitting next to Janice, said, "Ouch! That put you in your place, sir."

"I deserve it," Tyler said with a sheepish grin.

"Anyway, let's put all that behind us and make a toast." DI Tyler held up his pint. "Here's to hard work bringing another good result. Well done, everyone."

A NOTE FROM D. S. BUTLER

Thank you for reading Deadly Intent. I hope you enjoyed it!

If you would like to be one of the first to find out when my next book is available, you can sign up for my new release email at www.dsbutlerbooks.com/newsletter

If you have the time to leave a review, I would be very grateful.

For readers who like to read series books in order here is the order of the Deadly Series so far: 1) Deadly Obsession 2)Deadly Motive 3)Deadly Revenge 4)Deadly Justice 5)Deadly Ritual 6)Deadly Payback 7) Deadly Game 8)Deadly Intent

I also write a series of books set in the East End under the name Dani Oakley. Please turn the page to find out more or take a look at the book page on my website.

www.dsbutlerbooks.com

ALSO BY D S BUTLER

Deadly Obsession

Deadly Motive

Deadly Revenge

Deadly Justice

Deadly Ritual

Deadly Payback

Deadly Game

Lost Child

Her Missing Daughter

Bring Them Home

Where Secrets Lie

If you would like to be informed when the next book is released, sign up for the newsletter:

http://www.dsbutlerbooks.com/newsletter/

Written as Dani Oakley

East End Trouble

East End Diamond

East End Retribution

ACKNOWLEDGMENTS

To Nanci, my editor, thanks for always managing to squeeze me in when I finally finish my books!

I would also like to thank my readers on Facebook & Twitter for their messages of support and encouragement. Thanks to Jacqueline for her careful reading of the series and helping to find the annoying typos.

My thanks, too, to all the people who read the story and gave helpful suggestions, especially my mum, and to Chris, who, as always, supported me despite the odds.

And last but not least, my thanks to you for reading this book. I hope you enjoyed it.